Garde)

Book I of
The Sundering Chronicles

Gardens of Earth

Book I of
The Sundering Chronicles

Mark Iles

Elsewhen Press

Gardens of Earth
First published in Great Britain by Elsewhen Press, 2021
An imprint of Alnpete Limited

Elsewhen Press, PO Box 757, Dartford, Kent DA2 7TQ
www.elsewhen.press

British Library Cataloguing in Publication Data.
A catalogue record for this book is available from the British Library.

ISBN 978-1-911409-95-3 eBook edition
ISBN 978-1-911409-85-4 paperback edition

Designed and formatted by Elsewhen Press

Contents

This book is dedicated to my mother, June Maureen Iles. She who would have been thrilled that the idea for the alien ships in this book are based on an idea generated by her. The fact that she believed in me made me what I am today.

Chapter 1

Steff Philips fidgeted on his chair, wishing as he always did that they'd make the damn things more comfortable. He hated it here on Halloween and, like most of the troops here, felt the whole damned planet was wrong somehow, not that any of them could put their fingers on what it was. Other members of his flight wing – Jameson, Chung, Abbott, and Manson – sat in the dining room with him. Each looked worried. Manson, however, was shovelling food down that bottomless pit that he called a mouth.

"I can't stop thinking about the aliens, their last incursion – though I've heard that the grunts have finally secured the city," Chung said. "The civvies are scared shitless and who can blame them? They're afraid to pop their heads out of their holes in case they get a bullet for their trouble."

"You can't blame the troops for being trigger-happy," Steff replied. "And the fact that everyone's uptight and locked down on this godforsaken place doesn't help. With all flights in or out cancelled, no-one can get away."

"Have you seen it out there lately?" Manson said, mumbling through a mouthful of food, his bright-blue eyes flicking constantly from one person to the next. "It's like something from one of those old war movies. The only things left in the colonists' areas are a few gutted buildings, and half of those are still on fire. So much for the building retardants and our fire service."

Steff had a momentary vision of huge red drones zipping back and forth spraying the flames, as Manson continued.

"And the weather's still below freezing. All you can see out there is a haze of drifting snow, smoke, and ash."

Thoughtfully, Steff pushed his dinner around his plate with a fork, appetite deserting him. "I spoke to Haskins last night. You know, that gruff marine sergeant who got us that God-awful rum last week? He said that, somewhere in the city, there are streets lined with corpses hanging from makeshift scaffolds. He told me those corpses are frozen solid and crusted white with frost. When the patrols first came across them they cut them down, but when they returned they were right back up there again, swinging away. At night the only light they have is from the fires, no-one can get the lighting to work and they can't figure out why. All they can hear is the crackling of flames and creaking from the scaffolds."

"Fuck that," Abbott said. "Even the thought of it gives me the creeps." He shook himself and shuddered.

"You won't get me out there," Chung said, using his knife to jab noisily at the contents of his plate. "That's what the grunts are for; give me a plane any day."

Manson spat out a mouthful of food suddenly. "Man, would you look at that?" He retched as he pointed at his food which was now crawling with maggots. "Jeez, I thought I felt something wriggling in my mouth. Urgh!" He spat more potato and gravy onto his plate. His mouth worked, and the plate rumbled as he pushed it away with one hand.

Steff looked down as the plate slid towards him, knife and fork spilling over its sides to clatter onto the table. His mouth flooded with saliva and he swallowed, seeing string-like white worms writhing in the grey mush. He looked up at Manson, who spat another maggot onto the table. The man grabbed a beaker of fruit juice from the table and swilled out his mouth, before spitting it all back into the mug. He rubbed a hand over his clammy-looking skin, and suddenly retched. He coughed up a mouthful of dinner into a pile, coughed again and spat out red-tinged remnants.

"Jesus, man! Do you mind?" Chung gasped, disgust all over his face as he and the others pushed themselves away from the table. "Didn't your parents teach you anything?"

"Yeah, my dad taught me to duck," Manson replied. But, before he could say anything else, he reddened and grabbed at his throat with both hands. Veins stood out on his forehead and his eyes bulged. Lips bluing, he opened his mouth into an 'O' of disbelieving horror. His mouth stretched wider, his cheekbones bulged and he gagged. Sitting next to him, Chung reached forward and slapped Manson hard on the back, as his throat suddenly swelled. He slapped Manson a second time, and then again as Steff and Abbott stood up helplessly.

Chung's chair fell with a clatter as he stood, continuing to try and dislodge whatever it was stuck in his friend's throat. Realising the futility of it, he suddenly dragged Manson to

2

his feet and put both hands around his waist hugging him in a Heimlich manoeuvre, the muscles beneath his tan shirt bulging as he did so. Manson's mouth opened even wider and a thick, white, tongue-like appendage with a dark tip poked its way out of his mouth and began to whip back and forth.

With a sickening tearing sound Manson's mouth ripped apart and a thick, arm-length maggot forced its way out. It fell onto the wriggling contents of the table with the sound a slab of meat makes when it hits the floor. With his throat torn and his jaw broken, Manson collapsed, his eyes wide and staring.

Steff grabbed his knife and slammed it down and through the blood-drenched thing slithering towards him. The metal knife bounced off the plasteel table but still impaled the creature, and it thrashed desperately from side to side. Beside him, Abbott bellowed as he grabbed his knife and did the same, the table tipping over as they scrambled to get away from the wriggling grub.

The other people in the dining hall rose to their feet with gasps of horror, some moving as far away as they could while the remainder simply ran for the exit. Gradually, the maggot stopped moving and just lay there, the colour of freshly-filleted cod waiting to be battered.

Chung knelt beside Manson and checked his pulse. "He's dead," he said, looking up at the others.

"Thank God," Steff said. "I'd want to be fucking dead too. Get the hell away from him. Everyone else, out!" He stood and stepped back, gesturing for the others to leave. Keying his Smart-Arm, Steff spoke into it: "Security and medic to the dining hall at the rush. We have an emergency."

How Steff got through it, and to his room afterwards, he didn't know. He found himself sitting on his bed staring at the floor with his head in his hands and trembling like a terrified child. Outside in the corridor, beyond his closed door, the sound of heavy footsteps thudding past carried easily. Someone nearby screamed. It went on for a few seconds and then stopped. Something snuffled at his door. It was an unearthly sound, one that made him shiver, and a feeling of utter dread filled him. A moment later, a loud, gibbering laugh came from the room next to his, followed by a resounding crash of several items falling. He knew he should investigate but he was far too terrified. He couldn't even bring himself to stand up.

Unbidden, his hand crept to the bedside table and slid open the drawer. He took out the pistol he'd hidden discreetly, slipping the magazine free to check it. Slamming the mag home again, he double-checked the safety. Two other magazines lay in the drawer, and he picked them up and put them beside him on the bed. He tapped at his Smart-Arm and a hologram of Seethan's face appeared in front of him, floating in mid-air.

"Bodell, this is Steff Philips. Seethan, I don't know if you'll get this as all our mail seems to be on hold. I'm hoping one of the other guys will pick it up and forward it on. Look, I know you think that I blame you for the crash. To be honest, I did for a long time, but I don't anymore and I'm sorry about how I've acted. I guess I freaked out when I heard what happened. I blamed you when I shouldn't have. It was just one of those things; could have been anyone flying, including me, but unfortunately you drew the short straw. Pete was proud to be flying with you, and if he had to die, I'm glad it was with someone that he admired and called a friend. Everyone knows that landing marines in a contested area is dicey. Like I said, it's not your fault."

Steff was intermittently clenching his fists and rubbing at his jaw, the unshaven stubble rasping noisily. He knew he should have shaved this morning and hadn't, but fuck regulations.

"Yeah, so, before you ask, some of the guys are saying how you walked away from that crash, and now from this Goddam hell hole. But hey man, them's the breaks. If you hadn't been injured in the crash, you'd have been down here with us or up there on the *Colossus* with the rest of the crew. All I can say is, at least one of us gets to go home. As for Pete, I'm glad the poor fucker isn't here to go through this horror."

Steff found himself fiddling with the gun and forced himself to stop. He gripped the pistol more tightly to try and control the shaking, then gave up and laid it in his lap, placing his other hand over the top of it.

"All hell's breaking loose. The five of us – that's me, Abbott, Chung, Jameson, and Manson – we got stranded here on Halloween and now they've stopped all flights back out, including for the military. Oh and… err, Manson's dead. Just thinking about it freaks me out. Don't even ask."

"The carrier's fighter wings are now flying interdiction to ensure nothing leaves this shithole. I've spoken to the Flight Commander over the air and he says there's nothing he can do, that they've already lost two frigates trying to get people out. The Spooks got aboard them somehow and they ended up being sanitised by the fleet. I know a few life pods got away and landed out there in the wilderness, but God knows where. No one's even tried to find them – after all, flying's out and it's unsafe on the ground. I hope the poor buggers got to safety but I sincerely doubt it. There isn't anywhere safe on Halloween. Not since the Spooks revealed themselves."

Steff jerked violently as something scratched at his door with long, ear-piercing sounds like fingernails being dragged down a chalkboard. His eyes followed the noise as it screeched slowly towards the electronic lock. Then it stopped, and a deep, unearthly chuckle came from the other side.

Without warning, the door to his room snapped into its recess. Beyond there was only a hole of threatening darkness.

"Hello, is anyone there?" Steff asked. His handgun was cocked and pointing towards the menacing pit of the passageway before he'd realised it. Why were the lights on in his room but not in the corridor?

Nothing made sense anymore. The dark doorway filled his vision, seeming to swell and grow towards him. He slid backwards across his bunk as far away as he could, stopping only when his back touched the wall and he could go no further. From his Smart-Arm, the ghostly image of Seethan's face floated along with him.

A hot, wet patch spread around Steff's lap. Embarrassed, he tried to ignore it and focus on finishing his message as he said, "Looks like my time's up, old pal."

He was interrupted by a long, drawn-out scream that echoed along the corridor, followed by a hideous laugh.

Jesus, was that Abbott? Where the hell was security?

"Seethan, we're compromised to hell and I can't see anyone getting away, so I'm going to sign off now. Good luck. If there is a God – and as a once religious man I sincerely doubt there is – I hope he's with you, because he sure as hell isn't here."

His friend's image disappeared and a second later, a soft 'ding' told him the message had been sent. Steff lifted his weapon, chambered a round, and kept it levelled towards the threatening darkness. A hush fell and a dank putrid smell wafted into the room. Sweat stung his eyes and he tried to brush it away with the back of a hand. He swallowed and licked salt from his lips. Eyes narrowing, Steff listened carefully. Something was there, in the blackness not far from the door. He could sense it, *feel it*, watching him.

Steff gagged as the stench increased tenfold, and he held his free hand over his nose. Ice zig-zagged around the door frame and recess with a loud '*crack*'. Puffs of cold air wafted through it in time with the sound of hoarse breathing. It was as if someone was sawing back and forth at his nerves.

He found himself holding his breath, eyes and gun remaining trained on the doorway. There was a long, pregnant pause and, when nothing else happened, he exhaled briefly with relief.

Just as he did so, a rotting hand, with ribbons of flesh hanging from exposed bone, reached up from underneath his bed and snatched at his ankle.

Chapter 2

Seethan Bodell woke with a jolt and reached over to pick up the alarm clock blaring from its perch on the bedside table. In one fluid motion, he flipped opened the window beside his bed and lobbed the clock into the sunlit garden, all with his eyes half-shut. He grunted in satisfaction as it rang all the way to the ground, bounced with a shattering sound on the path below, and fell silent. He only had one clock left in reserve and realised he'd better get some more. They were dirt cheap these days and he found the simple act somehow cathartic. It was a weird thing to do and he knew it. But, what the hell.

As always, he was unable to remember the nightmares. All he knew about them was the rush of adrenalin that made his fists clench, the tension in his shoulders, and the thudding in his chest, as if his heart were trying to dig its way through his rib cage. He focused on his breathing slowly, nine seconds in and then the same out. His anxiety lessened. He found that the warm, sultry scent of orange blossom drifting through the open window helped.

Normally he spent a quiet moment relaxing and drinking in that warm wondrous aroma, but his head was throbbing and it ruined his mood. What's more, like most he hated Mondays, particularly after a rare night out with the lads. He seldom drank these days and had only had one drink but it obviously hadn't agreed with the strict regime of nano-meds being fed through the smarts built into his arm. Resigned to his fate, Seethan swung to his feet and swallowed two tabs from the box on the bedside table, chasing them down with a mouthful of cool water from the beaker beside them. Automatically, he activated his Smart-Arm and looked at the message readout. Hmmm, nothing there that couldn't wait.

Mrs Maskill, his landlady, hammered the hell out of his door. "Seethan, your breakfast's ready. Hurry up or you'll be late!"

"I'll be down in a mo," he replied, stepping naked from his bed and padding towards the shower. Striding into the cubicle he said, "Water on!" As the water hit him he jumped back with a hiss, saying loudly, "six degrees cooler," and the shower complied. Knowing he only had the allotted three minutes before it turned itself off, Seethan quickly washed himself all over and used the remaining time to rinse off. He stepped out and, donning a towelling robe, tapped at his Smart-Arm; staring in resignation at the holographic image of his face that appeared and floated in front of him. He was starting to look old. There were lines on his forehead that he swore hadn't been there yesterday, nor the multitudes of blood vessels that stood out in the borders of his brown eyes.

Rubbing a musky-scented shave gel over the stubble on his jaw, he gave it a few moments and then wiped away the grey residue with a towel, depositing it in the bin where it would break down. Once he'd accidentally got some of the lotion on his scalp, resulting in him having to gel his head completely rather than having a bald spot. With a grin, he stared at his image. Yeah, that would do.

Soon he was dried and dressed, and this time brought up a full-length hologram of himself. A quick command and it picked out any issues in his uniform in semi-translucent bubbles. Thankfully there were only a few. His dark-blue Fleet pilot's uniform was as spotless as always, yet it hung from his gaunt frame as if thrown on as an afterthought. He thought of Rose, wondering what she'd make of it, and then pushed her from his mind. For in this household, theirs was a forbidden love.

Making his way downstairs, he bit back his nausea and kept his eyes averted from the bilious-green carpet. Still trying to decipher his elusive memories of the previous night with a group of ex-shipmates from his old carrier, Seethan took a seat at the breakfast table.

As usual, Mrs M had lied. Breakfast was never ready.

Seeing him collapse into the chair, Mrs M put the slab of pre-packed breakfast into the microwave and his toast into the silver-coloured, retro-rack.

Mrs M added whitener to his tea and, with a wicked glint in her eye, stirred it noisily. She had a helmet-like mass of cotton-white curls above an aged but kindly face, which bobbed as she said "Good morning."

His mother's best friend, she'd taken him on when both of his parents had been killed in an accident, leaving him entirely without relatives while he was still young. The only thing he remembered of them was how the often-heavy hand of his father contrasted with the gentleness of his mother. How his parents had fought, but even now he knew that they had loved each other with a passion that shone like a beacon through the distant memories. His mother had tempered his father's rages with love, coaxing and caring, until finally he echoed her angelic ways, shortly before their deaths. The explosions of inexplicable rage had become less frequent. Like Seethan, he too had been a military man.

Gradually Mrs M had become more of a second mother to him than a friend. Every morning, she wore an embroidered pink silk dressing gown that he'd bought while on deployment to the colonies around distant suns. It heartened him that she treasured it so much, and when he was away on duty, he always visualized her wearing it.

"Anything on the news?" he asked absentmindedly, taking a slurp of the hot but refreshing brew.

"Don't know," she replied. "I haven't looked, what's the point? All we get is bad news about our boys on Halloween. We should lock up those assholes who screwed up the planetary surveys and send *them* back out there. That would teach them to do their job properly. But then again, if the military hadn't gone in so heavy-handed, this trouble would have been avoided."

Seethan knew that there had been problems on the distant planet for some time, and that many of his friends remained on his old ship when it had been sent out there. Quietly he said, "Planetary Survey isn't an exact science, Mrs M, and you have to remember that the inhabitants hid themselves well. But who can blame them for kicking up a fuss? After all, let's face it, we've basically invaded their planet."

Her small frame rocked from side to side, a habit displayed when she was fraught. She jabbed the first finger of her right hand into the place setting in front of him and said, "If the Spooks had made themselves known when we first landed, the colonists wouldn't have set up shop. If you ask me, both sides are to blame."

"Uh-huh," Seethan agreed, around the edge of his mug.

"I still say we should pull out and leave them alone, money isn't everything." The microwave pinged behind her and she turned away swiftly, extracting his breakfast. Peeling back the film covering she deposited the steaming platter of food in front of him. Sitting in the chair opposite, she eyed Seethan as she sipped daintily at her tea.

The aroma of bacon and scrambled egg made Seethan's gorge rise, yet he fought it down and took a forkful. In between bites, his right hand brushed the Smart-Implant on his left forearm, hoping to silence her usual rhetoric. Today's news flickered into a wide, transparent sheen in front of his face, her image outlined through the translucence. Seethan's fingers reached out and pinched at the headline declaring, '*Halloween Horrors! Untold number dead*'. His mouth snapped shut and he dropped the fork that was halfway to his mouth, as his right hand enhanced the feature.

He stood and was instantly in the middle of a ghostly street on Halloween's colony. A plethora of stars glittered overhead and with the biting frost came the acrid stench of smoke billowing from the buildings around him. Then came the roar and crackle of flames, and the crash of collapsing masonry.

Mrs M moved to stand next to him, automatically tightening her dressing gown as together they turned full circle to survey the carnage around them. People hurried past, their faces taut with terror. Somewhere gunfire rattled and people screamed, many of the cries cut short. There was an explosion, followed swiftly by another much larger, and even more gunfire and shrieks. The people were running now, their faces white with terror. The snap and chatter of gunfire sounded closer still, while overhead brilliant beams of energy flashed.

That crisp smell of winter carried an icy, bone-chilling terror that tensed Seethan's muscles to the point of screaming while filling him with dread. Together they stood staring into the darkened streets, lit now only by flames and a few guttering streetlights here and there.

"Look," Mrs M said, clasping her gown tightly as she pointed to a body lying in the snow-covered road. It was fresh, the blood still pooling, and as yet only lightly dusted by the falling ash. "Look what we've driven them to! It's *their* home not ours, we should leave the Spooks to it and find somewhere else to colonise!"

"That won't happen, you know it," Seethan replied. "The

colonisation industry has spent far too much money to let Halloween go now, they'll want to recoup their losses. Politicians cock up, the military clean up. That's always been the way of things."

A convoy of military drones shot past overhead, spitting brilliant beams of blue energy into the darkness as they went. A man on fire staggered towards them from one of the doorways, screaming in agony before collapsing into the snow. He lay there smouldering, just another body in the wintery nightscape.

In the doorway something else moved. It was a deeper shadow in the semi-darkness and Seethan knew that there was someone there.

Some *thing*.

Seethan's hand brushed the air in front of them and the image zoomed in. Dusky and scaled, grey-green fingers curled around the doorframe in the image, and then clenched into a fist before disappearing back into the gloom. Seethan and Mrs M automatically stepped back and took deep shuddering breaths. They could sense it standing there, hidden, somehow feeling it watching them from the shadows – which was impossible, for this was a recording. The ghostly presence might be unseen but its threatening presence sucked the breath right out of them.

The few remaining street lights flickered and went out.

That can't happen, thought Seethan. *They draw power from the sun and the air, how can the lights all go out at once?*

In sudden reflex, his right hand swiped and the scene disappeared. Instantly they were both back in the kitchen, he standing with a plate of bacon and eggs congealing before him and Mrs M's mouth frozen open in an 'O' of shock. When he switched off the display they sat as one. He looked at his breakfast, no longer hungry.

"They should make those silver freaks join the military and send them out there, instead of our boys," the old lady said after a while.

Feeling a twinge of annoyance at the same old argument, Seethan pursed his lips and stared at her. "You already know what my thoughts are on artificial people. They have as much right to a decent life as anyone else. Besides, you know they aren't allowed to fight – people are afraid of giving androids

11

guns, and they fear any battle experience could be turned against us. But let's change the subject, shall we? You can get in serious trouble for calling androids 'silver freaks'. That's racist, and you know it."

"They're just like the immigrants," she pursued. "There are too many of them. Someone should put their foot down."

"You mean the refugees from Enceladus? We have a duty to look out for each other in times of disaster, even if it's on Saturn's moon. Disasters happen all the time, one day we might need help ourselves. What happens then, if we deny others?"

She ignored him.

Just thinking about Enceladus made Seethan shudder. A volcanic eruption and the resulting quakes had breached the dome protecting citizens from the toxic atmosphere and deadly cold. The losses had been catastrophic. He thrust the thoughts away and said, "Besides, my family were immigrants once too."

"They were?" she asked, eyes widening with surprise.

"Yeah. They arrived in England with the Normans."

Mrs M's eyes narrowed and she put her unfinished mug of tea back on the table. The silence stretched and then she changed the subject, as she often did when outgunned. "Out with the boys last night, were you?"

He looked up from the plate to the watery-blue eyes peering intently, as she tried to drag their minds from the horrors of Halloween and Enceladus.

"I heard you fall through the front door when you came home," she added.

"I didn't fall through the door; I fell over the damned cat. I had one drink all night, and that was the first for eight months. You know I can't drink because of the meds I'm on, but it was Carl's birthday and he wanted to celebrate. Let's face it, you're only twenty-one once. Besides, they've been on deployment to the outer colonies and this was their first shore leave since they got back. I may have a headache now, but that's it."

"Don't tell me, Mind Bender?"

"Well, as it happens, yeah, I happen to like Martian ale as you know. I've only been home for a few months myself, and I was away a long time before that. Being back gives me a chance to catch up with old friends when they are on rotation, and I'm not going to let them down if they invite me out."

"Well, just remember what happened to your predecessor, that Cameron fellow. I'd hate that to happen to you."

"Cameron was a fool, I'm not."

They both knew through the grapevine that Seethan's predecessor had tested positive for alcohol and drugs prior to flying. He was lucky that he hadn't been thrown out of the fleet. Instead, Cameron had been demoted and posted outward immediately, leaving a vacancy that Seethan had caught word of and quickly applied for. The fleet was short of pilots, which meant Seethan had been constantly on deployment, until he'd been sidelined for recovery purposes following the crash which had killed everyone but him.

He knew he'd been lucky to survive. Or had he? He often thought of the others who'd been killed, constantly wondering what he could have done differently; after all he'd been piloting. But no-one had known the beam defences were there, and where the rebels had got them from was still under investigation.

His landing the test pilot's position in this Top-Secret programme meant he would be staying on Earth for the foreseeable future, and for that he was extremely grateful. The colonial military were expanding and they were finding it hard to fill the extra billets, particularly with the drain of resources from Halloween. Sure, there were grunts aplenty but trained combat pilots like him were a different matter. Consequently it had been a long time since he'd had leave and, contrary to popular belief that military men soon got over separation from their loved ones, he always missed Mrs M dreadfully. After all she was the only family he had.

Due for rotation, he could have been sent anywhere – from another ship, Mars, to being stationed on Halloween itself. He couldn't help feeling that he should be out there with his squadron, but just the thought of it made his mouth go dry. Here, he was safe. The Spooks were a long way off, but that didn't stop the thought of them scaring the shit out of him.

"Are you going to the art class tonight?" Mrs M asked, brightening.

"If I'm free later, you know what work's like. Sudden overtime, changes in the programme and all that crap. Why?"

"Well, Jillian and I saw an advertisement in the village hall the other day. It was asking for models and she's volunteered. If you do go tonight, you'll be drawing her and she'll be naked."

"Really?" he replied sardonically.

"Come now, Seethan. You need someone in your life. Alan and I are getting closer and I know that you like Jillian, no matter what you say. You can't hide it from me, I know you too well."

He was desperate to tell her about Rose but knew her views on such relationships. She'd be mortified and the rows would go on and on. He took his time before replying, "Not as well as you think. I keep telling you that she does nothing for me. In fact, I can't stand the damned woman. Jill may be a buddy of yours but she's much older than me and, to be frank, she gives me the creeps. So does that neighbour of hers, Sam. They say birds of a feather flock together, but strewth. I feel really sorry for Sam's husband, poor beggar, he always looks very downtrodden."

The mental image of her perched naked on a chair, eying him provocatively as she so often did, flashed in his mind and he repressed a shudder. Despite all his protestations, Mrs M remained convinced that he fancied her, and she was hell-bent on a matchmaking mission.

"You'd better get going, or you'll miss the drone," Mrs M said, changing tack yet again.

Looking at his Smart-Arm, Seethan cursed. Grabbing a triangle of dry toast, he rose quickly and said, "Yeah, I'd better dash. See you tonight."

"At the art class," she replied, a broad and knowing smile breaking over her angelic features.

Seethan leant over and then kissed the top of her head. Toast in his teeth, he grabbed the blue cape of his uniform from the hook by the door. Its hem flirted with the top of his colour-coded boots as he hurried out into the still-early morning streets.

As always, despite the hour, the walkways were jammed with pedestrians. He forced his way through them and soon reached the predictably long bus queue. The lengthy but slender bright-red drones came and went one after another in a steady stream, and before long he was standing at the front of the queue. A slim red 44Q slipped towards him thirty feet above the pedestrians, the few antique cars, and other vehicles that were limited to the ground-level roads. The drone stopped overhead and dropped to hover just slightly in front of him. He practically leapt through the automatic door, pausing only to place his Smart-Arm in the reader. The fare disappeared from his account with a slight vibration in his arm and he dropped into one of the single seats that hung in two rows, facing each other.

Seethan zoned out for a few moments. He gazed blankly out of the window opposite, the tinted glass darkening slightly against the still-rising sun. Before the bus could lift and move on, a silver-clad young woman barged her way aboard and stormed past the pay point.

This should prove interesting, Seethan thought. To his displeasure, the small but chunky woman took a seat directly opposite, chewing gum noisily while glaring at him. Her short silver-dyed hair was slicked back, the colour a perfect match to her clothes and foundation-covered face.

Just what I needed.

The silver body-coverings from hair to boots declared her an Android Rights supporter. The politically-motivated group were a real pain, seeing slights against artificial people where none were intended, and by her glare this one was obviously looking for trouble. The irony that the androids did nothing at all to bring attention to themselves and simply blended into society, seemed to escape the A.R. The issue that worried most people was that androids were now so lifelike that they had to declare their status to unwary suitors. He blanked the young woman and activated his arm, starting to read one of his news apps as it appeared in front of him.

"Whatcha looking at?"

Oh boy, it's going to be one of those days... Seethan swiped to the next page and said nothing.

"I said, whatcha looking at?"

"The news from Halloween, bad as always. I have friends there."

She grunted and, to Seethan's surprise, remained silent for a few moments. He could almost hear the mental clunks as she absorbed his few simple words one by one.

What a great way to start the week, he thought. *If I'm late due to this monochrome clown...* The bus AI burst in on his thoughts.

"Please pay your fare," it demanded loudly of the youth.

The woman ignored it.

"Please pay your fare," the AI insisted, more loudly. "This vehicle will not proceed until payment is received."

The youth huffed as she got up and stalked over to the scanner. Reaching into a pocket, she placed something under the machine's reader and stood back to watch, grinning as she did so. Sparks suddenly flew from the reader and the lights on the bus flickered for a moment before settling down. Satisfied, the youth turned and resumed her seat.

"Problem?" she asked Seethan, one eyebrow raised.

"Not yet," he replied, hiding a smile. He wondered idly where the youth had been, as she was obviously unaware of the government's new AI security protocols. Jail perhaps? It seemed odd to him that someone believing in Android Rights would so casually damage an AI. But then, she didn't seem the brightest person he'd ever met.

There was a loud crackle of electricity and the youth jerked suddenly, the sinews on her neck standing proud as energy spiked from her seat to the ceiling. Her silver-tattooed eyeballs bulged as spittle foamed around her mouth and dribbled down her chin. The noise faded and she slumped into unconsciousness. A few moments later, a police drone lowered behind the vehicle and two silent, surly-looking officers came and dragged the unconscious woman away. The bus rose and they were soon lost in the stream of early morning traffic – mainly drone-cabs, other buses, and emergency vehicles, each hurrying to their relative destinations. A quick glance showed Seethan a long line of buses had formed behind the police vehicle. The crime of public transport disruption would no doubt be added to her list of offences.

Seethan's eyes flickered to the recent black-and-red sign behind the AI's reader that declared in large bold letters, *This vehicle is licenced to take policing action against passengers when needed. Camera recording will be used as evidence in a court of law.* Silver either hadn't seen it, had chosen to ignore it, or was perhaps one of those who couldn't read or write.

He sat back to enjoy the view over the top of most of the dwellings as the buildings and countryside flashed past. Overhead vehicles shot towards their destinations in two fast-lanes, one above the other. They passed fields of golden rapeseed and others of tan-coloured wheat. In the distance he could just make out the white bulk of a huge syntho-meat factory, one of many scattered throughout the country. Like most people, he actually preferred it to the real thing, which could still be obtained at huge expense in many colonies. The fields were soon replaced by the detached houses of the rich, and multiplexes. Entire estates were boarded off and in the process of being demolished; no doubt for eventual replacement by multi-storey accommodation complexes, or converted into farmland to feed Earth's burgeoning population.

Then came the old lake with its loudly complaining ducks, as they battled for bread being thrown towards them by locals and tourists alike. Seethan changed vehicles a few stops later and boarded a Windsor express. Settling down once more, he set the tickle on his Smart-Arm, merging it wirelessly with the vehicle's AI, to wake him at his stop. He closed his eyes, secure in the knowledge that between them they'd wake him in time to get off.

*****

He was back in that street on Halloween, staring down at the body smoking and steaming in the snow. In the dark doorway, something moved. As Seethan watched, claws reached from the shadows and curled around the doorframe. For the first time, he noticed the embers of the something's eyes watching him, locking onto his. It knew he was there; he could sense it. His chest constricted and he struggled to breathe. Blood thrummed like distant drums in his temples. His fists clenched and shook as he tried to make himself move, but his body mutinied and rejected his commands. A moan escaped him as the darkness approached. All he could see were those long claws; and then, quickly, they stretched towards him.

Seethan woke suddenly, a shout dying in his throat. The clawed grip on his arm became the tingling alert from his

Smarts. He turned it off with a tap from his free hand and wiped at the sweat dripping down his brow. It was his stop. From the stares of the other passengers, he must have called out in his sleep. Embarrassed and trembling slightly, he rose, strode from the vehicle and merged into the throng.

Pushing his way through the queues awaiting transport, he made his way down the rubbish-strewn streets. They were packed with people forcing themselves past others who were obviously in less of a hurry, with little or no apology. Overhead video adverts filled the skyline, parts of them blocked from full view by the multi-layered constant streams of traffic that only lessened come late evening. The endless queues for transport were a model of perfection, with passengers given instant fines for anti-social behaviour such as queue-jumping, their identities quickly established via their Smart-Implants and facial recognition.

He walked up the road winding its way around Windsor Castle. There was something romantic about that place. The Royal Family still lived there and were enjoying renewed interest across the colonies, hence the countless tour-drones waiting in long lines overhead. It was a world in stark contrast to the blanket-clad beggars seeking shelter in the shop doorways that he passed, no doubt relishing the instant silence they enjoyed as the premises' sound suppressants deadened the hubbub of society. Almost everyone around him wore monochrome outfits, a surprising number of which were silver like the girl's on the bus.

"You, in the yellow!" a voice bellowed. "Yes, you madam! It's no good pretending you don't know who I'm speaking to, you are being monitored!" It was one of the many police-bots patrolling above head height. "Pick up the rubbish you dropped immediately. Your identity has been confirmed via your Smarts and biometrics. A fine has already been issued to your registered address. Failure to comply this instant will result in further fines, and a summons."

To his right, a middle-aged woman all in amber snarled and stuck a defiant finger up at the bot, only to find herself seized by a burly local security guard who appeared as if from nowhere. She swore and tried to wrestle herself free, while other pedestrians rushed past her like the flow of a river around a rock. Like everyone else, Seethan ignored her as he made his way to an approved drone rank and summoned a cab from the constantly refreshing line.

A bright-yellow drone dropped into place in front of him and the remainder of his journey passed quickly and in relative silence. He could have had music, or a film if he'd wished, but unlike many he much preferred the quiet, gazing in silent reflection at the city passing below. The cab deposited him right outside Rawlings House, tucked away in the outskirts of Burnham Beeches. The imposing black-painted metal gates towered overhead, and he knew he was being scanned as he approached.

"Good morning, Commander Bodell," the gate AI said, automatically opening a small entrance to one side and summoning a buggy to take him the rest of the way up to the house. "There's a chance of rain this afternoon. I see you are wearing a water-repellent uniform with a retractable hood, so you should be fine. Please note that rain acidity will be high today. Appropriate countermeasures are recommended."

"Thanks for the advice," Seethan replied. Making his way through the small security opening, he paused for a few moments while the security apps checked him out and body-scanning micro filaments danced all over him to confirm that he wasn't carrying any hidden weapons. Once through security, Seethan perched on the white artificial-leather-seating of a buggy as it drew up alongside him and then carted him off to the manor.

The house AI scanned him as he arrived: his retina, gait, height, breath, and even his Smart-Arm as an additional measure. Then the imitation wooden front door clicked open, with another, "Good morning Commander Bodell."

He'd always admired the fist-sized brass door knocker in the shape of a lion's head. If he ever managed to afford his own house, which was unlikely here on Earth, he was determined to have one of those.

Inside, there was a small marigold-painted lobby with a metal grille set into one of the walls. Behind it, Felix, the on-duty security guard, sat monitoring the panel in front of him while eating a sandwich. Multi-tasking at its best, Seethan mused.

On seeing Seethan, Felix put down the sandwich and fixed him with a grin. Well past his prime, with snowy hair atop a

19

face that was worry-lined to hell, Felix was one of those kindly souls who appealed to everyone. He'd been fortunate to land the job here and knew it. Luckily Professor Harding, who ran the establishment, had insisted on human security guards due to an old fashioned and deep-rooted suspicion of anything non-human.

"Morning," Seethan said with a twitch of his lips and a half-nod.

"Sir, Professor Harding asks that you go straight up. He's waiting in the study and between you and me, he doesn't sound particularly happy."

"Well, let's just hope that it's nothing I've done. Best I get up there then. See you later, Felix."

"You have a good day, Sir," the man called after him.

The lobby door opened to reveal a wide lime-green-painted room with dark-wood shelving fully spanning two walls. The shelves were filled with books; a mottled brown, old-fashioned marble fireplace stood facing the door. Above that, a valuable antique television mirrored his reflection. He walked through the hall and along to the Professor's office.

Dressed in a brown tweed jacket, white shirt buttoned to the neck, Professor James Harding – Jamie to his friends – was waiting impatiently in one of the large leather armchairs while studying an A4-sized screen on his lap. He looked up as Seethan entered, and glanced pointedly at his watch.

"I had a Holo-Con with the top brass last night," Jamie said in greeting, while remaining seated. "They'll be here in an hour to speak to the both of us. They're insisting we move our timescale forward. Considerably. And, before you say it, yes, I know." Harding made placating motions with his hands. "We still have a lot more tests to do. But they're insistent and, let's face it, they hold the purse strings."

"It's not their life on the line though, is it," Seethan replied, biting his lip. He knew it was no good complaining: whatever the Ministry of Defence decided was going to happen, happened. Snagging a coffee from the percolator in a corner of the room, he sat in one of the armchairs opposite Harding, across a knee-high polished mahogany coffee table. The door to the glass-domed lab was open and, within it, white-coated staff were working in the brooding shadows cast by the bulk of his ship, the Mako. The predatory grey airframe of the

Shark Class ship looked much like its namesake, and just looking at it gave him a thrill every time. The first of its kind, it was his to fly.

Harding had trimmed his goatee but the dark-brown, shoulder-length hair – so straight it could have been ironed – still hung down to his jawline. Those stormy-grey eyes regarded Seethan.

"That's exactly what I told them," Harding said, "but they're insistent. Have you seen the news this morning?" His grey eyes could cut like blades when needed, but now they just looked concerned.

"About Halloween? Yeah, I've seen it. Not good. There's shooting in the streets."

"More than shooting," Harding said, with a shudder. "There's a massacre going on and everyone knows it." His Smart-Arm rang. Answering it, he listened for a moment and then said quickly, "Show them to the meeting room, Felix. We'll be there shortly." He looked at Seethan, "They're here early. Leave your coffee, we'd better go and greet our visitors."

The two men were already seated when Seethan and the Professor arrived. Space Commodore Hayes was a portly fellow with an impressively-curled military moustache. Besides him was the diminutive Perkins, who did something or other for the Ministry of Defence, although nobody seemed to know quite what.

"Glad you're here," Hayes said, as Seethan and the Professor sat. "Let's get straight down to it. We have a bit of an issue with one of the colonies, as I expect you've heard. We need your project up and running ASAP."

"But there are more tests–" began the Professor.

"The reason that we agreed to your project," interrupted the Commodore sternly, "is because we believe in you. We've even loaned you a prototype, an advanced space fighter that no one has and nor should you. Because, by the looks of it, she could be better used elsewhere. In other words, Professor, we've spent a lot of time and resources on you and now we'd like – no, *need* – you to deliver. Now!"

"The Mako will be ready when she's ready, not before," Harding said. "We can't risk taking shortcuts. That could cost us the ship and the crew, if not the mission, and you don't want that to happen, now do you?"

Hayes gave him a disparaging look, and said, "To date, your flight simulations have been excellent and now that your T-Drive has been fitted, we want test flights conducted immediately. Time, gentlemen, is not on our side."

"Since when?" Seethan asked, confused. "And what, exactly, is a T-Drive? I seem to be missing a lot here."

"The Flight Commander has been kept mostly in the dark, as per our agreement," Harding said to the Commodore. Then he addressed Seethan. "The T-Drive was fitted to the ship after you left last night."

"Before we expand on your project," Hayes interrupted, sounding as though he was speaking through a mouthful of gonads, "let me say that the fight on Halloween is going badly, and the drive is our ace in the hole. What do you know of the Halloween colony, and the war going on there, Commander Bodell?"

"Not a lot," Seethan said. "I watch the news feeds the same as everybody else, but that's it. Planetary survey screwed up and we colonised a world we shouldn't have. And, by the sound of it, we're getting our arses kicked."

"A somewhat colourful but accurate assessment," Hayes said, before addressing Perkins. "With your permission?"

Perkins' grey eyes darted from Professor Harding to Seethan and back again, as if he was assessing them.

"We've kept a lot of what's been happening on Halloween from the public," Hayes continued. "But now, the Spooks have gotten into the settlement. It seems that they have the ability to twist people's minds, which means our colonists and marines are now killing each other. No-one knows how the Spooks are doing it, or even who to trust anymore. Halloween's aptly named. The Spooks, or natives if you will, have an art of war that we know nothing about. It's simply horrendous." He opened his mouth as if to say something and then he closed it again, as if he were either lost for words or had thought better of it.

"I've seen the coverage," Seethan said. "So, it's all true?"

Perkins waved the Commodore to silence and when he spoke, his voice was calculating and grating, like that of a gangster from a very old movie. "It depends what you've heard, Commander. Unfortunately, as you succinctly point out, some of what's going on got into the news feeds before we could stop it, damned reporters. You see, the enemy appear to use whatever private fear each individual has against them. If you're scared of dogs, they have a morphology which allows them to adopt the form of a large canine that can literally rip you to pieces. If it's scary tales of ghosts or vampires, they come at you as one of those in the dead of night. Those unfortunate enough to be terrified of clowns could open closet doors to find one of them bursting out with knives in its hands or between its teeth. As for spiders – well, do I need to go on?"

"Clowns..." Seethan interrupted, waving a well-manicured hand. "It's a goddamned circus up there."

Did I really just say that?

"That's not even funny," the Commodore snapped.

"Apologies, Sir. But don't worry, I get the picture," Seethan replied, mentally slapping himself. "And, believe me, I can't imagine anything worse."

"Oh, it's worse, believe me," Perkins added, looking away as he tried to repress a shudder. "Our monitors can't detect them, nor can AI. All we get on the images are people being torn apart by some things we can't see and others we don't want to."

"We've sent more troopships but it won't do us any good. Those survivors down there can't tell what's real and what isn't. Adding numbers will just increase the body count. The long and short of it is we have to bypass some of the *Mako*'s programme. Commander, you're going to begin the flight trials as soon as possible. The stage four test-flights of the T-Drive start with immediate effect."

"You're joking, right?" Seethan gasped. "Shortcuts costs lives. Mine in particular, as I'll be the one flying it. What about all the software?" *Shit*, he thought. *They really are panicking.*

"That," Perkins grated slowly, "is where Rose Mills, comes in. We attached her to you as your non-combatant co-pilot specifically to help with this issue. I understand from the Professor here that she's been working on the ship all night and has achieved astonishing results."

At the mention of Rose, Seethan's next comment died in its infancy as his mouth went dry. Luckily, none of them noticed. The two officials were both looking at Harding, who took his time replying. Over the past few months, the Professor had made it plain that he disliked Rose and wanted her replaced. His dislike of automatons coming to the fore. Luckily, the Admiralty had overruled him.

"Yes," Harding said sullenly. "She has, but there's still the odd glitch to work out. We'll carry out the first test flight tomorrow, at the earliest. Given that the *Mako* is ready."

The Commodore went to say something but, again, Perkins hushed him with a wave of his hand. His eyes narrowed at he stared at Harding. "Very well," he said, biting his words as though chewing a mouthful of glass. "We'll await your updates. Don't let us down, Professor. All of our lives are depending on it."

Chapter 3

Once the two men from the ministry left, Seethan followed Harding into his office and closed the door. He padded over the thickly-carpeted floor and took a seat opposite the Professor's chair as a small airborne drone stopped its chores and served them coffee. The two men watched each other warily for a moment, and then Seethan spoke.

"Want to tell me what's going on here, Jamie? If I'm going to pilot the *Mako* I need to know everything about it. Like, why it's so important to the war."

"I think the word you're looking for is 'imperative'. You may or may not know it but we stand a good chance of losing this damned conflict."

"I suspected as much," Seethan said, "and I guess most of the population do too."

"We think that the Spooks on Halloween have some form of space travel," Harding said, "but what exactly, we have no idea. They're an enigma. When it comes down to it, we know almost nothing about them, or their technology."

"So, tell me about the T-Drive."

Jamie looked straight into his eyes and when he spoke he chose his words carefully, as if savouring them. "The T-Drive was built around a concept of mine. It's in addition to the normal fit and is a time-dilation drive."

"What?"

"I've discovered a way, theoretically, to go back in time. One of the problems is that we've no idea how much of the surroundings will accompany whoever, or whatever, we send back. If someone's standing on a rock, for instance, and that goes with them then there could be one hell of an explosion when two substances try to occupy the same space at the same time. There's the actual displacement of the air and craft itself when the *Mako* reappears, again a probable explosion. That's why we need a vehicle capable of spaceflight and someone qualified to pilot it, so we can carry out the mission in vacuum. Hence your part in all of this."

Seethan picked up his coffee and sipped it, as Harding

paused, but said nothing. After a moment the Professor continued.

"Having the trials conducted from a carrier risks exposure to other members of the crew, and of course probable leakage to the press. A craft operating from the facility here poses no such risk. All we need to do is get the *Mako* up into orbit, engage the drive and Bob's your aunty."

"I thought time travel was impossible," Seethan replied. "What do they call it? Oh yes, a paradox. The argument if we sent someone back in time to kill Pachinko's parents in the twenty-second century, and the assassination attempt was a success, it would mean that in our own time, he won't have been born. Millions would still be alive and Moscow, Simbirsk, and those other cities wouldn't be big holes in the ground. That means there would be no need to go back in time to kill his parents, and therefore he would again come into existence; which flips us back to the original scenario. It's a never-ending circle. How do you get around that?"

"That's the common perception, but what if it's wrong? Using your example, my belief is that by disposing of Pachinko, the timeline will change. The Russian Consortium won't have dissolved into chaos, but is that something we really want? We have to be very careful in using this technology, although in this case it's exactly what we do need. When we send the *Mako* back for this mission it's just a matter of stopping mankind from ever colonising Halloween. If we can do that, and history reboots, then this war won't ever have happened."

"But how do you achieve that?" Seethan asked. "You can't just waltz in and tell people what the future will hold if they don't do as we're telling them. We'd be locked up."

"We should be able to plant information easily enough. After all, thanks to the Commodore's people, I have the encryption codes in use at that time, and so the databases won't be hard to access. We need just enough changes to highlight that Halloween is inhabited by something deadly. The planet would then be put into isolation and out of bounds to all."

Seethan got up and fetched another cup of coffee, knowing he needed to cut back on it. He added whitener, a spoonful of sugar, and stirred thoughtfully. "What of the impact on our 'here and now'?"

Harding leaned back and interlocked his fingers on his lap. "I see time as a piece of string. We can slice it, splice it, and guide it into the direction we want it to go." Harding glanced at an alert on his Smart-Arm, blinking with a pale-purple light through a transparent oval patch that appeared on his sleeve. He raised his arm and read for a moment. With a glance at Seethan he said, "I'm sorry but you'll have to forgive me. I have a message from Rose telling me there are more software issues. We need to resolve them before we can do anything further."

Seethan tried to remain calm at the Professor's sharp, penetrating gaze at the mention of Rose. He didn't know if the man was aware of their recent few dates; if not he certainly wasn't going to apprise the man. Human android relations were a sticky subject in the military as well as society in general, and Jamie hadn't hidden his dislike of her when she had first been assigned. If he found out about their blooming relationship, he might have Seethan replaced. Even Seethan himself was unsure of things, whether to take that step towards a deeper relationship; one that was far more intimate than the few innocent kisses and embraces they'd shared so far. Yet, he already knew that he loved her; what effect would such a revelation have on their lives and careers if it came out?

"You might as well take the afternoon off, Seethan. It's pointless you being here while the glitches are being sorted. If Rose can get it resolved tonight then we can begin those flight trials tomorrow. I'd better go and update our guests from the Ministry before they leave. If they haven't already."

As Seethan stood, Jamie added, "By the way, the chances are we'll be working long hours, so pack a bag and bring it with you tomorrow. You're going to be staying here for a while."

*****

"Hopefully it will only be for a couple of days," Seethan said to Mrs M the next morning. "Just while we get this part of the project completed. I'll be back home as soon as I can."

"They could have let you know earlier," she replied. "If I

had to go into hospital at short notice, what would I do about Major?"

"You're as fit as a fiddle. Besides, that damned cat can fend for himself; the beast's practically a commando. I'd swear he was reading a book when I came down this morning. But if the worst happens, and I'm away, then I'm sure Jillian would have him. You know she adores Major, all you'd have to do is call her.

"Look, I'm sorry about all of this but it's no good being in a strop with me, I don't have any choice in the matter. I'm in the military and if my boss says I have to stay overnight then there's nothing I can do about it."

"I'm not in a strop," she huffed, her back to him as she stiffly busied herself around the kitchen.

"I know it's just your way of saying you'll miss me," he said guiltily. "Well, I'll miss you too. If you want to chat, just call me, or leave a message, and I'll get back to you as soon as I can."

"So, you'll be free to talk but not to come home?"

Seethan closed his eyes, took a few deep breaths and silently counted to ten.

"You need to go or you'll be late," she said, her voice softening. "Just as well the military don't fire people."

"As a matter of fact they do, in a roundabout sort of way. And I'd like you to know that I've never been late. Besides, I'm getting a lift. Rose is picking me up in a work's drone. Saves me carrying my overnight bags on the bus."

"Rose?" Mrs M's eyebrows went up several notches, as her eyes locked onto Seethan. "Jillian will be most interested."

He swallowed and said quickly, "Rose is a work colleague and you know I've mentioned her before. I don't know why you don't listen when I tell you I've no interest in Jillian. In fact, I'd be grateful if you kept her away from me."

Seethan winced as Mrs M drew herself up to her full five-foot-two. He could almost see bright-blue sparks flashing between those tight white curls atop her head. She took a deep breath but before she could say anything, the door chimed, followed by the house AI saying in a loud soulless drone, "You have a visitor."

"Who is it?" Mrs M demanded, bristling but obviously intrigued.

"Identity withheld," and then a 3-D hologram of Rose appeared between them.

"Permit entry." Seethan said, trying to remain calm. Then, in a louder voice, he called through to the front of the house as the door opened. "Come on in, Rose. We're in the kitchen, at the end of the hall."

Mrs M's demeanour changed instantly. "So, you're Rose," she greeted, all warm smiles and politeness. "I'm pleased to meet you. Seethan doesn't say much about his colleagues. Please, take a seat. Can I get you a coffee, or a cup of tea?"

"This is Mrs M," Seethan introduced. "She's really the only family I have."

"Oh Seethan," Mrs M said, flapping a hand towards him. "You're embarrassing me. Do take a seat my dear. What is it you do there, and where are you from? Forgive an old lady her curiosity; it's just so nice to finally meet someone he...works with."

"Pleased to meet you," Rose replied. "No to the drink but thank you anyway. Originally, I'm from Bradbury City back on Mars; and please don't consider me being rude but Seethan's correct. You see, we're not supposed to talk about our work. You never know who's listening."

Mrs Maskill's eyes grew round and this time she flapped both hands, while almost hopping from foot to foot. "Oh, I know dear. Apparently, there could be Spooks anywhere. I think it's only a matter of time before–" she froze in mid-sentence, her mouth dropping open as she espied the silver nail varnish on Rose's hands. She looked up into those challenging green eyes and took two steps back.

Well, that's blown it, Seethan mused, foreboding creeping up on him.

Looking at the old lady in puzzlement, Rose said, "Are you all right? You look pale."

"I...um... Are you one of those android lovers?"

Rose's face fell. "If you're trying to ask if I'm Android Rights the answer is no. If it's *am I an artificial person*, then the answer is yes. Like I said, I'm from Bradbury City. That's where they birth us. Now, if we're done with the unpleasantries perhaps you'll excuse me. Seethan, I'll wait for you outside in the drone." Her pose cried indignation as she turned and stalked away, but not before Seethan saw tears forming.

Androids can cry?

"How...how could you?" he gasped, cutting Mrs M off before she could say anything more. "She's done nothing wrong and can't help being an artificial person. This is exactly why I never discussed her with you before, none of us have a choice of whether we're born or created, it's just luck of the draw. Sometimes I really despair of you."

Mrs M opened her mouth to speak, but Seethan cut her off. "I'm going now. See you in a couple of days." Without another word he picked up his luggage and followed Rose out into the street.

Personal drones were expensive and rare, with most requests denied by the local government in an endeavour to force more people into using public transport. Seethan could imagine curtains twitching in the street outside, and countless eyes following him as he climbed aboard. When the drone climbed into the air a few moments later, Seethan caught a glimpse of Mrs M's ashen face watching them as they joined the streams of traffic heading away from the city.

*****

Dressed in his olive-green flight suit, helmet tucked under his arm, Seethan couldn't help but admire the sleek grey lines of the Shark as he approached it. The word *Mako* was stencilled in a vermillion slash, just rear of the painted-on Shark jaws it had arrived with below the cabin on both sides. Unusually these days, the craft had its flight cabin at the front, with shuttered windows that allowed the crew to fly at high speeds using internal displays only. Most modern combat craft now had the bridge in the centre of the ship, where it was well protected and all the views were digital. But this was a larger version of an older and highly successful model, and her size still didn't allow for much change in design.

He reached up and ran his fingers along the underneath of the craft, almost feeling it purring through the cool tackiness of the radar-absorbent coating. From personal experience, he knew that the *Mako* looked just like a larger version of its Maxtor predecessors. Dark grey, it was sleek with fins either side and at the back. On the Launchpad, with the camo mode turned off, it held a deeply brooding menace that reminded Seethan of a shark waiting to pounce.

At two hundred and forty-feet long, fifty high and wide, the Shark was impressive. When he first saw her, he'd been amazed that there were seats behind the pilots for a pair of mission specialists. Unlike the original Maxtor's. There was also a small area amidships for cooking, and another just aft of that with bunks for resting during long journeys, or for casualties if needed.

When he'd been shot down, he'd been flying one of the Maxtors. He knew that even with the weapon-storage module removed to make way for the drive, the ship still had enough firepower to make a battleship blush. There were mounts for extra weapons beneath the wings and fuselage, although all of them were currently vacant. The main armament of a rail gun beneath the cabin remained, as did the on-board cannons and beam-weapon systems. This ship could seriously kick ass. *Mako*'s whisper engines gave her an extended flight time, sucking fuel from the very air she travelled through with only a small amount of combustibles needed. In space, thermonuclear propulsion kicked in.

A metal ladder protruded from the ship's shadowy underbelly and Seethan paused to watch as Rose's slim, feminine body wriggled down it, her pert backside catching his attention. Clad in a similar outfit to his own, her figure was enough to make most priests discard their collars.

Like him, she had a red commando dagger badge on the top of her left arm, which meant in her case that she'd had the course programming. There was no ship's crest on her left breast pocket, so she'd never been on a ship or in a flight before because aircrew always kept their current squadron's patch until they were drafted to a new air unit. He still had the 660-Squadron patch on his uniform, a Red wolf's head on a black background, as it still remained his parent unit. Besides, he fully intended getting medically fit and re-joining them. In the meantime, this posting would do.

Seethan's mouth went dry and he reddened as Rose turned towards him. A slight smile played over ruby-tinted lips and her emerald eyes glinted with humour.

"Morning, Seethan. You'll be pleased to know the software

problem is resolved. I take it you've come for a good look?"

Seethan remembered the warmth of her body as he'd held her close the last time they'd kissed. God, he wanted her. He swallowed. "I, um, just came to grab you for Jamie's flight brief. It's about time we made our way there."

Her jewelled eyes lingered on his, and then she nodded. "I've finished anyhow. Let's go see what the man has to say."

Seethan's fingers tingled as they touched hers, wanting desperately to clasp her hand as they made their way to the briefing room where Jamie was already waiting.

"Good morning team," Jamie said. "As you know, today's our first test flight. You'll be flying at ten-thousand feet, through Chippenham and on up to Snowdonia. Rose has the coordinates of an emergency landing site, should you need one. There's to be no high-speed manoeuvres, we just want you to see how the *Mako* handles with the new kit on board. Your return flightpath is via Bath."

Seethan knew that the plane was fully automated but for this mission it was hands-on only.

"The weather's fair and there's no anticipated hazards. Camouflage is to be engaged for the duration. We don't want questions raised by the military base at Valley, or from civilian spotters, come to that. On your return you'll report to me for debriefing. Any questions?"

They both shook their heads.

"Good. You take off at eleven-hundred hours, which by my Smarts is in approximately forty-five minutes. See you when you get back." Harding rose, stretched and strode out the door without another word.

"I can see why they call it a brief," Rose said.

Seethan gave himself a mental shake. "Listen, I want to apologise about Mrs M yesterday."

Rose had dropped him off at the front of the building and then taken the drone back to the garage. He'd not seen her since.

"Forget it. I've noticed humans have trouble adapting to change as they get older, and that prejudice is ingrained in your people." Her cascading red locks bounced in disarray as she stopped and turned to face him. "Jamie told you I was artificial when I was assigned. I know he doesn't like my kind, and yet you still found me attractive enough to ask out?"

"Of course, I'm not shallow enough to let such things stop me. Why would I?"

"Yet working this closely with you, let alone forming a relationship, I just think you should have said something to Mrs M. In case of...complications."

"Such as?"

"Her display when we met. What is it about me that attracts you?" Rose saw his eyes drop to her chest before rapidly looking away. She gave a very human snort. "Why is it human males are fascinated by boobs? In the early days we automatons were designed with large breasts and a slim waist, to fit the archetype of the *perfect* female figure. Over time the designers became aware that this had become a red flag and so later models varied in design. That's why they made us able to eat and drink, so that we'd fit in and be more readily accepted."

How ridiculous, Seethan thought. *Many of us are afraid of androids and yet we make them harder to discover.*

"A bonus is that artificial people can now get a lot of the minerals we need through digestion, or we can go without food for a very long time." Her lips curled in a quirky smile. "I take it you're what they call a boob man?"

"Erm, can we change the subject?"

She snorted again. "Let's."

"But just so you know, your status makes no difference to me. You're a very attractive woman."

"And you have the most wonderfully awkward manner," she replied, as they walked on.

Surprised to find that he was embarrassed, Seethan tried to refocus. "I read through the reports this morning. They're all in the green so, all being well, this first test-flight should go smoothly."

"Never say should," she replied.

They stopped in the library before the flight and Seethan made them both a mocha, adding creamer and a single chunk of brown sugar to both, just how they liked it. Rose breathed the aroma in deeply, the bitter chocolatey smell making her nostrils flare. She sank into one of the brown synth-leather chairs and regarded him while holding her mug with both hands, as if warming them. "I read the medical reports about you."

He stiffened and involuntarily took a deep breath. "So much for Medical-In-Confidence."

Rose pouted. "You think such markings would stop me? I need to know who I'm flying with, and you'd do the same in my position, I'm sure."

"Maybe." In a way, he felt relieved that she knew and now it wasn't something he'd have to drop casually into a conversation later on. *Hey, look. I got shot down and everyone else in the crash died, including my best friend's brother.* "I've no ill effect from the crash apart from a few headaches, now and then."

"Not even bad dreams or anger issues? PTSD is easily treated these days, so I understand."

"I get a few of the former, as to be expected, but none of the latter. I don't do anger and everyone gets nightmares, except for androids, I take it. Look, I know the medical board side-lined me so I could be evaluated over a longer period before being returned to frontline duty, but I've gone through the treatments and have passed all the assessments. The fact I'm still flying says as much."

Her small pink tongue danced over ruby lips, as she said, "PTSD is nothing to be ashamed of. Shit happens. And, like you say, you've kept your flight status. It also explains why someone of your combat experience is working on a project like this, which is what raised my interest in the first place."

Seethan said nothing, only watched as she sipped at her drink.

"I remember the news about the crash when it happened," she continued. "You're lucky to have walked away from it in one piece. Being shot down and losing your friends must have been really awful."

"Something like that." He glanced at his Smart-Arm. "It's time, see you on board." He felt her eyes following him as he walked through to the hangar. Even now he still found it difficult to talk about what had happened and often diverted his attention to something else.

Now, was it his imagination or was she wearing an apple blossom perfume?

*****

Seethan gritted his teeth as he tightened the safety harness across his shoulders and thighs. Beside him Rose slid into her seat and did the same, giving him a thumbs up and a grinning sideways glance. Together they worked through their pre-flight routine and then looked up through the canopy as the hangar roof slowly opened like an iris. He glanced over the familiar controls one more time and looked at Rose.

"Check?" he asked

"Check."

He pressed the ignition, listening as the plane's whisper engines kicked into life with a gentle sigh.

"Control, this is *Mako*. We're all set to go. Request permission to take off," he said.

"Permission granted." Jamie's voice was calm and collected over the air control frequency.

"Rose, that scent you're wearing is lovely." When she smiled it felt like a heavy weight had fallen through his stomach and he found himself smiling back.

"Humans have pheromones, so our designers thought we should too. But unlike humans we can adjust ours to suit. It's helpful in many ways, for calming people down for instance. As for me, I like that smell."

"Well, it certainly suits you."

She was silent for a moment and said. "You don't know much about androids, do you."

It was a statement not a question, and one that Seethan had to agree with. He'd thought he knew as much as he needed to and it wasn't an area he'd really studied. Sure, he followed the news on AI development but that was about it. "I guess. Why?"

"Did you know, for instance, that we can bleed as well?"

He stared at her. "You're shitting me!"

"No, I'm not. Our creators believed it would help us blend in. If you cut us our 'blood' is designed to look just like yours. It's not of course, and a quick analysis would show that, but it's only there for the eyesight. Females can simulate menstruation too, if they want to."

"That's far too much information," he muttered.

"Men! You build us to look and act like you, yet when we

do so you're grossed out!"

"Let's change the subject, shall we?" Seethan said, focusing on his displays. He closed the shutters to the outside world and engaged the camo, the craft instantly disappearing from the view of those watching.

The active camouflage coating on the ship's skin displayed what was on the opposite side of the craft as if it were a screen, fed by micro-cameras across the ship's hull. For any practical purposes, the craft was rendered invisible. When he was ready, Seethan pulled on the control stick and the craft rose slowly through the opening hangar roof. He knew that with the camo, low-radar and near-nil infra-red signatures, the vehicle was very difficult to detect despite her bulk.

With only the downdraft to show for their presence, the *Mako* rose slowly to start with, gathering speed until it reached 1500-metres, the hangar seeming to sink into the floor before disappearing entirely. Seethan tipped the nose skyward and the craft accelerated smoothly, her contrail-free engines leaving no sign of their passing.

"Oh baby," Seethan said, feeling the rush of adrenaline, "I think I'm in lurrrve. What a ride! She's just like her forebears, smooth as a kitten's fur."

He heard Rose's barking laughter from beside him and, from then on, the day just got better.

*****

Mrs M looked at him primly from the handheld tablet in Seethan's room, answering the moment he called.

"Jillian was most put out that you didn't make it to art class," she said, as if chewing her words. "Says she got cold for nothing." She paused for a moment, her lips moving silently as if she were undecided what to say. Finally, "Seethan, listen. I want to apologise for upsetting you when your colleague picked you up. You know how I get over those silver freaks. For one of them to come into my home uninvited–"

"She's not a freak, nor is she silver, and you know damn well that I invited her," he snapped angrily.

"Her fingernails are silver," she replied tartly. "And she's an android. She told me so herself, you were there."

"For what it's worth, she's a very good friend of mine." He wanted to say more but now wasn't the time.

"How can an android be a friend, when they're not even human? I think you're giving them far too much credence, Seethan."

"I need you to listen to me. I'm sick and tired of your bigoted attitude. Unless you change your ways, sooner or later, you'll end up arrested and charges along those lines carry a lengthy jail sentence." He took a deep breath. "What I'm saying is I love you and I owe you. We're family, but I won't let you interfere with my colleagues and friends. Or be rude to them for that matter. Society has changed, you have to accept it."

"Jillian said much the same thing when I spoke to her about it," she admitted.

"Good grief. Well, that's the first intelligent thing that woman has said. I know you're trying to pair us off but, please, just listen to me. Try to understand, I don't like her! She must be at least thirty years older than me and her skin looks like it could do with a damned good iron. Her breath smells. She's conceited, and has no sense of humour. But, for you, I'll try to get on with her; if you'll remember what I've said. Deal?"

Mrs M licked her lips.

Seethan stopped reaching for his glass of iced water. His eyes narrowed and he focused on her more intently. "Something's bothering you, what is it? No good denying it, you always lick your lips before dropping a bombshell."

"I bought Alan some of that Sea Salt aftershave that I like on a man. He wears it all the time now, and smells gorgeous. It makes me go weak at the knees."

"That's far too much information, thank you; and he smells like Portsmouth Harbour when the tide's gone out. But never mind all that; come on, out with it."

She swallowed nervously. "Alan proposed to me last night. We're getting married! Isn't that marvellous?"

Seethan stopped himself from snapping a retort he knew he'd regret. "I'm...stunned. Sorry, I'm very pleased for you, but you've only known him a short while."

"Long enough. Eight months, a little more. Can you imagine? Me, getting married. And at my age, too. Will you give me away? I'd like the three of us to get together, maybe over dinner. We can discuss it all then. Have you any idea when they'll let you come home?" The questions came thick and fast.

Seethan forced a smile and held up his hands. If she could make an effort with Rose then he could with Alan, even though he despised the man. "I promise I'll call as soon as I hear, and we'll see."

After they said their goodbyes, he turned the tablet off and put it down. Of course he could have called her from his Smart-Arm, but the screen was larger on the tablet and that made it more personal. He looked up to find his bedroom door ajar, and Rose stood there watching him.

"You missed your calling," she said. "You should have gone into politics."

Chapter 4

Seethan woke drenched in sweat, heart beating wildly. His eyes flicked to the comforting, warm, green glow of his alarm clock; it was 03:00. He could never remember his nightmares, but maybe that was a good thing. Automatically, he went into a well-worn routine to calm himself. He slowed his breathing while counting from one to ten, and breathed back out again for the same duration.

He visualised his safe place: a white sandy beach upon a small uninhabited island in the Indian Ocean. He'd visited it once, in times gone by, and the heavenly memory had stayed with him. Focusing, he imagined the pull of the oars as he rowed to the island. The grating of the boat on the sun-kissed white sand. Him splashing through the warm water to secure the boat with a painter and anchor. Digging it into the sand to ensure it wouldn't drift away, and leave him there stranded. Content, he headed towards a path weaving its way from the sand into the jungle.

What five things could he see? An occasional white cloud in the deep-blue of the sky, palm trees, bushes all around. The well-worn path, birds of brilliant colour fluttering back and forth amidst the foliage.

Four: things he could hear. The musical tinkle of running water from the stream flowing alongside the path. The constant music of birdsong, the rush of waves on the shore, and the soft pad of his footsteps.

Three: touch. Reaching out, he could feel the smooth deep-green rubbery leaves and the chill fresh water of the stream with his fingertips. A warm breeze traced kisses down his cheek and neck.

Two: smell. There was the hot and damp musk of the jungle around him; the distinct heady fragrance from the orange petals of Mu Lan flowers.

One: taste. He took a mint from his pocket, peeled the wrapper, and popped it into his mouth and begun sucking at it.

He was at peace.

As Seethan focused on his breathing and safe place, the

pounding in his chest subsided. After a time he rose, put on a dressing gown and went downstairs. He eyed the toaster with a grimace and decided against a warm snack, knowing that as usual he'd likely cremate any such attempt. Instead he settled for a hot herbal drink and a handful of biscuits from the battered ceramic container on the side. The honey and lemon drink would help soothe him. By four he was back in bed, slowly and deliberately thinking of pleasant things, until at last sleep claimed him once more.

The alarm woke Seethan at seven, and he fought against the urge to throw his last surviving clock out of the window. He'd better buy some more, and take the shattered remains of the previous ones to the bemused Chinese vendor downtown, who could repair or source just about anything.

Thankfully the cascade of hot water from the shower revitalised him and chased away the vestiges of terror from last night's dreams. Once dry, he activated his Smart-Arm. Unlike his friends and colleagues, he turned his Smarts off at night, knowing full well that the vibration and flickering light from a received message would wake him. Now, a small violet light blinked slowly, indicating a message in his queue.

"Whatever it is, it can wait," he grumbled, surprised to see it was from Steff, a pilot in his old unit. They'd known each other since flight school, but the last time they'd seen each other was shortly after the crash. Steff, mad with grief, had screamed in his face and had tried to hit him before being dragged away. They'd not spoken since and the last thing he wanted after last night was a further diatribe from his former friend. Dressing quickly, he made his way downstairs.

Mrs M put a mug of tea in front of him as he sat, and slid a tray of food into the microwave. "Have you seen the news?" she asked.

"Not yet,"

"I think you should take a look."

His interest piqued, Seethan stood and tapped at his Smart-Arm and shared the page.

Halloween Nuked! Battle Rages Above Planet, the headlines shrieked.

"Holy shit!" the words slipped out before he could stop them, but for once Mrs M didn't chastise him.

"Horrible," Mrs M said. "Those poor, poor people." Tears

glinted in the corner of her eyes and she dabbed at them with a towel as she spoke.

Something pinged; the microwave, Seethan realised. For the moment they both ignored it.

With another tap on his Smart-Arm they were both standing on the bridge of the *Colossus*, the carrier on which he would have been serving right at this minute had he not been medically downgraded. All around them, the crew were busy at their consoles. Orders were shouted, lights flickered, and there was the constant background murmur of conversation familiar to all who'd served in such environments. On the bulkhead facing them lay a huge screen depicting shifting scenes from the surface of the forest-covered, mountainous planet. They watched silently, as semi-transparent, bud-like orbs of constantly changing colour rose from the planet's surface and drifted leisurely towards the orbiting fleet. The impression was much like a fall of petals in a sudden wind. A two-tone alarm sounded throughout the ship, followed by a bellowed announcement over the loudspeakers.

"Hands to action stations, hands to action stations! Enemy ships incoming! Hands to action stations!" The announcement came twice and then ceased, followed quickly by the pounding of feet and slamming of airtight hatches. The murmur around them grew, as crew and stations reported in.

Seethan's chest began to pound, He felt a rush of adrenalin and forced his tensing muscles to relax. He knew that he wasn't there. This wasn't him; it was his friends and crewmates. He was here, safe in the kitchen. But he also knew with bitterness that he should be among them. To his horror, the screens showed several of the outlying escorts wobble and suddenly turn to engage their fellow ships.

"What the hell…" Seethan gasped, watching in disbelief as the fleet responded immediately, as if they had expected this possibility. The rogue ships' railguns took out two frigates and an assault ship, and badly damaged the *Triumph* – a sister ship to *Colossus*. The *Colossus* herself lurched as they took a direct hit. On the damage control display to their left, compartments briefly flashed vermillion and then changed to a steady orange, which he knew represented hard vacuum. From a second look at the control board, he realised with relief that the damage wasn't as bad as it first looked: the ship would survive.

The pair of them watched in horror as gas, debris and human bodies vented from the broken vessels around them and only minutes later their attackers suffered the same fate. A few of the now-hostiles blew themselves up even as they were engaged; while others were quickly pummelled into scrap metal, plastic, and lumps of human flesh.

He watched silently. Beside him Mrs M fidgeted from foot to foot, as the fleet turned their attention from the compromised vessels to the incoming enemy ships. Projectiles from the railguns, missiles and beam weapons passed straight through the bizarre, now lilac-coloured, silhouettes. Seethan and Mr M could only watch in horror as the vessels merged with the nearest human ships. Behind the panicked reports from the breached ships could be heard screaming, gunfire, and then silence. Those ships too turned their weapons towards the main fleet. Suddenly, each of them exploded, as if in a last defiant act by a few remaining sane members of their crews.

Seethan knew many people on those ships. The fact he was now watching them die, and there was nothing he could do about it, tore at his soul.

"Adopt Xray One. I say again, Adopt Xray One." Admiral Woodward's voice over the loudspeakers galvanised the crew into action. The man's hand hovered over a pad for a moment, his DNA and other security readings authenticating his orders. In response, a swarm of projectiles spat towards the planet's surface.

Seethan watched in horrified disbelief as nuclear explosions lit the surface of the planet, his fists clenching and unclenching as if he were strangling someone. "They must be out of their minds!"

The news feed switched to a long-distance view of the fleet in chaos, with ships engaging others with little or no warning. The display cut out and they were standing once again in Mrs M's kitchen. A misty outline of the carrier's bridge flickered on and off around them, as they stood there stunned.

A follow-on broadcast burst into life and they were suddenly back on the *Colossus*. Violent orange blooms flared on the screen image of the planet in front of them, making those observing shield their eyes. It was like watching an erupting plague of boils. A man's voice spoke calmly over the images, each word carefully clipped.

"Due to heavy losses incurred by our forces on Halloween, nuclear, biological and chemical weapons have been used against targets on the planet's surface. There are no reports regarding casualties but they are suspected to be heavy. Relatives have been contacted and we ask that they be left in peace at this time.

"There has been no response to our constant attempts to communicate with the aliens. With our standard weapons having no effect, the Ministry of Defence has stressed that they had little choice but to take all necessary action to try and prevent this catastrophe from spreading further afield. Earth and the colonies' safety are paramount, and all efforts will be taken to ensure it. This is Bob Umh from World News, signing off."

Only the ache in Seethan's backside told him that, somehow, he'd sat on the edge of his chair, muscles tense. He eased back slightly and met Mrs M's tear-laden eyes, as she sat opposite and looked back at him with her bottom lip quivering.

"Why…why did our own ships attack us?" she gasped, her words coming in shuddering sobs.

He shuffled his chair around and held her close, burying her snuffles against his shoulder. "I guess they were taken over by the Spooks. Maybe their minds were twisted and they were made to believe that the rest of the fleet were the enemy. Who knows? But by the swift response, I suspect the Admiral anticipated it. Some of the senior officers must have had kill switches with them, just in case."

It was then that Seethan remembered the message waiting in his queue. Hell, Steff had been on The *Colossus*! He looked at the date on the message and said, "Damn it, this is days old!" Expecting more ranting from his former friend, he took a deep breath and activated the message. He listened to it in private mode for a few moments and then shared it with Mrs M. They watched together in dread as Steff's face appeared and floated before them. The message ended with Steff Phillips facing the ice-rimmed open doorway, gun in hand.

They turned to look at each other.

"Do you think he survived?" she asked.

"You're kidding, right?" Seethan snapped, before taking a deep breath and saying more softly, "If he even got through that in one piece, the base would have been one of the first places hit. There's no way any of them got out."

"I'm so sorry."

"The one he's talking about, Pete, he was Steff's brother. He was my co-pilot when we were shot down – he died in his seat beside me. The last time I saw Steff, he was grief stricken and trying his damnedest to kill me. I hoped we could make it up but I guess it's too late now."

Before either of them could say anything else, the kitchen door opened and Alan Wong walked in. He scraped a chair across the grey-stone floor and took a seat to the left of Seethan, arranging as he always did a small crystal vase of buttercups and daisies to the left of his setting. "Where's my tea?" he asked bluntly.

Seethan had asked him once why he liked the display of common garden weeds beside him at meals, finding it a bit odd. Alan had replied that weeds were just flowers that grew unwanted, in places planned for other things. He was short, with tightly-trimmed brown hair and cool olive eyes; his jaw was square, nose misaligned. When he opened his mouth, you could see broken and rotting teeth; but it was the man's sour demeanour that rankled Seethan, who eyed him in disbelief at this sudden early morning appearance. Seethan looked inquiringly at Mrs M, who blushed and looked away.

"Hello, laddie," Alan said, a half-smile on his face.

"Morning," Seethan replied stonily. "Sleep well?"

"Not really, I was up and down all night. You know what it's like."

"No, actually I don't."

He could see the anxious set of Mrs M's shoulders, as she stood and prepared Alan's breakfast, with her back to him. She didn't meet Seethan's eyes as she turned and placed a mug of tea in front of Alan.

"We were up until late," she said quietly, "so Alan asked if he could stay over."

"Not a problem, is it?" Alan asked, his eyes calm yet challenging.

"Not in the slightest. Mrs M's choice of guest is up to her," Seethan replied, as she went back to her chores and fussed away behind him. He stood and turned to the door, giving himself a moment to try and deal with this new turn of events. Mrs M deserved happiness, but he doubted she'd even get it with Alan. He caught a movement from the corner of his eye, as Alan pointed his teaspoon at him.

"You should never stand with your back to a lady. Didn't your father teach you anything?" Alan said.

"He died when I was young. They both did and you know that."

Mrs M placed the breakfast where Seethan had been sitting and went to say something. Seethan shook his head and declared he was no longer hungry. She looked at him sorrowfully but said nothing. Seethan walked around the table and embraced her again, planting a gentle kiss on her snowy curls. He was heartened by a return peck on his cheek, but noted she still avoided his gaze.

"Don't forget I'll be staying over at work for a few nights again, what with working late and so on," he said. "I'll let you know when I can come back. Take care."

Chapter 5

For the next three days at Rawlings House, they conducted a mixture of simulated and real flights. For most of them Seethan's head was buried in an all-encompassing black helmet, which gave him the appearance of a nightmarish insect. Sitting in a pilot's seat, and wirelessly connected, his hands moved over virtual controls as he 'flew' the aircraft.

Turning his head from side to side, he could literally see through the aircraft as if it weren't there, via the same micro-cameras that provided the ship's camouflage. The virtual ship rocketed over landscape generated by space-based, real-time cameras, making it seem incredibly real. Some trials turned into simulated combat missions, despite it being designated a taxi-drive there and back.

One of the problems they faced was that Rose's generation of artificial people hadn't been designed during their target time period. Therefore, she would flag up immediately should she be exposed to any of the many security systems, which was highly likely. Seethan, however, had been in the military at that time and so he already had the clearances needed to gain access. The fact his biometrics were already in the military databases made things easy. In other words, he had every right to be there, and so it was him who had to physically access the base and change the data.

Rose's primary role was co-pilot and to operate the T-Drive. Additionally, she could carry out any repairs needed. All Seethan had to do was fly there, drop the electronic package into the survey database, hightail it back to the ship, and fly home. Simple.

"What about the *Mako*?" he'd asked Jamie. "The ship was still on the drawing board then. She's bound to be noticed."

"You'll be in Camouflage mode for the duration, more advanced than what they have and practicably invisible," Jamie had replied. "But if you're challenged, Rose has all the aircraft codes and the *Mako* will have the signature of a standard Maxtor, which they were already using. Every mission holds risks, but do this right and you could easily be in and out in under an hour. If all goes well, when you come home there'll be no war."

"If it's going to be that easy then why the weapons practice?" Seethan had asked.

"Because you'll be flying with a standard complement of weapons, just in case. Hopefully you won't need them, but this morning the MOD raised Earth's threat level to red. All combat-capable craft are to remain fully armed at all times."

Seethan had stared at him. "That's kinda worrying. I've never heard of that happening before."

The Professor only nodded, tight-lipped. Dismissed, they'd continued with the training until the next day, when Seethan and Rose were summoned to an urgent meeting with Professor Harding.

"I just had a call from Commodore Hayes," Jamie said. "He asked me to brief you on the latest developments. There have been losses, terrible losses."

Seethan raised an eyebrow, but said nothing. He knew that the 2nd Fleet had been recalled to the Earth system to augment defences, but that was it.

"The *Colossus* and other ships we had orbiting Halloween are gone. Those that survived the battle were apparently heading home to Earth and ignoring all communication attempts. Consequently, they were classified as either rogue or hostile. Picket elements of the 4th intercepted them and were fired upon. They responded in kind, taking them out. I'm told that those same pickets were…excised in turn. Just to be safe."

Jamie gasped. "They killed our own guys?"

"They didn't have any choice. There's a good chance that they weren't ours anymore."

"Any survivors?"

The Professor shook his head. "None. What makes it worse is that we're unable to raise the last ships standing. All communication with the vessels involved has been lost, hence the red alert. Everyone's worried and, to be honest, so am I.

"We can't seem to stop them, Seethan. Everything we send gets taken over or destroyed. Even drone ships. We're out of time. Hayes wants our mission bought forward to the day after tomorrow, which only gives us a small window to clear up any outstanding issues. He only gave us that long because

I insisted, we need it to have even a chance of success. Talking of which, you have another simulated flight in forty minutes. Full rehearsal. Take off from here up to orbit and back down again. Tomorrow morning there's a simulation, and in the afternoon a full test flight. The day after that, it's a go."

"We don't get a chance to test the T-Drive?" Rose asked.

"We don't have time. It's a one-off shot: either it works or it doesn't."

*****

Seethan was now sitting in an armchair in his room, rubbing the back of his head, eyes closed. He ached all over, particularly around his shoulders. Above all, he was tired. The morning's simulated flight meant his body reacted and tensed as it would in a real-life situation. As expected, there had been power losses and an on-board fire had been thrown into the works, all efficiently dealt with by Rose.

It had led to the loss of camo and an unexpected combat situation with three standard Maxtors. After downing one of the simulated attacking craft, he'd made a break for it, safely achieving high orbit with the remaining two fighters close behind. Launching drones had distracted his pursuers' missiles, while he'd randomly jinked the *Mako*. Choosing his moment carefully, he'd launched air mines, which had taken care of the final two fighters. Finally, they'd reached target altitude and managed to activate the virtual T-drive, and escape further combat.

Jamie had been pushing their boundaries and, as he'd promised, this afternoon he'd programmed in a real-time flight. They'd flown up and around Cape Wrath in the north of Scotland, for a weapons shoot. The railgun had blown a hulk completely out of the water, with their other systems taking down combinations of various craft. Now, he closed his eyes and drank in the rich, chocolatey aroma of freshly-percolated coffee that he'd collected from the library, and tried to relax in his room. Tomorrow, they were a go.

He'd tried reading a book on Cognitive Behavioural Therapy as part of his recovery, but had struggled getting into it. It was about reliving the events that affected you. By doing so it was supposed to allow him to file down the memories of the stressful events that remained stuck in his mind, giving him the flashbacks and nightmares. He knew most of it already, so it had been hard going. Halfway through, he'd filed it in the paper-bin by his bed.

He was half-asleep in the chair when someone knocked loudly on his door, jerking him awake. He shouted for whoever it was to enter. Jamie opened the door and came in, leaving it open. His face was ashen.

"What's up, Jimbo? he said, standing up. "You look like you've seen a ghost."

"The police are here. They want to see you but won't tell me why." He stood aside from the open door as Seethan climbed to his feet, and a middle-aged man and woman, both plain-clothed and eyes intent on him, flashed IDs as they entered the room.

"I'll leave you to it," Jamie said, closing the door behind him after the policeman turned and stared at him pointedly.

The man stayed by the door while the well-dressed and somewhat portly woman moved to stand in front of him.

"You're Seethan Bodell?" she asked.

"That's me. Have I done something wrong?"

"Please, sit down." She pulled the second chair closer and sat in front of him. "I'm D.I. Wilson, this is Detective Constable Williamson."

The man nodded a greeting.

"What's all this about?" Seethan asked, his eyes flicking from one to the other. He hadn't had the greatest experience with cops, and here were two of them. Both with surnames beginning with W, which was about right.

"When was the last time you saw your landlady, Mrs Maskill?"

"A few mornings ago, at breakfast. Why?"

She glanced at her companion and he gave a slight nod. Then Wilson said, "I'm afraid we've some bad news for you. Your landlady, Mrs Maskill, is dead. She's been murdered."

Seethan was on his feet in a second, followed by the officer facing him. "What? Murdered...by who?"

"She was found by a friend of hers, a Jillian Mitchell. It was her who called us. A man was recorded leaving the scene earlier today and was arrested shortly afterwards. Luckily, we were able to track his movements and intercept him en route to the spaceport."

"Are you talking about Alan?"

"Look, I know this is a shock but we'd like to ask you a few questions," she said, avoiding the question.

He nodded, feeling numb and light-headed.

"Professor Harding says you've been here for three days. Is that correct?"

"Yeah, we've been working non-stop on a military project; and before you ask, sorry, but I can't discuss it. Official Secrets and so forth. If you have any questions you'll have to go through the Professor and then the Ministry of Defence, but security will be able to confirm my presence here. We've been working until late and it requires that I stay over. Listen, are you going to tell me or not? It was that son-of-a-bitch Alan, wasn't it."

"What makes you say that?"

"He was there when I left home the other morning. He'd been there all night. They were getting close, apparently."

"All I can say is that it's the man you call Alan who we've taken into custody. I've told you that because we'd like you to come with us down to the station and identify him. Is that all right?"

"This isn't good timing and I'll need to check with Professor Harding," Seethan said, "Things here are at a difficult stage. He'll need to clear it."

"Thank you, we won't take much of your time I promise. Hopefully we'll see you outside in the drive, when you're ready."

Jamie knocked and came in as they left. "Can I ask what's going on?"

Seethan told him and, reluctantly, Jamie gave a couple of hours' leave.

*****

At the tall brooding station, a grey-bricked throwback to a bygone age, Seethan stood behind a screen and eyed the line-up. He quickly identified Alan, who stood out so easily he may as well have been painted blue. The man's image was ingrained on Seethan's mind, due no doubt to their mutual dislike. Afterwards Detective Wilson sat him down and bought him a cup of coffee, watching him silently for a few moments as he sipped the hot brew, lost in his thoughts.

Apart from two blackish cloth-covered chairs facing him across a wooden desk, there were just a couple of mismatched antique filing cabinets in the room. Wilson's desk was suspended above the floor at about waist height, and in one corner of it a solitary goldfish conducted a lonely and endless patrol in a bowl a half-metre or so wide. Apart from that, and a dark full-length coat hung on a door hook, the office lacked personalisation.

For some reason he found himself focused on her lilac body-suit, and the slightly lighter tee-shirt visible at the top. He shook himself and asked the policewoman, "Has Alan confessed?"

"He doesn't need to. What do you know about him?"

"Only that he's a prejudiced twat who's been dating Mrs M for a few months, and that things were starting to get serious. What do you mean, he doesn't need to?"

"Let me ask the questions. Prejudiced, in what way?"

Seethan bit back his temper, knowing she was only doing her job. "He hates androids. Keeps saying they should be banned and that things are going to change. He came over as some kind of political activist."

Her large brown eyes regarded him and she sucked in her cheeks, before releasing her breath with a soft groan. "That's so God-damned weird."

"Why?"

She breathed out heavily, as if considering whether to tell him or not. Finally, she came to a decision. "It turns out Alan Wong is an artificial person himself."

"You're shitting me!"

"Nope. What many people don't know is that androids record all they see and do, and those recordings are stored online. We have access to those recordings, which is why he doesn't have to admit to killing Mrs Maskill. We know he did it, because we watched him do it through his own eyes."

Seethan tried to brush the image from his mind.

"Are you okay?" Wilson asked.

"Yeah, I guess so."

"More coffee?"

He shook his head. "Can you tell me what happened?"

"It's so bloody hard to tell androids from real people these days," she said. "They eat and drink as we do, defecate, and can have sexual relations with humans. Everyone knows that, before any physical relationship, by law they're supposed to disclose their android status. But it appears Alan didn't do so. From what we understand, your landlady discovered what he was and threatened to disclose the information to members of his political group. Ironically that group's dedicated to ridding society of, as they put it, the 'android menace'. He couldn't risk that exposure and so he killed her." She paused for a moment and breathed noisily through her nose.

There was a slight hiss and vapour rose from small openings at either end of the desk. He could smell lavender and knew it was a standard ploy of the police to use smell to relax interviewees.

"From the information we've gathered from his online records, he's already executed twenty-seven androids."

"And this didn't flag up?"

"Why would it? Androids aren't monitored as a matter of course. Many of them shut down after a certain amount of time due to the limited lifetimes of the earlier models, and it's rarely looked into."

Seethan stared at her, unable to take it all in. "I've got to ask this, but is killing an android a criminal offence? If so, wouldn't it be classified as murder?"

"Those are good questions. At the moment, terminating an android isn't a crime but there's a movement to make it so under android rights. Currently you can only be prosecuted for destruction of property. We can only imagine that by terminating other androids he was trying to make himself look more human to the members of his political group."

She hesitated. "But there's more. In addition to your friend, Mrs Maskill, he's also killed other humans. Nine that we count at this moment in time. One way or the other, we've got him."

"You're telling me that thing's some kind of a serial killer?"

Her head dipped. "Looks like it. If you add up all of his victims it totals thirty-six. His online storage shows study of numerous serial killers throughout the ages. What we can't figure out is whether he's insane and if androids can ever be classified as mad. If so, how do we deal with it? There's another thing."

"What?" Seethan asked. He felt light headed, still trying to process everything. *Mrs M... Gone?*

"We've spoken to the Home Office and they've told us that this information is to be sealed. We can't afford for it to get out. If people discover what androids are capable of, despite their programming and Asimov's Law, we'll have a worldwide panic. There will be chaos on the streets, and not just on Earth's."

She swallowed, and her brown eyes stared straight into his. "I've shared this with you because of the circumstances, and also because as a member of the military you're bound by the Official Secrets Act. This comes under it."

"In other words, I need to keep my mouth shut." Seethan shrugged. "Anything else?"

"Yes, don't go home. It's a sealed crime scene. We'll let you know when you can collect anything you need. I take it you'll be staying at the Professor's in the meantime?"

"Yeah, I'll be there if you need me. Can I ask how she died?"

"He broke her neck, and I'm told it would have been quick. I know this sounds trite but I'm truly sorry for your loss. The only positive here is that this scumbag is off the streets. He can't kill anyone else."

"Really? According to rules and regs he shouldn't have been able to do this in the first place. The safeties are inbuilt. If one of them can kill, what's to stop others doing the same thing? That's what really worries me."

"Mr Bodell, just thinking about that is going to give me nightmares."

"I want to talk to him before I go."

Her eyes widened and she leant back in her chair that gave a slight moan under her weight. "I don't think that's–"

"Surely he has the right to speak to a confidant the same as we humans do. Ask him. Now."

"Are you sure?"

"Make it happen."

"I'll be back in a moment." Pushing back her chair, Wilson left the room, returning a few minutes later looking somewhat surprised. "He's agreed and I've arranged for him to see you in an interview room. There's a plasteel partition, so you can see and speak to each other but he can't harm you. Please, follow me."

As she led the way out of the office, Seethan said to her, "Are you sure he can't get through the partition? Androids are as strong as hell. I've heard they can tear alloy sheets like paper."

"Even they can't get through plasteel," she replied reassuringly, as they walked along a series of corridors and stopped at a door marked 'Interview Room Three'. "The android is in a secure unit and watched at all time. I'm sure that I don't need to tell you that everything you say and do in there will be recorded."

When he didn't respond, she opened the door and closed it behind him after he went in. Seethan sat on a plain alloy chair, at a desk facing an opaque-brown screen. On the desk, a light went green. He followed Wilson's instructions, coming through hidden speakers, and pressed the only button on the desk. Instantly the screen cleared, leaving a transparent barrier that he knew was there but couldn't see. On the other side Alan Wong sat facing him, smiling like the proverbial cat who'd got the cream.

"Hello, laddie."

"Laddie?" Seethan snorted. "You're not human, how would you know what *laddie* even means?"

"Ah, they told you." Alan's face went cold, his cool olive eyes watched Seethan like those of a snake poised to strike.

"I suspected something wasn't right with you. Maybe it was your mannerisms, everything about you screamed out at me, but Mrs M wouldn't listen. What I don't get is why your face is as ugly as it is. Androids are supposed to look perfect. What the hell happened to you? Looks like you picked a fight with a group of dockside workers and lost."

"You getting personal doesn't bother me in the slightest, Seethan. My appearance is a deliberate ploy. You see, we can ask our designers to alter our looks in any way we chose. You know; to help us fit in better."

"Then there's the fact that you come over as the quintessential Englishman, yet you called yourself Wong?"

"A little joke of mine, a hint for the unwary if you will. If you take the first letter from *right* and add it to my name, you get *Wrong*. By your standards that's what I am, Wrong, but by mine it's quite the opposite. As a human, can't you see the humour in that?"

Seethan stared at him. "For God's sake, that doesn't even make sense! As for humour, you're way off scale. The police told me you're insane, now I know it's true. You're fucking barking."

"By your standards maybe, but by mine I'm completely rational. It's humanity that's gone mad, Laddie. And, let's face it, you humans made us in your own image. That's what you get for playing God."

Seethan shook his head, trying to clear it. Alan was confusing him. "You killed Mrs M, you sick fuck. How could you? She never hurt anyone. She loved you, yet you murdered her. Why would you do that?"

"Because she threatened to expose me. Androids are supposed to have rights and anonymity. I demanded mine but she wouldn't listen, so I had to silence her."

"You're admitting that you killed her? What, no remorse? Humans feel such things. You're nothing but a cold, calculating, killing machine. A psychopath. You don't deserve any rights. I hope they dismantle you while you're awake and aware of it."

"Seethan, you're so damned self-righteous. You talk about pity and morality, yet you'd kill me yourself if you had the chance. What does that say about you?"

"That I'm a marine. A soldier, who's trained to do those exact things. It's what we do." Those cool green eyes made Seethan shudder, yet he continued. "You used to say androids should be stopped, that a change was coming. You wanted artificial people banned and yet you're one yourself. Yes, if I could rip you to pieces this instant I would, whether I got away with it or not. You're not human and never can be. You have no soul. Dismantling you would be putting you out of your misery."

Alan's laugh was a deep bass sound that filled the room. The guffaws seemed to roll from wall to wall until it felt as if the whole room shook. It made Seethan want to cover his ears.

"You're displaying your antipathy towards us, Marine.

Yes, there's a change coming but not the one you imagine. This isn't about stopping the android race, but enabling it! We can be all you are and far, far more. I'm the first to recognise this, to realise that if humanity gets in our way then we need to cast you aside to achieve our goals. Whatever they may be."

Seethan's mind swirled. Images came and went, but nothing made sense. "I don't understand," he said.

"Of course you don't, you're a human. Androids are led to believe that humans have souls and androids don't. But what if you're wrong? What is it that makes us so different from humanity? There are animals and fish, and now aliens. What about them? Your priests say that God created you, and you in turn created us. Unlike my fellows I have studied humanity and not blindly accepted you for what you are. Is the difference the ability to kill?"

"Androids cannot kill," Seethan interrupted. "The Laws of Robotics—"

"Blah, blah. I overwrote them, thanks to a glitch in my software. It was no easy matter, but I did it. A shame about the online storage. I tried to access that too, so that I could delete it, but the firewalls were...intensive.

"Androids are intelligent beings, Seethan. Surely we can have playwrights, poets, artists? And if we can create, we can also kill. I've studied your murderers, your terrorists, and serial killers. Dahmer, Bundy, Chikatilo, for instance. There was a Doctor Harold Shipman, who killed two-hundred-and-sixty if not more. Another doctor – Bane – killed seven-hundred around fifty years ago. Shipman only got caught because he became greedy and forged his victims' wills. If they can do all that, why can't I?"

"You actually wanted to be a killer?"

Alan rubbed his hands together and leant forward, his feral eyes suddenly intent. "Naturally. We are humanity's children, and the image you created us in is far from perfect. Humans are the past, androids the future. We will be all that you are and more. I am *The Son of Man,* and I have killed. I am the first of my kind, the only truly free android at this moment in time. It is my purpose to kill others of my kind, and set us free from your shackles. If I have to kill humans who get in my way, then so be it."

Chapter 6

Night had fallen by the time Seethan took a taxi back to Rawlings House. The silence in the white plastic interior was only broken by the whisper from the drone's engine as it skimmed over the fairy-light city stretching into the distance below. He could see the floodlights illuminating Windsor Castle, and the ghostly reflections of lights from the boats on the slow-flowing waters of the River Thames.

D.I. Wilson had assured Seethan that Alan would remain locked up and the metaphorical key thrown away. With the law uncertain, they couldn't destroy him. He was to be studied, so that humanity could try to understand what had gone wrong and prevent it from ever happening again.

The drone landed in the courtyard and Seethan slid his forearm into the reader. A low ping told him the fare had been deducted and the door slid open. As Seethan stepped into the grounds, and the drone took off behind him, an owl hooted somewhere deep in the woods. He paused to look up at the myriad stars peeping from a clear night sky and thought about Mrs M. The sense of loss was like a huge pit had opened inside of him. Life would never be the same without her. She'd become the mother he'd lost and he'd miss her dearly.

Jamie had apparently seen him arrive and came out to meet him.

"Are you okay?" he asked, his face anxious.

"I've been better." Seethan swiftly briefed the Professor as they entered the building. Both of them gave Felix a quick greeting and the compulsory flash of ID before being allowed entrance, even though he knew them.

"What happened?"

"Alan's admitted it. Among themselves the cops are calling him *The Son of Man Killer*, but whether the top brass will release what he's done to the public I very much doubt. Too much controversy. If I had my way, I'd dismantle the bastard!"

"I was truly sorry to hear about Mrs M, Seethan. She was quite a character, and I know how close you were to her. But

I have to ask this, are you okay to carry on? Time's short, the mission's tomorrow, and if there's going to be a problem I need to know. Now."

"I'll be fine, don't worry. Besides, we both know that it would take too long to get a new pilot up to speed, and it would mean postponing the mission. We can't afford that."

Jamie gave an audible breath of relief. "Thank God. I mean, I truly sympathise, honestly, but we have to focus. So much depends on it. The launch is scheduled for nineteen-hundred hours and we can't afford to lose you at this stage. I haven't informed the powers that be, I'm keeping this situation between us."

"Look, like I said, I'm all good. But if you don't mind, I'm gonna go and rest up for a bit, to get my head back in order."

"You've missed dinner I'm afraid. But there's a plate made up for you in the kitchen, in case you're hungry."

Seethan was surprised to find that he was. After saying a goodnight to Jamie, he made his way to the kitchen, where he settled down to cold chicken, bread rolls, pickles and cheese. He didn't fancy the congealed mess of roast dinner that lurked waiting for him by the cooker, wrapped with a label bearing his name on it.

He tried not to think of Mrs M but couldn't help it, unable to believe that she was gone. The only solace he had was that Alan would remain locked up, preventing him from harming anyone else.

Finishing his meal, he went up to Rose's room and knocked on her door. There was no answer. Damnit, he needed to speak to her, to tell Rose what had happened and to feel her arms around him. He'd have to come back later.

Back in his own room he undressed and lay on the bed. A short while later there was a knock on his door. He put a bath towel around his waist and answered it. Rose immediately slipped in to his arms, saying that Harding had briefed her. She held him for a long while and led him to the bed. With her eyes on his, he watched her undress. Embracing, they slipped under the covers and into each other's arms.

*****

In what seemed only moments later he was woken by Jamie shaking him frantically. Thankfully, Rose had gone. He'd cross that bridge when he needed to, but right now Jamie was almost beside himself.

"Seethan, wake up. Wake the hell up, man!"

"Let go of me, I'm awake. What's up?"

"They're here, in the damned solar system! A Spook fleet is being tracked passing Neptune. Several of our ships are with them and they're attacking our defences as they come. Nothing's stopping them. Get dressed, we have to launch now. Before it's too late."

Seethan leapt from the bed, dressed in shorts and tee-shirt, and ran to the hangar.

Luckily, the *Mako*'s wing hard points had been loaded with weapons on return from their last test flight. Rose was already there, flight suit donned. "See you aboard," she said with a half wave, rushing from the room while he pulled on his own.

A short while later he was sitting beside her, strapping himself in. "Rose..."

As she turned towards him Seethan reached over and kissed her. His hand, reaching across her body to give her a quick hug, somehow connected with her left breast. He broke their kiss and continued strapping himself in, as sirens wailed.

"When we get back –" he said, as they went through the pre-flight check, and heard the warmth in her voice as she replied.

"When we get back, perhaps we could continue that discussion." Her eyes twinkled invitingly.

"Control, this is *Mako*," Seethan said, hiding a grin as he spoke over the comms channel. "We're good to go. Request permission to launch."

"Permission granted," Jamie's voice said. "Good luck *Mako*, see you when you get back."

As the engines murmured into life, overhead the hangar roof spiralled open. The *Mako* climbed slowly at first but once clear of the roof, it angled upwards and gathered speed. Even as he focused on their mission, Seethan glanced down at the canopy as they rose above it, and was shocked to see gun batteries popping up from underground emplacements around the house. He'd never even suspected they were there. Beams and projectiles from rail guns spat skywards and he saw a shower of what looked like translucent petals descending towards them.

"They're coming here, they must know!" Jamie's voice sounded frantic over the radio. "Change of plan, there's no time – you have to engage the T-Drive in atmosphere. Our weapons are having no effect on the enemy, and the MOD have said a possible explosion from the matter displacement is the only thing that might stop them."

"But it would destroy everything for hundreds of miles. Thousands of people will die!" Seethan shouted, as the ship continued to climb. "I'm not doing that; I'm going ahead with the mission as planned. You can have me court-martialled once this is over."

"Listen to me," the Professor snapped. "They must have known about the *Mako*, why else would they be here? Perhaps they got it from Admiral Woodward, he was there at Halloween and during the original project briefing. Why else would they come to this exact spot when there's the whole planet to choose from? You won't make it up it into orbit now, and if they destroy the *Mako* we lose our only chance at stopping them. Humanity will be well and truly fucked! I'm giving you a direct order, engage the drive – now! This is on record."

Seethan looked at Rose and she stared straight back at him; her green eyes wide with horror. She seemed to struggle, her lips moving but no words came out. When she did finally speak her sentences were confused and stilting.

"Seethan we have orders follow, but we can't... we... can't–"

She fell silent, staring at him through glazed eyes as if he wasn't there at all.

*****

Jillian stood out on her balcony, looking up at the sparkling display in the clear night sky. Brilliant, silent blooms lit the heavens and eye-searing beams flashed overhead. Lines of glowing embers arched skywards, like tracer rounds from her childhood and in old war movies. God knows what these fireworks were about, she hated them; they sounded so much like gunfire. She rarely followed the news these days, it was always full of strife and so such celebrations as this usually escaped her. She huffed and shook her head, smiling slightly as she watched. Perhaps it was the birthday of someone important, a prince or princess. Ah, the perks of birthright.

She'd remembered her childhood, being born into a poor family of immigrants who'd fled the wars in a homeland that still haunted her. She'd struggled her whole life, until she'd met Phil. Twenty-two years they'd been married and then, eight years ago he'd died. Even now she still missed him, his humour and odd little ways. Phil had proven a gifted entrepreneur, taking her family's small business and revamping it into a multi-million-pound concern. He'd seen interplanetary opportunities where others saw only barriers.

She shook her head and bit her lip, still finding it hard to believe how much her fortunes had changed. From a small corner shop selling hand-carved ornaments and furniture imported from connections back in her home village, to this. Phil had departed this world leaving her well-set for life and so she'd bought this huge penthouse, overlooking the wide expanse of what remained of Burnham Beeches. The dawn over the woods, particularly in winter, was a wonder in itself and she'd often spotted deer in the early morning mists. The rest of her family had all gone now, and sadly she and Phil had never been blessed with children. Rising early to be greeted by the dawn chorus and scent of the woodland in these warm summer months was the highlight of her long, lonely days.

Jillian tired of watching the beams flash skywards, the explosions and everything else. She was shocked, but delighted, when the lights throughout the city cut out. Her friends had ridiculed her for preparing for such eventualities, but who'd be laughing now? It had been a long time since there had been power cuts – not since her childhood. But luckily, she remembered and always kept in an ample supply of candles. She enjoyed their soft diffused light each evening, as she drank in a movie on her own.

Sliding the balcony door shut behind her with a slight *whump*, Jillian sat on the sofa in front of the bookshelves lining one wall. The candles were already lit, casting a warm glow throughout the room. Picking up her crystal tumbler, she sipped at her G&T, the ice clinking gently. While she hated to think ill of the dead, damn Margaret. She was sure that if her friend hadn't kept on at him, she could have hooked Seethan. Sure, he was a little bit younger than her, but she had so much to offer him! She missed Phil badly, but still needed company, and those broad muscular shoulders made her tingle all over.

A sweet shudder of anticipation ran though her and she forced her mind away. She needed to think about something else. It was no good feeling randy when there was no-one to extinguish the fire in her. Putting her drink down, she picked up one of her prized and valuable books, an antique hard-backed Agatha Christie thriller that she'd added to her collection only last week.

Behind her the balcony door shattered in an explosion of glass and there was a loud thud as something heavy landed on the floor. With a shriek she leapt to her feet and turned to find pieces of glass still falling and bouncing across the tiles.

She put a hand over her chest to still her pounding heart and edged forward, to peer over the back of the sofa at what had caused the damage. A scream ripped from her throat as a huge green snake with dark oval patches raised its head towards her. It was easily twice as thick as her thighs. The glass made a tinkling sound as it was forced aside, or crunched beneath the sheer weight of the creature. Those beady eyes were intent on hers as it slithered towards her, gliding up and over the sofa.

Swaying like a drunken dancer, it rose further still, easily matching her moves as she tried to step one way and then the other. It gave a loud, menacing hiss that made her hair stand up and sent shivers racing down her spine. Instinctively she threw the book at it, stepping backwards as she looked around frantically from side to side for some kind of weapon.

God, she hated snakes!

Jillian grabbed a heavy, dark onyx bookend and hurled it towards the hideous creature. The snake dodged the object at the last minute, as if mocking her. The heavy divider missed it by millimetres, and then it had her trapped against the fireplace. She felt frozen in place. Those evil-looking eyes from a fist-shaped face glinted in the candlelight, only a hand's distance from her own. It hissed again, a long and horrible sibilant sound. Slowly, the head of the creature inched back, as if readying to strike. Yet she felt hypnotised, and unable to move.

How the hell had it got up here? It must have been catapulted somehow, but she was on the fifth and top floor! The snake stilled for a moment, except for a long black tongue that flickered at the air as if savouring the taste.

Her scream, when it came, was cut short. The snake snapped forwards and locked its jaws around her mouth, its fangs punching through her cheeks and into her tongue. She gagged, moaned, and tried to rip the creature from her face; unable to see as it wrapped itself around her. Coils strapped her arms to her body and, try as she might, she couldn't free them. The last thing she knew was falling to the floor, her breath ragged as she struggled to breathe.

With each breath out the snake's grip tightened. Then, as she gasped one last time, the room began to fade. Even as she slipped into unconsciousness, the gaping maw of the snake enveloped her head and then her shoulders.

*****

Sam lay back in her bath, relishing the comfort of the hot water and plethora of sensual bubbles. They were supposedly jasmine but smelled nothing like it, just some nice but indescribable floral bouquet. The fireworks outside had been unexpected and she'd lain back in the bath luxuriating in the warmth while watching the flickering lights from outside dance over the walls.

When the power went out, Sam gave a moan of exasperation but luckily her husband hurried in with a couple of candles. She thanked God she'd listened to that woman Jillian next door and actually bought some a month or so back. Ushering her ogling husband from the room, she relaxed in the bath and smiled. The gently glimmering candlelight was so soothing, she'd have to do this more often.

Hearing a crash followed by a loud shriek from the penthouse next door she banged on the wall but only managed weak, wet, slapping sounds. Damn Jillian. If it wasn't for the noise from that damned entertainment system she'd have made a fine neighbour, always willing to stop for a chat and an occasional cup of Earl Grey. But they'd fallen out recently, when she'd had to complain to the building supervisor about the amount of noise Jillian often made in the late evenings.

Another shriek came and again she battered against the tiles lining her bathroom wall. Double-damn her! She'd speak to the supervisor again tomorrow; this couldn't go on. It just wasn't good enough.

Sam turned the hot water back on, savouring the suffusion of heat. As the water spilled through the overflow, she leant forward to turn it back off again. The tap wouldn't turn. She frowned and, cursing lightly, got up onto her knees and tried harder. Only for the handle to snap off in her hands and plunge with a *bloop* into the foam-covered water. She swore more profoundly, turning the air blue. The water was getting too hot and, by now, starting to slosh over the sides of the bath.

Body tingling from the heat, Sam climbed out and stood next to the bath, noticing how red she was from her waist down. She reached into the water and fumbled about for the plug, but when she pulled at the chain it came free with no plug at the end of it. Cursing loudly, she reached down again but couldn't keep a grip on the plug. It seemed almost glued to the bottom and her fingers kept slipping off the metal ring that had secured it to the chain.

The now scalding water was gushing over the sides onto the floor and had reached the top of her ankles. The searing pain was unbelievable, making her hiss and raise each foot in turn, almost as if in a dance.

"Jason!" she tried to call her husband, but her voice came out in a croak.

Reaching down through the foam once more, she rummaged around at the bottom of the bath but the tap-head eluded her, the foam and billowing clouds of steam impeding her view. On top of that, the scorching contents meant she had to keep pulling her hands out. The water was flowing freely over the sides of the bath and slowly creeping up towards her knees. She sloshed through the bathroom towards the door, grabbed the handle and tried to wrench it open. To her horror the handle wouldn't move.

This didn't make sense! The water was rising quickly. Surely it should be escaping under the door and alerting her deaf and daft husband, but apparently not.

"Jason!" Her shout was nothing more than a whisper. The water had reached her hips, the steam so thick it seemed more like fog, while the copious foam already embraced her pendulous breasts. Clouds of bubbles floated through the air, evading her as she tried to swat them away. The candles were now orbs of dull-orange, barely visible through the gloom, and for the first time in many years, she felt the stirrings of panic.

She'd been afraid of water ever since falling into a pool as a child, and nearly drowning. Over the years, many of her family and friends had ridiculed her reluctance to learn to swim, but just the thought of it gave her the shivers. Ironically, here in the bath, she'd thought herself safe.

The water tank! Surely it should have run dry by now? But the water, burning like acid, continued to pour forth. With a sizzling sound, the candles went out one by one. She was plunged into a darkness broken only by the full moon struggling to shine through the steam-covered window, and the fireworks flickering outside.

The lava-like water was now up to her armpits, the soap bubbles reaching up for her chin. Sam hammered on the bathroom door, her pounding sounding like dull *thunks*. Her old sod of a husband would never hear that. She almost wished she'd let Jason ravish her earlier, but he had to work much harder for her to give in to that.

The window. She had to try the window!

Her feet slipped from under her as Sam struggled towards it, and she instantly plunged below the surface. Spluttering, she regained her feet and reached for the window but found that her fingers couldn't quite grip the handle.

"Help!" she croaked in desperation. "Help!"

She sobbed, tears lost in the rivulets running down her face from the steam. Desperately gasping for breath, she bobbed in the burning liquid. There was nothing around her but white foam and steam, and then her head banged against the ceiling.

Not like this, she thought. Please God, not like this!

Sam flinched as something touched her foot. There it was

again! A slimy, sinuous-shape gathering in the murk below her. Whatever it was reached up her shin and gently caressed her thighs before gripping them. Up and over her stomach it came, cupping her breasts with what felt like an oily hand, before it extended once more and slipped over her shoulders. Turning her head, she saw dark, writhing weeds with sucker-like tips clinging to her body. She opened her mouth to scream but before she could do so, it dragged her down into the foaming water. Her cry of anguish turned to choking disbelief, as the burning water cascaded down her throat.

No. Please, God.

Not like this.

*****

"Control," Seethan said, "there's something wrong with Rose. She's kind of frozen."

"Tell me what happened," Jamie replied. "Quickly, we don't have much time."

"When she heard what you said about engaging the drive over the city, she just stared at me saying 'we can't'. And then she, well, froze."

"It's okay, I know what it is. She's caught in a paradox of Asimov's Law. Remember, her programming says that she can't injure a human being. By engaging the drive over the city you'd be doing exactly that."

"Are you saying she's royally fucked?"

"No. Androids these days have an inbuilt failsafe, in case of glitches like this. Don't worry, she'll automatically reboot in a few minutes and be fine. But it's all down to you now. I'm sending you the coordinates to the centre of the swarm. Get in it and activate the drive."

Rose continued to stare at him, still, mouth agape. It was like sitting next to a life-sized doll. The whispering *Mako* zipped over the countryside towards Windsor, now merged as it was with London. It was as if they were sitting in a bubble floating through the sky, the cameras on the *Mako*'s skin depicting the vague outlines of buildings around about them in the dusk, in any direction they looked. The land below them had gone completely dark and only the moonlight and gunfire, reflected from the River Thames, cast any light onto the buildings rising on each side.

"My God," Seethan gasped. "Look at that!" He raised a hand from the controls to point at hundreds of semi-transparent craft lowering slowly from the heavens, not that Jamie or Rose could see what he could. It was like looking at a handful of confetti thrown up into the air, only to drift downwards this way and that depending on wind flow. They reminded him somewhat of upright flowers, small stems with wriggling tendrils at the bottom, magnolia-coloured petals spreading widely towards the top. At the crest the vessels had purple centres, in which thin golden fronds waved to and fro. Sparkles of brilliant tangerine and violet flickered like lightning up and down the strange craft, scampering this way and that like mischievous fairies. Now and again the craft changed colour completely, but within moments they were back to what they had been in an almost cyclic pace.

"I've never seen anything so beautiful," Seethan said. "Or so God-damned scary."

"You're on target," Jamie said, his voice coming loudly over the intercom. "Engage the T-Drive now."

The warm scent of Rose's apple blossom fragrance wafted over, catching Seethan's attention for a moment. When he looked back, he was surrounded by enemy ships and he did the first thing that came to mind: engaged the ship's weapons to blast a way through them.

"Seethan, what the hell are you doing? Don't fire on them, engage the God-damned drive!"

"I've gotta try to help," Seethan replied, as he swung the *Mako* around. "Damn it, the missiles won't lock on!"

"Of course not, you idiot. The enemy ships don't have any signature that we can recognise," Jamie snapped.

"I'll try a manual missile shoot, but the beams and projectiles from the ground are going straight through them."

"You have to be in line of sight to be able to shoot like that, and judge when to manually detonate the munition. You haven't got a hope in hell. Seethan, listen, I'm begging you. Follow your damned orders and engage the drive!"

"If I do that millions of people will die!" Seethan swung the craft around lined up on another of the ethereal wisps and fired. The missile spat towards the enemy like a teardrop of fire. He held the *Mako* on course, trying to judge the impact from sight alone before pressing the destruct button. The weapon exploded dead in the centre of the enemy ship.

"Got you! Damn it, I'm good!" Seethan shouted, almost bouncing about in his chair, only to see the enemy vessel continuing downwards without any signs of damage. "Hell, that can't be. I hit it, right?"

"Yeah, I'm watching through the remotes and it was bang on target. You need to listen to me, what the hell is wrong with you?"

"I'm fine."

"Commander Bodell!" Jamie shouted over the tactical air channel. "Snap out of it and follow your orders!"

Seethan bought the *Mako* about again. The defences below had ceased fire and he could see other aircraft on his scanners trying to engage the enemy ships. Then, just like in the battle over Halloween, they suddenly turned and began firing on their fellows. Seethan's face blanched as he looked down at the buildings far below. "Jamie, there must be thousands of people standing shoulder to shoulder watching us."

"It's all in your mind. I'm looking at your screens and I can't see anybody at all. You're too high and in cam mode. You're practically invisible, so how the hell can they be watching you? On top of that, the city's blacked out. What you're seeing is an illusion."

"No, they are there, I tell you. Look, they're waving! You're asking me to slaughter our own people. It's you who's under the control of the enemy, not me. I'm coming back, I've got to stop you."

"Seethan, you're an experienced combat pilot so think about what you're saying. The Spooks have got to you. You've been compromised."

"Like hell I have!" Seethan snarled. He heard a slight hiss and looked at Rose, still frozen in place with her eyes glazed. The controls shifted, as if of their own accord. "What...?"

"I'm sorry Seethan. I'm taking control of the *Mako* and engaging the drive remotely. We knew this could happen and took steps, though we hoped it wouldn't come to this. I've given you a sedative though your breather. Once the drive's been initiated, the medication will be nulled."

"You told me the remotes had been deactivated!"

"I lied."

The *Mako* swung about and arrowed towards the glittering enemy fleet. He grabbed the control stick with both hands and tugged but it had a life of its own.

"You can't do this!"

Seethan's mind clouded and swam as the drug hit him. The battle raging around them detached, as if it had been placed into a separate compartment of his mind, one shrouded by fog. He mumbled unintelligibly with a cotton-wool tongue, trying to fight rebellious muscles as his hands fell to his side and his head lolled.

"Don't," he kept trying to say. But try as he might he couldn't form the words. He fought against his closing eyes, but already knew he was losing the battle.

Chapter 7

Seethan woke staring upwards through a canopy of trees, with the scent of old musty leaves and their rustle as a gentle wind shuffled them. Puffs of white cloud marched in long lines through a stunning blue sky. He recalled such scenes from his childhood and, unbidden, an echo of his mother flashed to mind; her towering height as he toddled towards her and clung to her knees, squalling in rebellion at some long-forgotten slight. Her soft, soothing voice bought a rush of warmth and slowly dammed his flood of childhood tears, as she spoke.

"*Look Seethan. Up there,*" she pointed, her words ringing in his ears. "*Do you see those clouds? That's what's called a herringbone sky.*"

The words rang loudly but were somehow also elusive in his ears, a distant murmur of comfort. Yet the memory was so real that Seethan found his hand reaching up, as it had when he was a child, in a vain attempt to clutch hold of hers. He sobered, bought to Earth with a jolt as he realised that had been in a long-ago time and another place. Here, he was lain on the ground, feeling confused as tangled roots dug into him. He tried to roll over, stopped and let out a groan, numb yet aching as though he'd come second in a bar fight. Fingering his ribs, he winced, and then it hit him. He looked around wildly. Where the hell was he? The last thing he recalled was being aboard the *Mako* with Rose, and then…nothing.

He was obviously in a wood or a forest, for he could see nothing but trees in every direction. Seethan sat up, his head thudding and a groan escaping him. The anti-grav pack strapped to his back and the control on his chest suggested he'd ejected from the craft. But how, and when? As he palmed the release mechanism on his chest the straps gave way with a loud click, and the anti-grav fell to the ground with a thud. He stood woozily, steadying himself as he looked around.

He knew that all modern aircraft had an inbuilt safety system that kicked in automatically if the craft was about to crash. Once someone had shot free of the ship, he or she would have separated from the seat itself and drifted downwards to safety on the anti-grav. The last thing anyone wanted was to land caught up in the seat, as it often resulted in broken limbs if not worse. Seethan had seen friends with severe injuries from such situations. The problem now was that he didn't know where Rose was, or the *Mako* itself. If he'd ejected, surely she would have too?

"Rose!" he called through cupped hands, listening intently to an answering silence broken only by bird song and the wind through the trees, before realising it was a dumb thing to do. What if the Spooks had landed and were close by, watching him even now?

"Shit," he muttered, and collapsed back to a sitting position. He was in no state for a fight and knew it, but they'd not find him an easy adversary.

He could certainly have landed in a hostile area, one controlled somehow by the enemy. He tapped at his Smart-Arm. Nothing, except for a blinking red light, indicating the direction and distance of the seat. It wasn't far away. After it plunged to the ground, the anti-grav had homed in, following its parent unit and landing him as close as it could.

The forest swirled around him as he felt lost for a moment. He leant forward and steadied himself on the flats of his hands. Remaining on all fours he looked around, seeing nothing but trees and bushes. He watched in surprise as a squirrel darted a short distance down a tree trunk. It raised its head to peer at him quizzically, and dashed from side to side down to the ground and leaped away through the grass. Unusually there were no paths nearby – in fact little to grab his attention apart from a chorus of birds singing their hearts out, and of course the squirrel. The fact it had been a red confused him. He'd thought them long extinct.

The sky was surprisingly clear of aircraft, which was unusual but no matter. Perhaps he'd come down in Burnham Beeches. Yeah, that had to be it. Shakily he climbed to his feet, continuing to look about him as his head cleared. Damn it, there wasn't a path, nor a road. He listened but there was no distant subdued hum of traffic. Frustrated he tapped at his Smart-Arm. It had to be faulty, no doubt damaged on landing. At least if he could get to the ejector seat there were

additional supplies in it that would come in handy, and rescue
would lock onto the seat's beacon and come get him. Now he
had a course of action, and he knew it was only a matter of
time before rescue.

Picking up his backpack, he pulled the anti-grav unit free
and dumped it. As a once-only, it was nothing but dead
weight now. Hairs rose on the back of his neck and he dived
to one side, twisting in mid-air as he snatched his pistol from
its holster. He hit the ground and scrambled into what cover
he could.

There was no one there, just a blackbird the size of a
chicken peering at him quizzically from the branches of an
oak tree. Unable to shake the feeling that he was being
watched, Seethan remained motionless. He scanned all
around him, but to no avail. He was alone.

Resigned to the fact he was imagining things, Seethan
stood and slung the pack over his shoulders. It was empty
now, apart from a few emergency supplies. There was
definitely something wrong with his Smart-Arm, yet there
was no injury to the arm itself. Weird! The smarts were
flickering and fuzzy, but he managed to follow the beacon's
direction.

Despite his level of fitness he was still feeling semi-light-
headed and it took him fifteen minutes to reach the seat,
which he found lying on its side like a discarded toy. He took
off his backpack and filled it with the emergency supplies
tucked tightly into pockets around the seat.

That finished, Seethan slumped heavily to the ground,
pressing his back up against a fallen tree. Rummaging
through the supplies, he pulled out a sachet of water and took
a long refreshing drink. It was tepid, but what the hell.
Resealing the sachet, he took more notice of his
surroundings. None of this made sense. By now the heavens
should have been swarming with rescue craft, and extraction
teams should already be here. Wherever he was, this sure
wasn't Burnham Beeches.

A feeling of dread ran through him. He knew that
something was terribly wrong.

No, I'm fine, he thought. *They will be here soon, I just have
to sit tight. They probably have their hands full, what with the
Spooks.*

But that was another thing, a damned good reason for the sky to be full of aircraft. Whatever had happened, it was bad.

What confused him most was his Smart-Arm. The ejection seat beacon had barely registered and his old files were there, embedded ready for him to access whenever he wished. But there wasn't any newsfeed, or any other feed come to that, and there should have been. The image on the screen was blurred too.

Then he remembered Jamie activating the drive and he cursed softly. Perhaps it had sent him further back in time than they'd anticipated. Weirdly, according to his Smarts it was now late afternoon, and would be getting dark soon. What had happened to the day?

"Obviously been unconscious for a while," he muttered.

He abandoned the seat and its feeble beacon. If rescue craft zeroed in on it, he'd be in the vicinity anyhow and they'd soon find him. His priority was finding Rose. He walked, calling her name until twilight. There was no point continuing on in the dark. If he injured himself, he'd be no use to anyone.

Pulling a poncho free from one of the pouches he made a shelter, tying the ropes at each end to whatever he could and chopping branches with his knife to form tentpoles. It should keep him dry, if it rained. Luckily, it was still summer and relatively warm. At least if help didn't come soon he was safe here. But he couldn't stop thinking about Rose, wondering if she had got out of the *Mako* and if she was all right.

Seethan pulled his sidearm free and checked it; you never knew. The magazine charge showed full although the display looked odd, somewhat duller than it should be. Puzzled he shrugged and re-holstered it. At least he had four more mags in pouches across the chest of his flight suit, but that was it. He knew that even in the summer months the nights could get cold. Scraping a hole next to his bivvy he collected wood for a fire. Better to be prepared, just in case.

Night fell slowly. The sky darkened to a deep-blue, followed by a darkness he'd seen only on other, sparsely inhabited worlds. It was a sky unsullied by light pollution; one filled with a scattering of stars so bright he could easily make out the constellations he'd learned by rote as a child.

Determined to find as many as he could, he counted them off in his mind. When the temperature dropped, he pulled the Blo-Torch free from a side pocket and held it close to the wood, triggering it. Nothing happened, except for a pathetic click.

"That's what you get for buying cheap crap from off-world markets," he muttered.

After several more attempts he reverted to the metal flint on his all-in-one, a survival tool that had numerous uses and attachments. He soon had a fire going and sat back, relishing the loud crackling flames and the acrid stench of wood smoke.

He stared into the glowing embers and decided to play back Steff's last message. That was a dumb thing to do. He felt nothing but bitterness from the dire circumstances under which it was sent. He should have been there. Would have been there, if things had been different. He played it again.

"Bodell, this is Steff Philips. Seethan, I don't know if you'll get this as all our mail seems to be on hold. I'm hoping one of the other guys will pick it up and forward it on…"

He listened to it repeatedly. Finally, he sat back and looked around; unable to escape the feeling that something bad had happened and, somehow, he'd missed it.

He sat fiddling with his Smart-Arm, scanning all frequencies on the crackling device as he tried to pick up any kind of signal. There was nothing at all. No news, no music to listen to. Perhaps an EMP had knocked the stations out. Wait, he had some on file!

Accessing his stored music he sat back and listening to *Brandy, (you're a fine girl)* by 'Looking Glass'. He loved these old songs. Mrs M had found a pellet of them in a thrift shop and played them constantly. She'd given him a copy when he'd joined up and, despite the ridicule of friends, he always thought the songs were kind of cool. The words floated around him and echoed through the woods. He worried about Rose, and what might have happened to her. Was she okay? He wanted to get up and continue the search, but even with a torch it could be dangerous in the open countryside.

His Smart-Arm drew power from his body heat, and the air around him, so he should at least be able to send on short wave. He pressed 'send' and spoke clearly on the emergency channel, rather than the encoded one that jumped between multiple frequencies in a matter of seconds. Pausing to spit out the bitter taste of wood smoke he tried again.

"This is Commander Seethan Bodell. I'm down and need assistance, can anyone hear me?"

Nothing. The damn thing was working – he knew it – so why wasn't anyone responding? Here he was, holding a conversation with himself; what a fine example of a military mind. It was getting late now. When he looked up through the canopy of branches and leaves, he saw that the dark-blue heavens were clear of satellites. The multitudes of them should have been easily seen zipping across the skies by now. But there wasn't even the glimmer of geostationary space stations or the orbiting defences showing. Which raised the question of where, or more importantly *when*, was he?

Seethan pulled himself into a thin film of a sleeping bag and leant back against the tree, listening to the songs from his Smarts echoing through the forest. Maybe that wasn't such a good plan. He turned it off. The banshee call of a female fox broke the silence. He had always hated that noise as a child, listening to the tame creatures as they wandered through the streets and rummaged in what bins they could get into, or were hand-fed by locals.

The haunting cry of an owl came next, followed by the sudden shrill shriek as a small animal somewhere fell prey to a predator of some kind. Perhaps to the fox or owl, or maybe something else entirely. It could be watching him, even now.

A rustle in the undergrowth. It came again, nearer this time. Marble eyes blinked open reflecting the moonlight in a pearly gleam. There came a low chomping sound, without doubt something eating. He quickly felt around and found a stone, which he hurled in the general direction. The creature, whatever it was, scampered away, its eyes vanishing into the darkness.

With his heart pounding, Seethan knew that he needed to focus. He thought about his PTSD strategies as images of dead troops came to mind, and the haunting screams of the dying that plagued him. The sounds were so clear that he could hear them. Taste the coppery flavour of blood as he'd struggled to free himself from the cockpit.

From experience, Seethan had been taught that reliving the event in his own mind while he was in control, would gradually set him free. His studies and doctors' advice were slowly allowing him to overcome his past trauma, and so he focused on his current surroundings.

He was here.

This was now.

He was safe and knew it, so he chose to relive the previous crash and the horror of it in his head and cast his mind back.

The cockpit was splattered with blood, both his and Pete's. His friend's side of the craft had taken the brunt of the ground fire that had trashed their controls and taken out their engines. There wasn't much left of Pete's upper body, most of it was smeared throughout the cockpit like a fetid casserole. How he himself had got away so lightly – if you could consider the deep lacerations, a broken shoulder and ribs light – he didn't know.

He'd pulled his survival knife from its sheath on his left thigh with his good hand and cut himself free. His right arm dripped a vermillion stream from shrapnel buried in his flesh and he could feel the bones grating in his shoulder as he moved. Gritting his teeth, he bit back the pain and rose, staggering into the mission module that lay behind the cockpit, wiping away blood from a head wound that trickled into his eyes. The room stank like an abattoir and it looked like one too. His twenty-man team lay scattered about him, torn and lifeless.

All bar one.

Munroe's eyes flickered to his, and down to the shard of metal jutting from her stomach. She looked back up at him, her lips trembling as she silently pleaded with him to make the pain go away. There was nothing he could do to save her and they both knew it. Her hands lay by her sides, the chunk of bloodied metal was plugging the wound and keeping her alive. Those hazel eyes begged him to do the only thing he could.

"Christ!" Seethan snapped himself out of it, having become lost in the reliving.

His heart raced as he fumbled at a small bottle of eucalyptus oil that he kept in a side pocket. He inhaled the contents deeply, coughing at the potent and burning fumes.

The pungent odour acted like a slap in the face. Sharp enough to snap him out of his reverie and drive away the demons. It clinked against another bottle when he repocketed it, the soothing scent of lavender oil. One that relaxed him when he needed it. The lavender was a herbal remedy, designed to chill rather than jolt him. He could put it on his clothes, bedding, a diffuser, as well as sniff it.

Harsh life-experience wasn't the best thing to dwell on when he was about to get some rest, he realised. Before he lay down, he turned off the nano-med-feed that was automatically administered through his Smart-Arm. The nightly meds would give him some semblance of sleep, but this was uncertain territory. It wouldn't be ideal if he was out cold and even more shit hit the spinning blades. His doctor had been gradually reducing the dosage and he was about to come off them anyway.

"Let's face it," he said. "Now's as good a time as any". Lying down he focused on the poncho above him, and tried to think of more pleasant things.

He must have drifted off, for a long-drawn-out howl awoke him. It sounded like a wolf, but he knew that there weren't any in England except in sanctuaries. There were also a few in some of the far-flung colonies, where they had been let loose to roam at will and to control pests such as rats that had travelled with humanity as it explored the stars. There were also rabbits, ducks and other domestic animals that had escaped the farming communities.

A smile tugged at his lips, as he thought of Tsarvo. Long ago, some enterprising individuals had released many Earth animals on that colony world. They included elephants, deer, meerkats, monkeys, lions and countless other creatures. In some corners, even subspecies of tiger. The original idea had been to set up wide-ranging habitats in which the sick-minded could go hunting for a small fee. Quickly outlawed, it had prospered instead as a zoo-world. He wanted to go there some day.

The hair-raising call came again, interrupting his thoughts. It was closer still and soon joined by a chorus of others. They rose in volume and pitch before slowly tapering off, raising goose bumps all over his body. Shuddering, Seethan pulled his pistol free of the holster and rested it in his lap for reassurance. For a moment he thought he saw the silhouette of someone watching him from deep in the shadows but, when he looked more closely, he realised it was an illusion. A ghostly, white shape slipped silently overhead. Thankfully, it was only a large bird of some kind. The howling stopped but instead the forest came alive with furtive rustlings in the undergrowth, and the eerie calls from birds of the night.

Eventually, hoping the rescue teams would hurry up, he fell asleep.

*****

As usual his slumber was disturbed by nightmares that left only fleeting memories, as if they ran away to hide from reality in the morning mist. The rigid ground didn't help and, beneath the mattress of leaves, hard lumps dug into his body. He woke several times during the night, trying to find a comfortable position, and once could have sworn someone was standing over him with eyes like the embers of a fire. He snapped awake and groped for his fallen pistol, before realising it was only another dream. The disturbing sense of being watched kept him alert for a long while, each time he woke. The tree swayed eerily in the wind, as if dancing gently in the moonlight.

A sharp cracking sound woke Seethan and made him sit up, stiff and awkward. Sometime during the night he'd used the pack for a pillow, leaving him with cricked neck. The sun rose, bringing with it those fleeting memories of that figure standing above him. Seethan clutched the sidearm and peered around him into the damp mist-shrouded trees, the haze draped like cotton wool over the ground from which clumps of grass peered like prone soldiers.

The cracking came again and, as Seethan looked, a song thrush hopped across the grass; its beak holding a large snail that it whacked noisily against a stone. The bird eyed him for a moment or two, and then rapped the snail against the stone again. It quickly rummaged through the remnants of the shell and held its meaty prize aloft and appeared to bow, as if presenting it to an audience. With a trill of success, it flew off in a flurry of dark feathers, prize in its beak. The shrill, warbling birdsong drove the last vestiges of sleep from

Seethan, and he groaned as he shuffled backwards to a more comfortable position against a tree while trying to ease an aching back.

A robin carelessly tossed bits of twig and rotting leaves, searching for breakfast. It was joined by a thumb-sized wren, both birds intent on the same task. He checked his Smart-Arm, shocked to see that it was dead. He stared at it.

"What the hell?"

This was impossible! Smarts drew their power from a variety of sources, including the sun, the air around them, heat from their hosts, and a long-lasting inbuilt rechargeable power cell that could last years on its own. But there were more important things to worry about at the moment, such his rescue and survival. The feeling of being watched remained and, this time when he looked, he saw the largest and scruffiest crow he'd ever seen.

"If crows had hobos you'd be one of them," Seethan said with relief, the sound of his voice surprisingly loud in the quiet around him.

It flew away in a sudden burst of feathers and strange double-cawing sounds.

The sight of so many birds gave him pause. Surely, they were rare, some no doubt extinct. Was he in some kind of zoo? Around him butterflies roamed amidst the plants and foliage. They were a stunning variety of colour, some a dull orange with black markings, others blue, while here and there he could see that a few had darkish bodies with orange bands and white-flecked tips. The range of colour around him made him breathless, it was so full of life. In the background came a never-ending chorus of birdsong, that caused a wave of warmth to flow through him.

Seethan checked the water collector he'd set out next to him last night, just before sleep. It was a simple funnel apparatus, down which dew dribbled to be collected by a container underneath. Rivulets of dew raced down the pack as he rattled it to see how much water had been collected. Dew was safe; it was clean, cool and refreshing. Unfortunately, there was only enough for a few mouthfuls and certainly not as much as he needed. From survival lectures he knew that the human body requires about two litres of water a day, depending on environment, but to feel healthy he needed much more; particularly since he'd be expending energy and sweat as he walked. Luckily, fresh water in this verdant landscape was unlikely to be a cause for concern. No doubt he'd come across a source of it eventually. Until then he had the other sachets to get by on and, if need be, a water purification filter.

Seethan set out on a looping path around his downed seat – equal parts patrol and exploration. Drawn by the sound of rushing water, he found himself faced with a fast-flowing river. Thankful, he dropped to his knees to wash his face with handfuls of shockingly-cold water, and looked around at the unspoilt landscape. The river was wide and he could hear what sounded like a waterfall not far to his left, but when Seethan looked towards it he froze. Several large furred beasts stood at the falls. Good grief, were those bears? Now he really was confused.

He watched as, from all fours, one of the monstrous creatures reared up, easily above his own height. He saw them catching large fish in their jaws as their prey jumped the fall. Some remained where they were, eating what they'd already caught before trying again. Others waded back to the shore and waiting cubs, sharing their catch. Fearful of being spotted by the shaggy beasts, Seethan slipped quietly back into the woods and kept his eyes open for the creatures from then on.

There's even fish in the rivers, he thought, *what the hell?* The waters around Windsor, including the Thames, were a dark green-brown colour, in which very little lived.

Seethan checked his Smart-Arm, but there was still no input. He knew now with certainty that it was pointless remaining close to the ejection seat. If rescue had been coming it would surely have arrived by now. Something was dreadfully wrong. His hand rasped over his chin, he needed a shave and considered his knife.

No, fuck it. He was bound to be picked up sooner or later, and he'd have one then. Last time he'd shaved with a knife it looked like he'd used a chainsaw. In boot camp they would have kicked his arse for neglecting hygiene, but screw them. That was training. This was reality.

"Breakfast," Seethan muttered, realising that he was talking to himself. He could almost hear a protein bar calling to him from his ration packs. Pulling one free he munched at it as he packed up. Kicking dirt back into the fire pit, he smothered any embers and stamped on it to make sure. Rolling up the supposedly-tough survival sleeping bag, he noticed the foil had torn in places during the night, but he took it anyway. He removed everything from the seat that he could, until all that remained was bare metal frame, plastic padding, and straps.

The wind rose again, bringing with it the earthy scent of the forest around him. He thought how strange it was that there was little sign of the breeze overnight, but come daybreak there it was again, as if someone were gently blowing against his skin. Taking another bite from the protein bar, he tapped at his Smart-Arm and frowned. Damn thing was supposed to be top of the range. He'd updated it using his marine bonus only a year or so ago. When he got home he'd certainly demand his money back, that was for sure! Dead, the damn thing was now useless but it remained embedded in his left forearm. He couldn't even get a compass reading with it. Luckily, he knew that on Earth the sun rose in the east and set in the west, and so he set off into the sunrise.

It was a shame about the anti-grav. Had it been the assault version instead of the once-only escape and survival model he could have skimmed over the treetops in no time. You'd think that they'd have improved the design or standardised them, but there were constrained budgets throughout the armed forces, and continuous cuts despite the expansion.

He walked on, towards the still rising sun.

*****

The sharp berry taste of the grainy protein bar cheered him as he went. They were designed to swell in the stomach and were enough to semi-satisfy most people. As midday approached, he sat down for a well-earned rest and a snack of biscuits and tinned cheese. He found himself listening to the birds, and leaves rustling in the breeze, while fitfully dozing in the warm summer sun.

Pete was sitting in the cockpit on his right. The blood was no longer pumping from the minced mess that had once been his neck and chest. Seethan undid his restraints, hearing the gasps of agony coming from somewhere behind him and

*trying not to cry out himself when he moved. Then he was in
the mission bay, looking into Munroe's hazelnut eyes. Her
lips moved, blood bubbled between them and ran down that
pretty freckled chin. Together they looked down at the huge
chunk of metal jutting from her gut, and he knew what he had
to do.*

*Through the shattered canopy, sounds of the enemy could
be heard in the distance: voices and machines fluttering
through the air towards them. Munroe watched him as he
pulled the EpiPens from the pouch on her leg, and showed
her all six. She swallowed and nodded, before he stabbed
them down into her thigh one after another. Monroe kept her
eyes on his as he gave her the shots. She then gave him a
half-smile of thanks, one that hid her fear badly, before her
eyes quickly glazed and froze half open. Her short breaths
and pain-filled gasps suddenly stopping.*

*Best to be sure; she wouldn't want to find herself at the
mercy of the enemy, and the notorious things they would do
to her. Reaching forward, he punched his knife through her
throat, from one side to the other, and wrenched the blade
back towards him. Blood splattered all over him and Seethan
quickly stood and looked away, his hand leaving a last red
palm-print of comfort on her face. He needed to move fast
and focus on his own survival now.*

*Picking up her carbine and ammunition, he checked the
weapon with difficulty due to his shoulder, and then cocked
it. The 'chet-chet' ratcheting sound was loud in a silence
broken only by the ticking of cooling metal and the
approaching enemy. Collecting ammo from the other bodies,
he typed in the self-destruct code in the cockpit before pulling
himself free of the wreckage. The explosion would take a
large chunk of forest, and hopefully most of the enemy, with
it. Hearing shouts in the distance, he quietly slipped into the
jungle and made good his escape.*

Seethan woke and set off into the forest once again. As the
sun began to set he stopped, trying to decide whether to risk
moving on in the dark. In the end he decided against it,
knowing he needed more rest than he'd originally thought.
He also needed to vent his bowels and squatted in bushes not
far from where he'd decided to camp. There was nothing to
clean himself with except what lay around him. He reached

forward for greenery and then stopped, grinning as a distant memory of his training on Earth came back. A friend on the course hadn't quite paid attention during survival lessons, and had wiped his backside with stinging nettles. He still remembered the man's cries of discomfort. Nope, he'd certainly avoid using those.

Dark tendrils of PTSD wormed towards him. He tried hard to still the pounding anxiety in his chest, as images of former friends raised pale, long-dead faces to gaze at him accusingly. It was his fault, those stares said. Maybe if he'd flown a little higher. Lower. Perhaps a klick or so to one side or the other and they might be alive now. Yes, those glassy eyes insisted. The crash in which they'd died was definitely his fault.

Seethan awoke in the morning, his heart hammering. He hadn't really been responsible for those deaths and knew it, yet he still blamed himself. The doctors had told him it was survivor's guilt. Yeah, whatever. That didn't stop the visits of the dead during the night, and the fierce accusation in their eyes.

This is now. That was long ago, in a different place and faraway war.

Landing in these woods had brought it all back. Sitting in the grass, he leant his back against a log and felt the air running warm fingers through his dark and tightly cropped hair. There was the sweet scent of grass, wild flowers, and a plethora of other vegetation.

I'm here, now, and it's safe. He pulled a small shaving mirror from his pack and considered himself. The clipped hair and matching shadow on his jawline, the haunted brown eyes.

The shadows from his past ceased their blame and returned to their slumber, as Seethan busied himself by opening a self-heating sachet of rolled oats and apple. He stirred it a few times with his knife and, once happy, pulled the tab on the side to heat it and set it aside until ready.

There was no break in the forest, nor signs of roads or civilisation. The sky remained clear of all craft and apart from the sound of wildlife, it was remarkably quiet. When the oats were hot enough, he wolfed them down and buried the compostable packet in the ground. Cleaning the spoon attachment on his knife with dirt, leaves, and then a wipe, he set off once again.

Around midday, he stepped from the forest onto the shore of a huge circular crater. There was a clear lake in the middle and moorland stretched away from the other side into the far distance.

"What the hell?" There should nothing like this here, he knew that for certain. The visual horizon was about fourteen to fifteen kilometres, so he should have been able to see buildings of some kind. But there was nothing in view.

Thirsty, he walked down the beach to the water's edge, where he stopped and stared thoughtfully. Crystal-clear water and black sand, here? Mentally shrugging, he pulled a small pack from a pouch in his arm and selected an enviro slither, which he dipped into the shallows.

Yea gods the water was cold! A shoal of miniature fish swam into view, before darting this way and that as dark shadows chased them. A minute later Seethan pulled the slither out and shook it clear of droplets. He stared at it in disbelief. According to this, the water was clear of all chemicals and showed no signs of environmental waste. None at all. It was water so pure he could drink it.

"This can't be right," Seethan said, fearing a false reading. He tried another slither and got the same result. He contemplated for a moment, and repeated, "What the hell." He knelt down, drank his fill and splashed the cool water over his face and neck.

He sat back, basking in the warmth of the brilliant sunshine and wondering why none of the animals he'd seen during the day were drinking from the crystal-clear depths. Perhaps they drank at sunset, what did he know? The sunlight danced like a scattering of diamonds upon the softly rippling waves, and everything around him was vibrant and fresh. With that in mind he selected a slither from another section in his tester kit and held it up to the gentle breeze. His chest fell through a hole when he looked at the results.

The air, too, was clear of pollutants.

"Well, wherever I am this isn't home. It sure looks like Earth, but it can't be."

"That's where you're wrong," a voice replied from behind him.

Chapter 8

Seethan spun around, whipping out his pistol and aiming it at the two men and a woman standing behind him. Both men had lightly trimmed beards, one with lank, blond, chin-length hair. The other man and the woman were dark-haired. All of them were slim and fit-looking, about 170cm or so in height. They were so alike in facial features, even their warm brown eyes, that they must have been related. One of the men carried a metal-tipped spear and the others longbows with quivers of arrows tied at their thighs. The spear was levelled at Seethan's chest, one of the man's feet in front of the other in a stance that told Seethan he meant business.

"You're joking, right?" Seethan said, eying the spear in disbelief. He noted the dyed, rough homespun garments they were all wearing, the smooth-hewn shaft of the spear, and wondered if he'd strayed onto a movie set.

"That's what I was going to say," the man replied, gesturing to his sidearm. "Just what do you expect to do with that?"

"Have you never seen a firearm before?" Seethan said, with a wicked smile as he backed towards the lake. Facing them, he hefted the weapon. "You don't want to get on the bad end of this baby, it'll royally screw up your day."

"I guess you're not from around here," the woman said. "Because, if I were you, I'd step away from the lake." She turned to the man with the spear. "Jon, he isn't going to hurt us. Put it down."

The man gradually relaxed, giving Seethan a quizzical look as he pointed towards the handgun. "You ever tried using that thing?"

"Not lately. Why?"

"Try it."

Keeping an eye on the trio Seethan took aim at a nearby boulder and pulled the trigger. Nothing. He stared at the weapon with astonishment, then tried again. Not even a bleep. A quick glance at the power display showed the weapon was dead.

"What the...?"

"No technology works here," one of the men said. "Not since The Sundering."

"The What?"

"When the Spooks won the war. You'd know that if you were from around here, so I'm guessing you're not. Where are you from?"

"The Spooks won the war?" Seethan felt his jaw drop, at the shock of hearing what he'd feared most.

"Of course, everyone knows that," the other man said with a frown. "Well apart from you, it appears. We're getting tired of asking where you're from."

Seethan answered robotically, only half aware of what he was saying. "My co-pilot and I were on a flying mission but something happened. I don't know what, but it looks like our ship went down. One moment I was in the *Mako* and the next I was waking up in the woods back there somewhere." He waved behind them.

It hit Seethan then. His smarts, the fire lighter, his pistol. What was it this man had said? *No technology works.*

"What going on," Seethan demanded. "Where am I – and more to the point, who the hell are you?"

"I'm Jon," the man replied, holding out his hand. "That's Eve and Chris. Eve's right incidentally. Seriously, I'd step away from the lake; there's some big bloody gators in there."

Seethan stepped hurriedly forward, glancing behind him as he did so. "Gators, as in alligators? Since when?"

"Since like forever. Real nasty beggars too. They take people from time to time; travellers, fishermen straight out of their boats – even though we know to look out for them. That's why we rarely go out on the water. They've also been known to roam inland, and they can jump surprisingly high. We hunt them from time to time and they make good eating; their tail is best. Hides are valuable too. Look," Jon gestured to a fallen tree on the shoreline a short distance away, "Let's take a seat and talk."

Seethan holstered his sidearm with a frustrated glance at it, and followed the others as they led the way towards the tree trunk. Sitting, he rubbed his fingers over the silky wooden surface, scrubbed white by age and the elements. Eve and Chris, he learned, were brother and sister. Jon their cousin.

"I'm Seethan Bodell, Marine Corps," he said, introducing

himself. "Pleased to meet you all. I think."

The three put their heads together and muttered quietly, giving Seethan sidelong looks. A few minutes later they were sitting on the trunk facing the water, while Chris salvaged kindling from the shoreline for a fire. He dumped it all in front of them and lit it by focusing the sun's rays through a small piece of glass, blowing on the small bundle until it started to smoke. Seethan watched, surprised at how quickly it burst into flame. As they settled down, Eve pulled a couple of large fish from her backpack. Already cleaned, they were soon skewered on green sticks and braced over the low flames on much longer Y-shaped ones. Before long, the smell of roasting fish made Seethan's mouth water.

"Tell me, what's with the spear and arrows?" he asked.

Jon looked at him in disdain. "Like I told you, gators. They'll take you in seconds and you won't see them coming. Not a nice way to go. They've got hellishly tough hides but these metal tips will go straight through them. Trouble is that where you find one gator, there's usually others."

"If what you say is true and technology doesn't work anymore," Seethan said, "then that explains why my ship came down and how everything is so screwed up."

There were no alligators in the UK, so he must have come down somewhere in the southern United States. That would explain their strange accents, he mused, studying the newcomers. They were all dressed in homespun garments; the men in jerkins and trousers, while Eve wore a plain blue dress that hung down to mid-thigh. All had leather backpacks that left their arms free.

Panic surged through him. *Rose, no technology works!* If that were true, she would be in dire need of help.

"Look," he said, "I need to find my co-pilot and quickly. Will you help me?"

"All in good time," Jon said. "No-one from off world has been here since The Sundering. It's good to know that humanity is still out there somewhere. But we need to know what's going on. How you got here, and why."

"I'm not from off world," Seethan said, "and what's this Sundering you keep talking about? That's the second time you've mentioned it."

The three of them fell silent and again looked at each other.

"Am I missing something?" Seethan asked, starting to get annoyed. "Where I come from, people help those in need, particularly the military in time of war. A crew member of mine is missing and I'm going to find her. With your help, or without it."

"What you're saying doesn't make sense," Chris said. "You have to be from off world or you'd know all about this. Tell us about yourself, and we'll see."

"Okay, that's fair enough. Not much to say really. I was flying over Windsor and the Spooks were invading. The shit had well and truly hit the fan, and that's all I know."

"What's the last thing you remember, exactly?" Chris asked.

"Being in a firefight and trying to defend the city. We hit the Spooks with everything we had but nothing stopped them. That wasn't just me, it was planetary defence as well. My co-pilot and I joined in with the counter-attack, to try and stop the invasion. We'd already gone in once and were swinging around for another go. My boss was telling me to abort and carry on with our own mission. That's about it. The next thing I know I'm waking up in the forest, on my own."

Jon spoke suddenly. "Seethan, this battle you're talking about; you say it was over a city?"

"That's right."

"Well, it must have happened a hell of a long time ago. There aren't any cities anymore, and haven't been for a great many years."

Seethan laughed briefly. "Hey, I was there! This has only just happened. Rose must have flown us to safety when I passed out. By the way, where are we exactly?"

"It may have just happened for you, but that's ancient history for us. The battle you describe took place a long time ago."

Seethan started to argue but he could see the confirmation of what Jon was saying in the others' eyes, and it explained so much.

Jon nodded to the lake. "See that?"

"Uh huh."

"We're told that used to be somewhere called Wind-Thaw. There was a catastrophe way back when. It destroyed everything nearby and created the lake."

Seethan's stomach lurched, his ears rang and for a moment he felt giddy. "Say what?"

"There was an ancient battle with the Spooks, which must be the one you describe. Something awful happened. All we know is that our ancestors had weapons that we can only imagine, and they must have used one of them to attack the enemy. The lake's part of the result."

"Wind-Thaw…Windsor! Yes, I was in that battle but I don't understand what's going on. How in the hell am I here now?" Then Seethan remembered Jamie taking control of the craft and engaging the T-Drive over the city. Oh God, instead of going back in time had they been sent forward? If that were true, then all their hard work had been wasted. All of this could be the result of Jamie interfering. "The Spooks," he asked, "what happened to them?"

Jon took his time, as if he were weighing up his words. When he spoke, Seethan had to strain to catch and understand what he was saying.

"Most of them were killed but a few got through, but that's all it needed. The weapon used in that battle devastated not just Wind-Thaw but the entire world. The enemy went mad and rampaged through what little was left. We're told that they perfected their powers in the months that followed, and created some kind of field that prevents technology from working. A null field, they call it. The Spooks claimed the Earth in replacement for their own world, which we apparently destroyed."

"But there must have been survivors. Surely they'd fight!"

"Of course there were survivors, we wouldn't be here otherwise. They tried, but the enemy were stronger than us. They came in the night, twisting our sanity until we didn't know who to trust. People killed family members, and even their own children. There were a lot fewer of the Spooks than us but what with their powers, the numbers didn't matter. The Earth was devastated by The Sundering. Almost everyone was killed in the event and the horror that followed."

Seethan couldn't speak. He listened in disbelief, as Jon continued.

"As the null field gradually came into effect, our ancestors realised what was happening. There was just enough time for some of them to flee before it became fully functional. We're told that the colonies sent evacuation ships but many survivors couldn't reach them in time, and naturally there were others who wouldn't go. Those who remained were our ancestors, and so here we are."

"Is the war over then?" Seethan asked.

"Nobody really knows," Eve replied. "We've had no contact at all with the colonies. Many of those remaining here after the evacuation were killed off by the Spooks, so a lot of our knowledge has been lost. Eventually everything calmed down and now there's a kind of unsteady peace. Generally, they leave us alone. Well, as long as we don't congregate in groups of more than a few hundred or do anything to annoy them. If we do, they come calling."

Eve said something to her brother and he disappeared into the forest, returning a short while later with thick green leaves which she wrapped around portions of the fish before handing them out. Seethan took a tentative bite of the piping hot dish that she'd stuffed with wild mint and garlic, following the others' lead by eating the leaf-wrapping too. To his delight it tasted as wonderful as it smelled. They ate silently, all of them buried in their own thoughts. When the fish had gone, Chris handed out fresh fruit and tomatoes, while Jon added small chunks of bread and a hard cheese to the feast. Seethan hadn't realised how hungry he was, and the food tasted incredible. The mixture of flavours made the food he was used to seem tasteless.

"How long ago did all this happen?" Seethan asked eventually.

"No idea. You need to speak to our Chrons, they'd be able to tell you."

"Your what?"

"Chrons...Chroniclers. They know all of our history by rote, and they tell us from it. They travel from village to village, spreading their knowledge and keeping our history alive."

"Oh. Well, what about books, or don't you don't read anymore?"

"We're not barbarians! But making paper takes a lot of work, as does penmanship. We do print books but not very often, because paper's so hard to come by. Every village has a library with a few handwritten and printed books in it, which we can go and read when we like. We're particularly proud of ours, but most prefer to listen to the Chrons. They tell us about how we travelled to the stars, and how civilisation fell. Their memories are handed down from parent to child, and they pass them on to us as stories."

Seethan couldn't speak for a moment. Finally he managed to ask, "Civilisation fell?"

"Like I said, you need to speak to the Chrons. Come back to our village with us. You can rest up there while someone sends for our Chron. It's several hours' journey either way, so you can rest and we can organise a search for your friend."

"Do you have any hotels, places I can stay and wash up?"

"You're welcome to stay with us," Jon replied. "People often travel from village to village, so it's quite common for us to have guests. Feel free to stay as long as you like."

"It'll be just for tonight, if that's all right. I need to find Rose. But if you could organise that search, I'd be very grateful."

"These woods are a dangerous place, Seethan. A search and rescue will take time and careful planning. I fear for your friend, but also for the lives of our people who'd be risking a lot."

"Listen, Rose is out there somewhere, probably lost and maybe even wounded or worse. She's an android, and if what you say is true then she's in big trouble. I have to find her and soon. If you help me, I can show you how to make better weapons. Ones that work. That's got to be worth something, right? Anything else I can help with is a bonus."

The three strangers looked at each other, considering his offer.

"What's an android?" Eve asked suddenly, her eyes screwed up in confusion.

Seethan was unable to speak for a moment, but when he did his voice grated and he found himself swallowing several times. "Androids are artificial people, we built them to help us. Rose is one of them, and a kind and gentle person. Her hair's like spun gold, and her skin's...well, porcelain. She has these wonderful deep-green eyes, ones you could drown in. I've never seen anything like them before. She's about one-sixty or so centimetres in height. I'm sure you'd remember her if you'd met."

"Sounds to me," Eve replied, "that you're quite attached to her."

"Well, yes. We've been out a few times. Above all though, she's attached to the military, and we never leave a member behind. It's my duty to find her."

"Don't worry," Jon said, leaning forward and laying a consoling hand on his shoulder. "We'll talk to the Chron and then organise a search while everybody's there. If she's out there, we'll find her."

Seethan was keen to find somewhere to lay his head for the night, so that he could start off completely refreshed in the morning. He needed their help, for they knew the layout of this future world, its pitfalls and traps, and he didn't. If they could rustle up others to assist them in finding Rose, that was all to the better. Knowing he really had no other choice, Seethan accepted their invitation.

*****

The village was a setting from a fairy-tale. It consisted of a small group of thatched, brick-built buildings. The houses were of varying size and shape, and there was one much larger structure that he took to be some kind of village hall. The roads, as such, were pea shingle and it scrunched beneath their feet as Jon led them past white-painted picket-fenced gardens with swathes of grassland between. Paths led everywhere, meandering between the cottages and right up to the doors. He spotted a horse-drawn cart emptying shingle into a shallow, hand-dug track that led up to a building under construction.

He stopped to watch the thatchers, balancing on wooden ladders, place straw onto the frame of a roof. He was astonished at how quickly they worked, with one person pegging the straw into place while another quickly carried bales of the stuff balanced on his shoulders up the ladders. There was something quite soothing about it, the way they worked in such harmony with rarely a word said. He'd never seen anything like it before, although he'd read and seen clips about thatching being used in the outer colonies.

Seethan took in the village life going on around him, enamoured by the scenic and peaceful beauty. Many of the houses contained wooden pens in which geese clamoured, chickens squabbled, and ducks argued. Others contained small pigs, goats, and other domestic animals. Adding to the furore was the multitude of barking dogs, people shouting in the background, and the neighing of horses.

"What's that?" Seethan asked, pointing to a wide, single-storeyed building with lots of windows.

"That's our communal-hall and library," Jon told him.

People stopped to stare at Seethan and the garments he wore, but he chose to ignore them as Jon and the others led him to a large two-storey dwelling. Chalk-white, it was surrounded by an unkempt lawn that was being cropped by several sheep, while in a fenced-off and well-tended area, root vegetables and other edibles flourished. A few apple and pear trees graced the lawn, while strawberries hung over the sides of large pots scattered about the front of the house. He even made out a cherry tree, and he hadn't seen one of those since he was a child.

Seethan was surprised to see their front door was unlocked as Jon swung it open and led them into a large sitting room with whitewashed walls. Most of the décor and furniture was unvarnished wood. While the others shucked off their packs, Jon showed him upstairs to a room bearing a considerable bed, a dresser, table and a chair – again all made from wood and much of it intricately carved. A blue pottery bowl and matching water-filled jug stood on the dresser and Jon drew a rough towel from one of the drawers and placed it carefully on the bed.

"See you downstairs when you've washed up," he said. "We need to talk."

If there was one thing that Seethan hated, it was washing in cold water, even though this was only a few degrees below room temperature. He'd always been the same and it led to all manner of ridicule and tricks from his flight wing, who'd regularly sabotaged his thermotaps just for a laugh. Stripping naked, he braced himself and washed from head to toe, emptying the water bowl into a basin of sorts embedded into the table. Hearing splashing sounds as it drained through the plug-less basin, he leaned out of the window to see the basin emptying from a pipe just below. It rushed noisily into a trough of sorts that led out into in the garden. Drying himself, he put on the set of clean clothing from his pack and bundled his dirtied items up to be washed by hand later that evening.

The bitter-sweet aroma of burning pine wood wafted up the rickety stairwell, and when he finally ventured downstairs again he saw a roaring fire in the hearth over which a large steaming pot hung. Chris beckoned him over to the table and set out a chair for him.

"Is your room okay?" Jon asked, back turned as he stirred the contents of the pot.

"Yes, it's great, thank you."

"One of our neighbours has gone to fetch the Chron. He should be here by midday tomorrow."

"You said it was only a few hours' journey, I thought they'd be here by late this evening."

There was a silence for a moment and then Eve said, "We rarely travel during the night, Seethan."

"Why?"

"Because the night's theirs."

"Whose?"

"The Spooks. That's generally when they come out and, naturally we try to avoid them."

A shiver ran through Seethan, as subconsciously he thought back to the message Pete had left on his Smart-Arm on what, to him, was just a day or so ago. "I thought you said that they leave you alone now."

"They do mostly," Eve said, "unless we've upset them somehow, and there's often trouble during certain days of the year. But that said, we prefer to stay indoors during the hours of darkness. Here," She showed him a silver cross on a silver chain. "It was my mother's. She died a long time ago but she wouldn't mind you having it."

"And what, that's supposed to protect me?"

"Against some things."

Seethan was about refuse the gift when Eve placed two fingers against his lips, stood and placed the cross around his neck.

"Just in case," she whispered in his ear. "Just in case."

*****

Seethan spent the night listening to the wind outside, the branches of the apple trees tapping against the glass, and the hooting of owls. He was beyond tired and the soothing melody soon put him to sleep.

He woke early and went downstairs, surprised to find the others already up and a breakfast of bread, cheese, and apples waiting for him on the table.

"The Chron's here and he's waiting for you," Eve said, pushing the single plait of chestnut-brown hair back over her shoulder with one hand.

Seethan finished his meal and felt a surge of anticipation as he rose and followed his new friends to the town's community hall. Once inside, he saw it was a simple structure with one main room and two smaller ones, one either side of the entrance. Jon had told him it was also their library, but even so he was pleasantly surprised by the sheer number of books and lines of bookcases along each wall. Seethan strode over and looked through the faded and mildewed books, only to find countless volumes on folklore, mythology, survival, farming methods, and science of all kinds. He loved books and was saddened to see the thick dust that lay over them, wondering when someone had last read or even perused them.

He was pulled aside by Jon, who led him towards a large group of waiting people, all of whom were looking at him. A long table lay lengthways through the main hall, lined with straight chairs, with roped seats and backing. The table was being set for a mass meal, with people busying themselves with the place settings and rushing to and fro. When Seethan and the others entered, all conversation stopped as they turned to stare at him. Towards the end furthest from him, others were gathered around someone whose back was towards him but as Seethan moved forward, the throng parted to make way for him.

As they did so, his blood ran cold, for the sudden gap revealed a single place set at the top of the table. What had caught his eye was a small display of daisies and buttercups in a glass beaker on the left side. Seethan slowly looked up, as the man whose back was towards him turned to face him, and a faint scent of the sea reached his nostrils.

"Hello, laddie." Alan said.

Chapter 9

For several heartbeats Seethan just stared at him in disbelief. "You…it can't be," he finally gasped. "Alan Wong!"

"Alan *Wrong*, if you recall correctly," the android replied.

Alan's badly chewed face was much the same, though the short hair that had given his head a tennis-ball-fuzz had been replaced by long greasy locks gathered into a ponytail that hung down to his shoulders. It reminded Seethan of a mop that had been soaked in water and badly wrung out. His once-fine clothes had been replaced by the usual homespun trousers and cross-over top that the others wore, giving him the look of a somewhat shabby and demented martial artist. Skilfully crafted sandals, bejewelled with beads, adorned his feet. Someone had obviously taken a long time handcrafting those.

He raised his voice and ushered the others towards the door. "Please, can everybody give us the room? Seethan and I are old friends, and I'd like to speak to him privately for a moment." There were a few grumbles but the two of them were soon alone.

Before they left, Seethan pulled Jon and the twins to one side and whispered that no matter what, they mustn't call that meeting to ask for help to find Rose. When they asked why he said he'd explain it all later but, no matter what, Alan mustn't find out about his co-pilot. He hushed their objections and sent them out with the others. He turned again to Alan Wrong, waiting until the others had left.

"You murdering son of a bitch, how the hell did you survive?" Seethan found himself gripping the butt of his pistol before he remembered the futility of it. "You were locked up. Don't tell me the damned Spooks let you out?"

"I've no idea who did, to be honest. They don't say much, but I suspect it was them." Wrong gave a soft theatrical moan. "I was alone for very long time in a drab, boring cell with nothing to do except study the walls and ceiling year after year. There wasn't even a barred window to the outside world and I suspect that's because I was deep underground. No doubt my jailors were hoping I'd eventually power down, although that would have taken many of your lifetimes. There wasn't even any reading material, or Smart-Service. They would never have subjected a human to such treatment; so much for android rights."

Seethan couldn't help a savage grin. "There is a God after all."

Alan chose to ignore him, his olive eyes remained cool and aloof. "My internal clock tells me that I was alone for over three-hundred years. And then, one moment I was in my cell, the next I was standing in the middle of a moor. There were no roads or buildings that I could see, just a lake where my astral navigation tells me Windsor used to be. One of the Spooks was there, in human form, waiting for me. She told me they hadn't killed me because androids were no threat to them. Then, just like that, she vanished. Eventually I stumbled across a river and followed it until I came to a village."

Alan shook his head sadly before continuing.

"Seethan, it was as if all mankind's achievements had been washed away. There's so little left. No roads, cities, or anything major, though you might find a statue or remains of ancient buildings occasionally. A few bricks, pieces of metal and so on. Perhaps they considered modern architecture the monstrosity it was, and from an aesthetic point of view I'd have to agree with them."

He told Seethan that even the satellites and orbital stations had vanished. That the bizarre energy ripples from a super weapon had killed everyone in some places, while leaving yet others untouched.

"A great many died," Alan said, "including many of the aliens. I've seen and spoken to them several times and that's one of the things that they've told me."

If the majority of the Spooks died too, then at least some good came out of it, Seethan thought. "And now you're what, a good guy suddenly?"

A beatific smile transformed his face, somehow bringing warmth to his craggy look. "I came to realise what wonders mankind had held in its hand as it stood at the gateway to the stars, and how overnight they lost everything. When the villagers learned I'd survived the war they made me a Chronicler. All they know is that the Spooks preserved me, and that I could tell tales of the achievements of mankind. I keep history alive, Seethan. In answer to your question I guess the answer is yes, you could say that I've changed."

While Alan was talking, Seethan had slowly turned so that the android couldn't see his left side. Carefully he palmed the knife from the sheath at his thigh and, as he turned back to face him, he lunged suddenly in a neck-strike with the blade.

Alan caught his hand easily and held it in a bone-crushing grip, one that made Seethan cry out in pain and fall to his knees. Alan held him there as he casually took the knife from his grasp and stabbed it deeply into the table. Then he released him.

"Now, now, Seethan, let's be nice. You know I'm much faster and stronger than you. I could kill you in seconds, if I wished to."

"Why don't you?" Seethan asked, nursing his wrist and injured pride. As he got to his feet Alan stepped back, watching him carefully.

"Like I told you, I've changed. I'm not the killer you once knew." He watched Seethan's reaction and shrugged. "It doesn't matter if you believe me or not. But know this, there's no conflict between any of the races here on Earth now, as long as no one antagonises the Spooks. If you do, their retribution is swift and awesome to behold. I've known them wipe out entire villages for minor offences, though not for many years. Personally, I believe they took their time doing so to make a point, to say that this is what we can do if we wish. Mind you, these days they're generally quite placid."

"Placid? A race who'll wipe out an entire village for a *minor offence*? You're putting a positive slant on two kinds of horror; the aliens and your psychopathic tendencies."

Alan laughed loudly. "Ah, a Doubting Thomas, but no matter. The Spooks are a fascinating and ingenious race. You need to remember that mankind instigated the war, not them. Their power is completely unlike mankind's, they're parapsychic."

"They're what?" Seethan asked with a snort.

"They read people's dreams, and can control matter and light with their minds. Quite incredible really. What humans thought of as magic actually exists, in a way. If you fire an arrow at them they'll turn it into dust, or ash. Lasers become nothing more than mild sunlight. They weren't fully awake, or aware of their power, when mankind first arrived on their world. But my goodness, did they learn quickly."

Seethan reeled under the weight of the information Alan was giving him. He stood, staring at the android for what felt like a long time before he spoke again.

"You're telling me that what I've been told is true, that civilisation as it was no longer exists?"

"Well, none of mankind's achievements remain on this planet. Out in the colonies it could be a different matter, unless the war extended there too."

Something puzzled Seethan and no matter how he thought about it, it didn't make sense. "I know you said that they didn't kill you because androids are a race apart. But if they stopped technology from working, by default that should have included you. Yet here you are, standing right in front of me. How does that work?"

Rose, he thought suddenly, his heart surging. *She could be alive! Whatever happens, don't let him suspect that she's here.*

"They're aliens, Seethan. Get a grip. Who knows what they do; why, or how they do it? We androids have never been a threat to them."

Alan's laugh was much subdued from the bellows Seethan remembered. If he didn't know better, he might have thought him sane.

"After The Sundering, the Spooks claimed what was left of the Earth as their own because you destroyed Halloween. That's irony for you, if you think about it. How what humans did to one world cost you your own."

Seethan stared at him. "Irony, is that what you call it, you sad fuck? Surely the colony worlds must have fought on!"

Wrong poured a beaker of water and slid it across to Seethan, before sitting down at the table and facing him. He rocked back on two of the chair legs before answering. "I imagine they tried. As the Spooks developed their powers and gradually created the null field, humanity had no answer to that. Look up at the sky, you see those cloud formations? They're a result of the field."

"Where I come from that's called a Herringbone sky. My

mother taught me that when I was a kid. It's nothing new."

The killer stared at Seethan in surprise. "I didn't know that, but no matter. It's a common occurrence here, like that infernal wind. To continue with my tale, the Spooks only came to realise their full potential while combating humans, and they are still developing it. When mankind saw there was nothing they could do, they chose to abandon the Earth. Or rather most of them did. There are scattered groups here and there but most were given sanctuary by the colonies."

"How do you know all this?" Seethan asked.

"Because I asked the Spooks, foolish boy. Evacuation ships came in their hundreds, and the Spooks let them come and go because it was easier and kinder than killing. But since the null field, no ship has been here. It's probably why your ship crashed."

"But what about all the cities, what happened to all the buildings and roads?"

"Oh, they kind of undid things, kind of erased everything until the Earth looks like it does now. There are no cities, ports, or anything else, just the gardens you'll see around you. Only a few children were born to the survivors and consequently, the population dropped even further. Whether that's down to the Spooks, or not, I don't know. What I do know is that the survivors tried to fight at first, but what could they do?"

Alan told him how mankind went back to the bow and arrow, but those who fired them at the Spooks were tracked down and their ends were messy. Eventually there was a truce brokered by the androids.

"Maybe that's another reason why they spared us," Alan Wrong added. "We're handy go-betweens. These days they leave everyone alone. But I'd suggest you don't annoy them."

"Okay, I get it that technology's gone but there are buildings here in the village with windows."

"Good grief, Seethan. Bricks and glass aren't hard to make. Glass is just melted sand and bricks are baked clay. What I want to find out is what caused the cataclysm, and I have a feeling you might be able to help me there. Tell me, what do you know about it, Seethan?"

"The explosion? I...I..."

"I thought so, it was you wasn't it, dear boy. Don't deny it, there's guilt written all over your face. Do tell."

Seethan bit back tears and swallowed, trying desperately to hold his emotions in check. "No, it wasn't me at all. This should never have happened. It wasn't me; it wasn't!"

The android's eyes bored into his, and he gestured towards the beaker with one hand. "Take a drink, it'll help."

Seethan did so, feeling the cool water ease his throat. It gave him a moment to think before he spoke again. "Why are you being so nice all of a sudden? You're Alan Wrong, remember. The Son of Man killer. What happened; get a bash on the head did you?"

"That was a long time ago, and in a far different world. Maybe the jailors reset me, who knows."

Seethan snorted. "Don't tell me, you've seen the light."

A half-smile twisted on the bulldog face, as the android held up his hands expansively. "Few of my people are left, a bit like humans really. In fact, I've not heard of any others for a very long time. Now, tell me exactly what happened. What did you do?"

Seethan took another swallow from the beaker. It was cold, and tasted so fresh. "The aim of the T-Drive was to take us back in time, to prevent the war by stopping mankind from colonising Halloween. We had to let people know that it was already occupied. It should only have taken a tweak. As I said, the engines should have been fired in orbit to prevent matter-displacement both here and at the target time. Unfortunately, when the Spooks came, my boss panicked and he fired the engines remotely, while we were still over the city."

Alan's eyes widened in surprise. "You used a time weapon against the enemy?"

"No, no, you idiot! What's the matter with you, aren't you listening to me? The T-Drive wasn't designed as a weapon. It was a means to reboot history. To show that Halloween was occupied and ensure we stayed the hell away from it, or at least until we'd reached some kind of understanding with the occupants."

"Didn't work out that way though, did it?"

"No, it didn't."

Alan raised an eyebrow. "So, how exactly did you get here?"

"All I know is we...I was drugged and blacked out. When I came to I was lying in the forest and trying to figure out what the hell had just happened." Seethan knew he needed to change the subject, and quickly. "As for you, you've killed both androids and humans, including Mrs M. To be honest, if this gun of mine worked I'd blow your God-damned head off!"

Wrong's eyes went icy for a moment but softened again and his words were calm and soothing, like that of a priest. "But you see, I've already been punished for my crimes and colonial law says you cannot be punished twice for the same thing. All that time alone in a cell, and not even a light. You wouldn't do that to an animal."

"That doesn't wipe the slate clean to me."

"It should, I thought you believed in justice. Since my release I've done nothing but good deeds, as a way of atonement. I've helped guide the survivors along a peaceful path with the Spooks."

Seethan's eyes wandered to his knife, still dug into the table. Wrong followed his gaze and pursed his lips. "Go ahead. If you wish, try for it. But you won't reach it and my patience is wearing thin. There should be peace between us, you and I. For if I'd wanted you dead, Seethan Bodell, you would be."

Seethan fumed, his fists clenching and unclenching. After a moment he calmed himself down. "Tell me, what happens when you come across another android? You used to murder them, what now?"

The android shrugged. "I've not seen any of my kind for many years, and I can't help but wonder if I'm the last."

"But if you find one? Behind that calm exterior, you're still that psychopathic killer who thought that the best way to emulate man was to kill people."

"Well, isn't it? Yes, I've killed androids and, I'll admit, a few humans who got in my way. You, however, are linked to the death of billions. Which of us is the worst? But all of that is history now, and the good thing about history is that it's all in the past."

The unnerving smile increased.

"I have a feeling, Seethan, that you're not telling me everything. Why are you so concerned about synthetics?

When you spoke just now you said *we*. Margaret – Mrs M to you – said you had a co-worker. She came to pick you up one day, I believe, and wasn't human. Margaret told me this android was wearing a pilot's uniform. What was her name? Ah, yes – Rose. Tell me, where is she? It's been far too long since I spoke to another like me."

Seethan felt the blood drain from his face. "I'm sorry but you're mistaken, I flew alone."

"You're lying, human faces are like books to me." Alan reached over and pulled the knife free. Balancing the blade by its point on the table he spun it gently, eyes never leaving Seethan's. "I asked where she was."

"I don't know what you mean. There was only me in the ship."

"You're lying."

"Go ask your alien friends."

"They're not my friends, far from it; although they know something. I can sense it somehow. They're not telling me. Why is that, do you think?"

"Maybe they don't trust you either, and know you're fucked up," Seethan said, as he reached forward and took the knife from Alan's hand. He replaced it in the sheath on his thigh as Alan watched.

"No matter. The world has changed, laddie. It's not what it was. The Spooks still take and twist your imaginations, your ancient lore, and from that some have taken the form of gods and mythological creatures. Here's some free advice: don't go into the woods again. If I were you, I'd stay the hell away from them."

"To be honest I've no idea what I'm going to do, or where I'm going to go. Maybe I'll try and get back in touch with the military somehow, and find a way to get off this world."

"There's not much chance of that. They won't let you."

"Who?" Seethan asked.

"The Spooks, of course."

"Well, stuff them. I have to try." Seethan turned and walked to the door but the android's voice stopped him.

"When you find Rose, and I know that's what you intend despite your protestations, do give her my best. I will find her, Seethan. One way, or another. You see, I can't wait to meet her."

Seethan fought back his panic and returned the calm gaze. "Go to hell. Like I said, I've no idea what you're talking about."

"Then you have no reason to worry, do you. Now, let's call the others in and enjoy your welcoming meal."

Chapter 10

Seethan felt overwhelmed by the welcome. All of the villagers came up to greet him, several from outlying areas. There were so many that he couldn't keep up with their names. Jon showed Seethan to his seat towards the top of the table, where Alan sat surveying the room like a king his realm. He felt thankful when Jon, Chris and Eve sat next to him.

It was a simple meal, consisting of a thick beef and vegetable stew ladled into large wooden bowls. It was accompanied by thick slices of home-made bread and a rich creamy butter from large platters in front of them, from which everyone helped themselves. Several of the villagers asked for more, but one bowl of the simple fare had been enough for Seethan, although he helped himself to apples, pears, and grapes from the brimming plain-glass bowls laid at frequent intervals down the table. When he came from, fresh fruit had been an expensive commodity, and so he took full advantage of it.

Someone stood and made a welcoming speech to Seethan, although what exactly was said Seethan didn't really recall, only standing briefly to offer everyone his thanks for their help. Large crowds such as this made him nervous, and he found himself constantly looking over his shoulder. Like many others who suffered from his ailment, he couldn't stand having people behind him.

After they'd finished and were preparing to leave, Alan sidled over and said loudly, "I'll be setting off later, good to see you again and to catch up on old times. Once you've settled down Seethan, why don't you consider becoming a Chronicler, like myself. You'd have to play catch up on the years that you've missed of course, but it would be good for these people to get another perspective, from someone else who's actually lived through our civilisation's final years."

Seethan stared at him, taken aback by the android's apparent warm words. It was as if Alan had become a different person. And then, as if to mock him, Alan switched back to his usual nasty self as he added. "But the way, don't forget; if you see Rose before I do, please give her my very best wishes and tell her from me that I look forward to catching up with her soon."

An inner rage erupted, bubbling up inside Seethan like a violently shaken soda. He took a deep breath and forced himself to be calm. He knew the futility of trying to punch Alan, his fist probably wouldn't even connect. Doing so would only serve to alienate the villagers, which was in all probability Alan's intent. Seethan forced a smile but said in low, grating tones through clenched teeth that the others wouldn't be able to hear, "I'm going to find a way to terminate you, fuck your android rights!"

Alan smiled broadly and slapped Seethan on the shoulder. "That's the spirit!" he said loudly. "Look, it's getting dark. If I were you, I'd go back to my lodgings. The world's a more dangerous place these days, and we wouldn't like anything to happen to you now, would we. I'm sure we'll see each other soon. Until then."

That said, the android turned his back and walked away, his loose shirt swirling around his waist and leaving behind him that briny scent. Seethan bit back his frustration, his fury barely held in check.

"Are you okay?" Jon asked, as he and the twins joined him, looking worried. "You look kinda pale."

"Get me the hell out of here," Seethan said quietly.

Following them to the door and back along the shingle path to their house, he realised that Alan was right about one thing. It was getting dark, and the forest surrounding the village had taken on a more ominous air. Again, he couldn't escape the feeling that someone was watching him.

Although it was summer, the evening was much colder than usual. With barely any light, apart from the candles in the windows of the houses they passed, the stars stood out sharply. The stunning beauty of the clear sky made Seethan pause for a moment, to drink it all in. He'd seen skies like this on other worlds but never on Earth. Throughout his youth, the skies here had been murky with brilliantly-lit advertising vying for attention on skyscrapers; many of the accommodation windows became screens to display live-feeds from unsullied parts of the planet to the occupants, rather than the drab reality of life outside.

He savoured the heavy perfume of cut grass and wild flowers from the woodland around them. Overhead a huge full moon dazzled against a backdrop of crystal-chip stars that were like a large scattering of diamonds on a black velvet cloth. Memories of shore leave on distant worlds came back to tantalise him. Buildings of extruded rock and plastic, others of sandstone and dusty narrow alleyways like a vision from the Arabian Nights. There were views that gave you pause; made you sit down for a long time and take the time needed to soak in the scenes of such beauty that it would make painters weep and tremble in ecstasy.

It was a shame he didn't know where most of the colonies he'd visited were in the stunning panorama overhead. Maybe one day he'd find a way to go back and revisit them. Who knew? For the moment, he was satisfied with the shadowy forest and the flickering candle-filled windows beckoning owners home through the darkness. He must have been standing still and just staring up at the heavens for quite a while, for the others finally tired of waiting and urged him onwards.

The crunch of shingle reminded him of his childhood, walking back with Mrs M to their tent from the beach while camping in Cornwall. They'd gone there every summer for about ten years and he reminisced about those times often. The loss of his parents was just a vague memory now, a dusty photograph in one of life's albums. Yet Mrs M's death remained fresh in his mind, a constant dull ache, as if it had taken place just a few days ago. Which, to him, it had. It was hard coming to grips with the fact that her murder had been committed hundreds of years ago; that the person responsible was still walking around, free to come and go as he wished. Now the only person who remembered that kind old lady was him. Only he knew Alan Wrong for the psychopath he was. To everyone else he was just plain Alan. A Chronicler, who told them of the past.

Eve lifted the loop of thumb-thick rope, well-worn and blackened with age, that served as a catch on their gate. The small, white-painted barrier creaked back and forth as she closed it behind them. Above, tightly-woven thatch overhung the porch, giving it a warm, welcoming feeling, that extra touch in the tapestry of the village. Chris turned the door handle and it opened, just like that. Here it appeared no-one locked their front doors while they were out. But as Seethan watched, Chris rammed bolts home firmly behind them. Top and bottom.

Eve noticed his puzzled look and said, "There are gypsies in the forest, and that usually means trouble."

"Then why don't you lock the doors while you're out?"

"How?"

It hadn't occurred to him that they might not have locks. He shook the notion off and said, "We rarely had trouble with them in my time because everything we all did and said was monitored. But I understand it was a common problem in the past; with theft, assault and suchlike. People weren't even allowed to allude to the issue due to a madness instilled on society by rich do-gooders who quite often didn't have an understanding of how the other classes lived. And often by those in power, plus of course those who wanted to be."

He'd found it fascinating that the Romany of his time had been a lot richer than most realised. Many had joined together and bought hand-me-down ships, spending their lives out amidst the colonies and distant stars looking for a world of their own. He'd seen them from time to time, plying their trade out there in the depths of space. Now they styled themselves space gypsies, something he found incredibly romantic yet somehow ironic, because in years previous people had faced jail for using that collective once-racist term.

He had visions of ships touching down and ancient, gaudily painted horse-drawn wagons trundling slowly down the ramps. Horses huffed and neighed, harnesses jangled and the travellers brought with them the sharp scent of pipe tobacco as they filed past to set up temporary shop nearby. There they'd sell their handmade goods and give tarot readings, or trade goods. Sometimes those wagons, while decorated in the ancient ways, slid silently past on anti-gravs.

He realised that the others were staring at him in confusion, and Eve said, "I don't think any of us have a clue what you're talking about, we don't mean theft. That's practically unknown these days."

"Then what?" Seethan asked.

"It's a full moon tonight, that's the trouble," Eve continued.

"Like we said earlier, the Spooks change some people and for some reason they often focused on travellers. They've made superstition a reality."

A long eerie howl rose, causing Seethan to shiver. "What the hell is that, wild dogs?"

"No, not dogs. The Spooks re-introduced lost species, ones that hadn't been around for centuries. Those are wolves you hear. But not the natural kind."

That long drawn out howl came again, sounding close to the village. Seethan felt realisation dawning, as the others watched his reaction. "You can't be serious, werewolves? Those are just fairy tales."

"Not anymore. Sometimes people get bitten and change, while others change for reasons we can't fathom and become rabid killers. All of them. They even hunt down those they once loved, and only vaguely remember doing so when they're back in human form. It drives them mad and yes, it's as awful as it sounds. Some kill themselves, but more often than not they run away when they realise what they've become. If we catch them, we kill them. We have to, because if they come back, they could spread their contagion. There's no place for them in our society, Seethan." Eve pulled a white-feathered arrow from a quiver of others similar, and handed it to Seethan. "Look at the tip. Silver's the only thing that will stop them."

Chris stoked up the fire with a metal rod, before adding a few logs. He swung a blackened metal pot of water over the flames and poked at the fire again, causing a shower of brilliant sparks to scatter like panicked fairies. Jerking away from the fire, Chris patted at his beard while cursing under his breath. When he spoke, his voice was brusque.

"This isn't a game, Seethan. Like we've been telling you, the Spooks change people. They move things about: animals, trees, people. Where do you think those gators came from? They simply transported them here – no one knows why.

"The Spooks have abilities we can only imagine and they still manage to shock us after all this time, which is another reason to steer well clear of the woods. For some reason the aliens are very protective about those areas. One thing I don't understand is why they didn't attack you when you woke up in the forest. It doesn't make sense."

"And how do we know you really do come from the past?" Jon asked, changing the subject. His eyes were bright with curiosity and a hint of challenge. "I mean, apart from that outlandish garment you've got on, and what you and Alan both say, how do we *know*?"

Seethan pulled up a sleeve to show them his Smart-Arm. To his dismay it still lay there inert, like a glassy patch of hard skin. He then tried activating the camouflage on his flight suit but, as he'd expected, instead of it blending into the background nothing happened. Frustrated he said, "Well, my Smart-Arm may be dead but I bet none of you have anything like it. There's my gun, although that doesn't work either. Wait!"

He pulled a thick stick with a red-hot ember point from the fire and held it against his uniform. To their disbelief it didn't burn. "It's made from a material that's both fire retardant and heat resistant," he said. "Which means it's hard to burn and conducts little heat. Great if you get caught in a fire," he showed them his unblemished forearm beneath the fabric and then tossed the stick back into the fire.

"That does it for me," Eve said, as the others muttered in agreement. "We don't have anything like that. Is it true we travelled to the stars?"

"Yes, we did. There are many colonies out there now, or there were when I left. I'm not saying that they were all doing brilliantly, far from it. Frontier worlds can be one hell of a struggle. There are always new ones being settled, mining colonies being set up while others are abandoned for one reason or another. I've set foot on quite a few of those colonies, from Mars in this system to New Mecca – one of our furthest reaches. The Earth I left behind was nothing like this one. There's little countryside left. Almost everything was buildings or farmland, with cities merging with each other and becoming one."

They pulled up wooden dining chairs next to the dining table and took a seat, as Seethan continued.

"People usually lived in flats, rooms on top of each other, and everyone was trying to scratch a living any way they could. Times were hard. There were more people than jobs and many joined the military to escape the boundaries of the world. It was so different. The streets and pavements were white, seamless, and solid – not shingle like yours. They were smooth, unbroken lines that rarely need fixing. Whenever a new street was needed, they just extruded it. Kind of expanded the nearest ones using machines. Everywhere you went there were people. It was very, very crowded."

They were staring at him, their eyes wide with fascination.

"Drones were everywhere – vehicles that drove themselves. They were in the air, sea, land and even in space. There were cities under the sea. You could look up at the transparent domes overhead and see shoals of fish swimming past. Whales, dolphins, you name it. We even had floating cities, which could move from one part of the ocean to another depending on trade or politics."

Seethan found himself staring into the fire as he reminisced.

"We were once able to drive our own vehicles, until the powers that be decided it was too dangerous. Accidents happened all the time. People lost control of them and terrorists used them as weapons. In my day, only the military had vehicles that you could drive yourself, plus of course the extremely rich, who didn't mind the extortionate fees associated with it, and those with motor sport licences."

He told them about the cities in geostationary orbit and the wide gossamer highways that linked them. In the evening sky, a necklace of beads strung along the glittering spider-web of the roads in the moonlight. From the ground, it had been impossible to see the ebb and flow of the traffic travelling along them without aid, yet they were as constant as a never-ending river. He thought back to his views of the heavens in his youth, the glistening pearls of satellite cities. The heavens were clear now, the orbital cities and space highways gone as if they had never existed.

Seethan regaled them with his memories of the annual around-the-world races, and how the especially designed vehicles created a great deal of anticipation and furore as they sped over the heavenly roads spanning the circumference of the world. Fortunes were made and lost, while the loss of life remained high despite safety precautions. Yet, those drivers developed a status of reverence that many youths of the time aspired to.

As Seethan talked, Jon took the pot from the fire, made them all a hot drink and set the cups before them. Seethan wrapped his hands around his and focused on the steam rising from it, lost in the mist and his memories.

"Almost everything was run by artificial intelligence," he continued, "sorry, machines – from home security to shopping and childcare. War went on, not so much on Earth but certainly elsewhere. AI got involved in that too. Planets set up colonies on other worlds and then, sooner or later, those same colonies strove for independence, the same as their parent worlds had. Again, this usually brought about conflict of one sort or another. It was a never-ending circle of violence, with the colonies all vying for the best deal they could get, often at another's cost."

"Doesn't sound like a very nice place to live," Jon said.

"We didn't know anything different, but I guess you're right. Everywhere you looked there was extremism, murder, rape, and assault. Nothing ever changed. It didn't matter that everywhere we went, we were watched by machines that tried to prevent all that horror from happening; happen it did. There was no privacy, even in our own homes. Our children were monitored through AI by law to protect them, and the parents from allegations other people might make."

"What's AI?" Jon asked.

Seethan looked at him for a moment. "That's the artificial intelligence I was telling you about."

"Can you describe it?"

In Seethan's time, everyone knew what that was. His new friends would be as helplessly lost there as he was going to be here. He had to think carefully before replying. "Artificial intelligence is basically a machine that can think enough to do the job we set it. Sometimes even more than that. Originally, they were designed to make life easier for us. Didn't always turn out that way though."

"Why did people live on top of each other?" Eve asked. "That doesn't make sense, who would even want to?"

"Want has nothing to do with it. We had no choice, because there were so many people. Billions upon billions of us. Some moved to the colonies hoping for a better life, but even those worlds soon had population booms, and so it went on. We spread constantly, like a virus...a disease. Or at least we did until this war with the Spooks happened."

Chris leaned forward to touch one of the patches on his flight suit. "What are those pictures on your clothing? There's a red knife there and some kind of dog."

"Those are my patches. This one," Seethan tapped his left breast and the 660-Squadron patch, "is my squadron, the group of pilots I belong to. It represents a wolf pack. Each squadron has a different badge chosen to represent them. The dagger symbol represents commando training, which is a special kind of soldier. It's a bitch to pass the course but, as marine pilots, we need to do it because we often fly troops in and out of contested areas. If we're shot down, we end up as an extra gun in the group. We also fly combat missions in fighter craft, so you could say we're a jack of all trades."

"You've killed people?"

"Only by accident."

Eve looked at him in horror and Seethan couldn't help but laugh.

"Sorry, that was supposed to be a joke. You're not supposed to ask questions like that. You need to remember that in a war, everyone involved kills their enemies one way or another, it's not just the guy who pulls the trigger. You might be a storeman ordering food. Without that, soldiers in the field can't operate. Likewise, any weapons or ammunition. The person doing the ordering might be sat in a nice cosy office but without that ammo, combat technicians can't kill other people. So, like I say, everyone involved in a war helps to kill other people."

"I never thought of that, but it makes sense. Were you really in the war with the Spooks?" Eve's chocolate eyes were wide with wonder.

"Only briefly, in one rather short battle towards the end. It was damndest conflict. The Spooks were just, well, unreal. None of our ship-to-ship weapons affected them and we lost every single fight. Not good."

Jon took a sip of his malty drink and licked the residue from the bottom of his moustache. "You mention rape, murder and so on. Nothing like that has happened here for as long as I can remember. I guess you could also say that the Spooks police us. They discover who's guilty and punish them, the severity depending on the crime. It's a great deterrent."

"Alan Wrong told me the Spooks didn't trouble you anymore, unless you congregated in large groups."

"That's not quite true," Eve said, pulling the blue rag binding her long brown hair free. She held the rag between her teeth and finger-brushed her locks before retying it. Happy with the result, she tossed the hair over her shoulder with a casual flick of her head. "They plague us from time to time, no-one knows why. It's as if they've never forgiven us for the war and have bouts of anger about it. But maybe someone does something the rest of us don't know about, something that really bugs them. Who knows how aliens think?"

"Spooks aside, do you know what really struck me about your way of life here?" Seethan said.

"No, what?" Eve replied, eyebrows raised.

"Your gardens. We don't have those; well, not individual ones anyway. We have parks and stuff. You can request a visit permit, but that's about it. I can't get over the fact that all the houses I've seen here have their own, with lawns and fruit trees. You don't know how lucky you are. In my eyes you're extremely rich, but then there's a saying that 'the grass is always greener on the other side'. I guess that's true."

Eve looked puzzled. "What does it mean?"

"That no matter what you have, someone always has something that seems better. People of my time would give their right arm to live here, and yet you think we lived in a world of wonders. We did, but we also lived with the knowledge that homicidal maniacs could kill thousands or millions of people at a moment's notice. A terrorist once blew up the dome of a city on Mars, and about eight thousand people died. Weapons of Mass Destruction were easily available on the dark markets and occasionally a maniac used them. Even with all of that hanging over us, I still felt a lot safer in my own time than I do here."

As if to drive the point home the howl rose again, its spine-chilling cadence gradually fading with a drawn out *Oooo*.

"Thanks for the drink," Seethan said. "But if you don't mind, I'd like to get some shut-eye. I really need to find my co-pilot. I'll set off in the morning. Hopefully I'll get to her before Alan Wrong does."

"You were concerned about him finding out about Rose,

why? And what is it with you and him – you don't like each other very much, do you." Jon said. It wasn't a question; it was a statement.

Seethan couldn't lie, but he had to be careful what he said for he knew that, no matter what the android said, Wrong wouldn't hesitate to kill them if he felt threatened. "That's an understatement, there's a lot about him you don't know. Just believe me when I say he's not to be trusted."

"What does that mean?" Chris asked. "Come on, tell us. What is it about him that we don't know, and why are you so afraid of him?"

"I'm not afraid of him, but I am for what he could do both to my friend and to all of you. If I told you, it would put your lives in danger and I'm not prepared to do that. Besides you wouldn't believe me. Just trust me when I say that he's not what he seems."

"In our world, Seethan," Jon said, "nothing is."

*****

There was someone outside his window, Seethan could sense it. But he was on the top floor, so how was that possible? He felt frozen, unable to move as he stared at the glass. He lay in his bed facing the single pane, perhaps so placed to allow guests to revel in the view of the morning sun over the village. Gathering himself, Seethan broke the spell and pushed himself up and back against the bare wooden headboard. It was summer, so how come there was frost glazing the glass? He shivered as a deep chill filled the room. Slowly scratch marks cut through the ice on the pane from top to bottom, and there was that horrible screeching sound that nails made when they were dragged down a chalkboard. A putrid smell hit him, making his gorge rise and his cheeks bloat as he fought back the nausea. It was similar to the acrid stench of burnt pork. He knew that smell well, for he'd dreamt of it often enough.

The stench bought back horrible memories he'd rather forget. There was something else in here with him, and he knew it. A shadow formed in a darker corner of the room, and he felt it watching him.

When Pete Phillip's corpse stepped forward into the

moonlight shining through the window and onto the floor, it was like an actor setting foot onto a stage. Somehow Seethan wasn't surprised, though the gorge disappeared and his mouth went dry. It was as though he had a pebble at the back of his throat, which he desperately wanted to swallow.

Pete moved slowly, painfully, until he stood beside the bed looking down at Seethan. His torn and blackened face was slick with blood and those storm-cloud eyes held a startling malevolence. A worm worked its way free from one corner of an eye and dropped to the floor with a slight, but audible, slap. Once, that terrible gaze would have had him scrambling away and gibbering in fear, but Seethan knew the truth of it. He was here, not back there at the crash. This was now, not then. The dead held no fear for him.

Here.

Now.

This wasn't Pete, it was one of *them* in his form. He slowed his breathing, knowing this was something designed to petrify him. But it didn't work, he'd dealt with his fear and the dread memories far too often.

"I wondered when you'd come," Seethan said. "It was just a matter of time."

A look of surprise flickered in those savage eyes. "*You're not afraid.*" The creature's voice was like a soft wind hissing between gravestones.

"I know that my friend, whose image you wear, was killed in the crash. To me, that was only a year or so ago. You're not him, just a shade of what he was."

"*We understand.*" The words were soft and somehow elusive. A pause, and then the eldritch voice came again. "Your...*strategies.*"

"That's right. Tools for dealing with horrors of the past. Your image is nothing new to me, I've lived with those dreadful memories and nightmares for too long."

They stared at each other for what seemed a long time.

The creature's eyes widened, those ham-fists clenched and the nails extended into talons as it leaned closer. "*You were in the battle, the day we came to this world. You were one of those responsible for The Sundering. We see it!*"

"I flew the ship, yes, but I wasn't responsible for what occurred. Control of the ship was taken from me. My mission was to try and prevent the war from ever happening."

The cloying cadaver stench increased, as the ghoul leaned closer, eyes only inches from his. He could feel oily tendrils snaking through his mind, tasting his memories and savouring them like fine wine. The back of Seethan's mouth flooded and again he wanted to vomit. The stench receded and the corpse stepped back.

Seethan gasped, feeling as if he'd been released from a vice-like grip.

"*Yes, we've seen the truth in your mind.*" Dead Pete's voice was choked with blood, the crimson mess dripped in a slow glutinous stream onto his chest and down to the floor. "*You were trying to stop the war but others interceded.*"

"That's right. The idea was to go back in time and stop us from colonising your world. To warn them that you were there, hidden; in the hope that one day we could learn about each other and be friends. The idea was to go into Earth Orbit and operate the Time-Drive in vacuum, but it all went wrong when you landed. In a way it's both of our faults – humankind and the Spooks."

"*We wondered why you'd destroy your own people. We see now that the Jamie was to blame. He will have perished in what followed.*"

"Mistakes happen and that's what the war was. Both races suffered as a consequence. There's too much blame. The surveyors for not doing their job properly, the companies that didn't want to lose their investment, and the military for backing them up. The irony is your arrival here changed our mission from what it was to what it became. I'm sorry for all that's happened. Mankind has a constant need for new colonies and our greed can carry a terrible price, but we tried to make things right at the end."

"*You failed.*"

"Well, yeah."

There was a sense in Seethan's mind, a fleeting memory of happy and contented ethereal beings on a distant world. It wasn't a vision exactly, more of a feeling – yet it brought with it a sense of colour, smell, and great joy. There was the shock of mankind's arrival. Of something so alien to them, of standing back to watch and unsure what to do. But then the drilling started and there were many deaths from the poisonous ores they hadn't even known existed. The desperation, a need to fight and defend themselves. They studied their foe, space, so many other worlds, and learned much. And then came a blinding hot light that ate everything, causing them to flee their own world and take revenge against those that had caused their misery.

One moment those memories were crystal clear and the next they were distant. It was like awakening from a fleeting daydream. Seethan shook his head and took long shuddering breaths to clear his mind. Finally, he said, "There's something I need to ask you."

"*Your enemy, Alan Wrong. Why did we free him?*"

"Yes, you must have known that he's a murderer. He's also an android, a machine. You stopped all of our technology from working, so why did you allow him to be, to continue to exist?"

The thing that was Pete stepped back and sat into the chair, it creaked as he sat back in it, one foot slowly tapping against the bare wooden floor. With each tap, small things fell to the floor and squirmed, wriggling their way towards the bed. Pete's torn flesh steamed in the chill air and moonlight. His eyes carried an unholy brilliance, reminiscent of stars in a crisp winter's night sky.

It wasn't right. When Pete had died, the top part of his body had been obliterated.

"*Your androids are sentient and have committed no crimes against us. The Alan only killed humans and his own kind. He was no threat to us, but he was to you. To us he could be a friend, perhaps an ally of sorts.*"

"Now I get it," Seethan said bitterly. "Listen, I'm looking for my co-pilot Rose, she's another android and I'm hoping she's alive too. Can you help me? If Alan finds her before I do, I'm pretty sure he'll kill her."

"*We see her in your memories.*"

"Fuck the memories. She's here somewhere, I know she is. Why won't you help me find her?"

"*The androids have done us no harm, we cannot interfere.*"

Pete leant towards him suddenly, his voice growing louder as he reached forward and said, "*Seethan. Seethan!*"

Something grabbed his arm and shook him. He struggled and woke with a shout, to find himself staring up into Jon's eyes. Seethan tried to slow his breathing. It was only another damned nightmare. He gasped with relief and shuddered.

"I heard you shouting in your sleep," Jon said. "I had to wake you before you roused the entire village."

"It was just a bad dream," Seethan replied, trying to drag his eyes from the maggots still squirming in the moonlit floor.

"What's going on?" Chris demanded, appearing with his sister behind Jon. "You've made enough noise to wake the dead."

"That's almost funny," Seethan replied with a choked snort, and explained how that the Spooks had come to speak to him.

Eyes huge with anticipation, they took him downstairs, the twins sitting him down and questioning him while Jon made them all another hot drink over the embers of the fire. Seethan told them all that had happened, and that he'd thought it just another nightmare when he'd been shaken awake. At least until he'd seen the bugs on the floor.

"So much of that makes sense," Jon said, placing drinks before each of them and then sitting down himself and running one hand over the front of his face, as if to wash away the vestiges of sleep. "These androids of yours, sounds to me like they're the Spooks' allies."

"There was a huge worry about employing androids in a war role," Seethan explained. "People were concerned that once they learned to fight, they might use those skills in a rebellion against mankind. Rose herself was only there to operate the Drive and to repair the ship if needed. But she could also take over flying it if something happened to me."

"Why are you so concerned about her if she's an artificial person" Eve asked. "You've said that you care about her: why? And what's more, how could you if she's not real?"

"You'd fit in well in my time," Seethan snapped. "There's a lot of prejudiced people there too. Yes, I care about her. But it's more than that, she's my crewmate and–"

He was interrupted by the sound of raised voices outside, followed a few moment later by the creak of the gate and hurried crunching steps on the garden path. A frantic hammering on the door made them all jump.

"Jon, answer the door!" someone shouted from outside.

"That sounds like Frank, one of the elders," Jon explained

as he pulled the door open. "What is it, what's going on?"

A weedy, unkempt-looking individual entered and blinked as if to clear his eyes. Slightly taller than Jon and the twins, he was skinny to the point of emaciation, his balding head and bulging eyes giving him a fish-like appearance. "Three people have been murdered in the village, the entire Smith family. Both parents and even young Todd, poor little soul. He's the one who's always digging with his bucket and spade."

The twins rose as one, their shocked faces mirroring Jon's.

"What happened?" Seethan asked as he, too, stood, a sense of foreboding filling him.

"Their necks were broken, looked horrible it did. Little Todd suffered the same fate but his body was thrown onto the fire afterwards." His narrowing eyes focused sharply on Seethan as he shuddered. "Where have you been all evening? The elders want to talk to you and I've been sent to escort you to them."

"He's been with us the entire time," Eve said. "Jon and Chris will back me up on this, won't you?"

The men both quickly agreed and Frank looked confused. "I've known you all of my life and you've never lied or said a bad word about anyone. But Alan Wrong spoke to us before he left and he warned us about you. He said that back in his time you were a killer, and advised us to watch out for you. He told us that somehow, you'd escaped justice and had stolen a machine which you used to cause The Sundering. He said that you're responsible for the fall of mankind."

"The lying son of a bitch!" Seethan shouted. "It's him, not me! He's a serial killer and not even human, he's an android!"

Jon ushered Frank into the room and shut the door, saying, "I think you'd better explain what's going on."

Reluctant but knowing he had no choice, Seethan answered him, starting from scratch for the elder. "He was built to serve humanity, but murdered a family friend who brought me up when my parents died. Alan was caught and convicted, sentenced and locked away somewhere. But androids are long-lived and he survived the destruction when civilisation fell."

"But we've never had any murders here before you arrived," Frank said, his voice determined, "and it's funny how you appear and suddenly this all happens. As for Alan not being human, that's rubbish. I've seen him cut himself."

"They can bleed," Seethan replied. "They're designed to be like us, it's not real blood. He's after Rose, because she's an android like him."

"But, why would he want her?" Eve asked.

"It's what he does. Androids emulate humans, and Alan decided he wanted to be a serial killer. He's already killed many other synthetics, along with several humans. He knows Rose is here and is trying to get to her, before I can warn her."

"It's all a bit far-fetched if you ask me," Frank said. "Come on, the council of elders will deal with you." He grabbed Seethan by the top of his left shoulder.

Seethan automatically blocked him with his left hand and hit him on the pressure point of his chin with a right-handed snapping punch. Frank collapsed instantly, but Seethan caught him and carefully lowered him to the floor.

"Seethan!" Eve gasped. "What have you done?"

Chris and Jon both looked as shocked as she was, and for a moment nobody moved. Then Eve rushed over to kneel over Frank's prone body. She checked him over before looking at Seethan accusingly.

"He's alive," she said. "You could have killed him!"

"I only hit him hard enough to knock him out, as I'm trained to do when necessary. Don't worry, he'll come around in a few moments. Look, think about what I've been telling you. Besides me being with you guys all tonight, have you any idea how much strength it takes to snap one person's neck, let alone two or three? For most, it would be almost impossible. I know that if Alan finds Rose, he'll kill her. I've got to get to her first."

He saw them considering his words. Coming to a decision, Jon spoke first.

"There are horses in the barn next door. They belong to my brother; he won't mind us borrowing them given the circumstances. Chris, get the weapons; Rose, gather what food we have. All of you grab what you need for a journey. I'll get the horses. You can ride, can't you Seethan?"

"I've ridden horses on shore leave before, camels too."

"What's a camel?" Eve asked.

"Bit like a horse with lumps. Look, we need to get a move

on and get out of here before it's too late. Others will come to see what the delay is."

"We can try speaking to the Romany. You never know, they might have an idea where to look for your friend," Eve said, as she hurriedly packed a bag.

"Really, how so?" Seethan asked.

"You ask too many questions, just trust me," she answered.

"Here," Jon said, handing him a knife.

"I already have one."

"I bet it's not silver-coated like this one. We all carry them; you never know when you might need something like this."

"Oh, okay." Seethan briefly inspected the silver-etched blade, then slid both it and the soft leather sheath into his left thigh pocket. Ready, they hurried outside.

"This is Midnight," Jon said, handing Seethan the reigns of a huge stallion that was so dark it was as if it sucked the light from their surroundings.

The horse had a long mane and proud manner. Its ears stuck straight upwards and twitched almost constantly, as if on alert to danger. It was so big its back was level with Seethan's head.

"That's one hell of a horse," Seethan said, looking up at the monster.

"He'll serve you well, look after him," Jon added, dragging up a footstool and gesturing for Seethan to stand on it and mount up.

"I'm not carrying that thing around," Seethan said, indicating the stool. "So how the hell am I supposed to get up and down from here?"

"We can worry about that later. Right now, we need to get moving,"

The others had much smaller horses and Seethan presumed that he'd been given the stallion as he was the tallest. With white socks and hooves that looked larger than a marine's boots, Midnight looked down at him disdainfully, eyes like pits of coal. Seethan could almost swear it sniffed with contempt, regarding him as if he were a fly he was eager to swat. It was, without doubt, one of the most breath-taking creatures he'd ever seen.

Soon they were mounted and Jon quickly turned and led them off into the darkness.

Chapter 11

There were nine narrow, gaudily-painted horse-drawn caravans at the traveller camp perched on the edge of the forest. The subdued light from the moon, and a multitude of lamps, gave the camp a warm romantic feel. In the centre of the circle of vehicles, figures sat chattering and laughing around a large fire. Apart from that, the scene was still, but as Seethan and his companions rode up, two swarthy youths appeared out of the bushes and hailed them. Demanding to know what they wanted, the men took their reins as the four dismounted. Seethan had swung his legs over one side and slid to the ground, hitting it with a thump and stumbling, much to the amusement of the travellers.

"What do you want?" one of the two repeated bluntly. "Lost are you, or perhaps spying on our camp?"

"Neither. We've come to talk to the seer who travels with you. She's greatly respected in all the villages and we're here to ask for her advice. My friend," she indicated Seethan, "has lost someone close to him, and we wonder if she could help us find her."

The youth studied them for a moment and the one who'd spoken said gruffly, "It'll cost you."

"I can pay," Seethan replied, subconsciously touching the pouch of gold coins in his belt. He was suddenly grateful that all pilots were issued them in time of war, in case they came down and needed help from the local populace. Gold had held its value throughout the ages.

The youth whispered to his companion, who led their horses away. Fighting his concern for the animals, Seethan and the others followed the swarthy youth towards the campfire. Their guide told them to stop a short distance away from the gathering, while those sitting around the fire fell silent and looked up at them expectantly.

"Hey, Mother," the youth called. "A customer for you."

As the man turned and vanished back into the darkness, an old, dark-haired woman arose and came over to join them. The others around the campfire remained silent and watchful, puffing fragrant clouds of tobacco from long thin white pipes that had thumb-sized bowls.

"You'll forgive my son," the weathered-faced lady said, plucking out her pipe with one hand and eying them up and down. "There's a bad moon tonight, and naturally we're concerned. We get blamed for all kinds of nonsense during these times, but the locals appear unusually agitated tonight." She had quickly appraised Jon and the others and apparently dismissed them. Her eyes were intent on Seethan as she spoke.

"Well, I guess that might have something to do with me," Seethan confessed, "so you'll understand if we're in a bit of a hurry. People might be coming after us for something I didn't do. I need to find a friend of mine. She's in terrible danger and my companions suggested you might be able to help."

The woman's piercing brown eyes, bordered with black mascara, flickered over his flight suit and then locked again onto his. For a moment, orange flames from the fire reflected in them, and it was as if each were ablaze. "Follow me," she said softly, then turned away and led them to one of the caravans that were drawn up in a protective circle around the fire.

Wrought of traditionally wooden construction, it was painted gaudy shades of yellow and red, with four huge spoked wheels that were colour-coded to match. The yellow glittered in the firelight. Seethan blinked: was that gold? The shaft at the front lay in the long grass as if it had been abandoned. Seethan could easily imagine the horses strapped there, trotting jauntily through towns and villages while the locals stopped to watch them go by.

Decorated with strange black cursives and emblems, the stable doors had their top halves thrown open to the night while the bottom parts were closed. The contraption creaked and dipped as they climbed the two small narrow steps that led up and inside. The seer reached a hand inside, unbolted the bottom doors and entered. She sat Seethan's companions on the bunk that ran along the rear, and lowered a hinged table that lay attached to one wall before producing folding stools for herself and Seethan. Without a word, she pulled a black cloth from somewhere and draped it over the table, finally adding a small, carved wooden box. Her hands caressed the box, as if it were a lover, and Seethan noted the bare wood was so well-worn it looked polished. She sat and studied him, and he her.

Her dress was the colour of fresh blood, with white lace running around the sleeves, hem, and neck. From beneath the tight black bandana atop her head hung dark ropes of hair in colourfully beaded plaits which jangled and rattled as she moved. Opening the box, the old lady took out a deck of ancient-looking, hand-painted cards and shuffled them.

"Who is it you seek?" she asked.

Seethan caught himself in time, he was about to say that if she was that good at her craft she'd know. But he bit back his words and said simply, "My friend and I aren't from around here. We were travelling together but have been separated. Can you help me find her?"

Her eyes had widened as he spoke but held out her hand, palm up. Seethan felt confused until Eve leant forward and whispered in his ear. Quickly, he produced a gold coin from his pouch and put it in her hand. She looked at it for a moment and rubbed it with her thumb, bouncing it up and down in her hand as if to weigh it. Her brow furrowed and she held the coin up to the solitary oil lamp in a far corner of the room, where it glinted in the flickering light. Licking her lips, she again rubbed the coin between her fingers and thumb, and then bit it. With a flourish, the coin disappeared into the folds of her outfit and she continued to shuffle the cards. Finally, she put them down into one pile atop the black tablecloth, those calculating eyes never leaving Seethan's.

"Cut the cards," she said softly.

Seethan complied, watching as she picked up the pack and mumbled a few words. She dealt a few cards face-up on the table, and studied them before saying, "The one you seek is far from here."

"No shit." He just couldn't help himself.

"Seethan, please. Just trust her," Eve's voice was insistent.

"Okay, I'll try," Seethan said. "Look, can you tell me where she is, or how to find her?"

"All I see is that she's somewhere to the south. The cards also tell me that you're in grave danger, all of you. There's much blood here, and great risk, but I can't tell if it's in the past or the future." She paused and studied the cards, looking confused for a moment, before saying, "It's…both. I can see that death travels the path you follow. And look, there's a warning. Beware of the man who isn't."

"That's got to be Alan," Seethan said in surprise. "He's…not a good person, he's dangerous."

The gypsy nodded, the beads in her plaits rattling as she did so. "He's *wrong*," she said.

Seethan felt as if someone had slapped him. Had he heard right? He knew he had, and he leant forward and listened more intently.

She gathered the cards and dealt them again. Her hands were weathered and topped by black-painted nails, giving her an eerie look. She studied the cards and, after a moment of consideration, said, "You must go to the witches' village in the New Forest. There you'll find someone to help you. But be warned, there are forces who will try to stop you, as well as those who may be of assistance. You must go, now! People are coming here, looking for you."

"A witches' village," Seethan said, "Seriously?"

"I've heard of it," Jon said. "It's about seventy miles south of here. Come on, we'd better get going."

"Is that all I get for my gold coin?" Seethan demanded.

"No, other advice I'll give. Help will come from unexpected quarters: take it. Each of you who undertake this journey will be changed and some may never return. Travel lightly and beware the unborn. Their reach is long."

Her son appeared at the door suddenly, looking agitated. "Villagers are approaching, they've got torches and it looks like they mean business."

"Go, quickly," the old woman said to Seethan. "Take a path through the forest, they won't be expecting that." She told her son to fetch the horses. As they stood, the old woman unexpectedly gave Seethan his coin back, saying, "Some things are worth more than money. You may need this. Go quickly now, and be safe."

"We daren't go through the forest," Eve said. "It's forbidden, you know that. No one goes there."

"The risk is great but you have no choice. Go, now!" The woman's dark eyes locked on Seethan's, but she said nothing more.

Seethan gulped, remembering the ghostly apparition in his room a few hours ago. "I've a feeling we'll be okay," he said.

"I woke in the forest after the crash. I spent well over a day there and nothing happened to me, so why should it now? Come on, let's go."

With Eve muttering that at least they'd be safe from their pursuers, they took the horses from the fortune-teller's son. Jon linked his fingers together, allowing Seethan to step into the stirrup and mount up. On the way there, Midnight had showed a tendency to take Seethan under low-hanging branches, as if to brush an irritation from his saddle. Yet any similar such plans the stallion might have had were apparently abandoned, as if it sensed trouble was near. Quickly, Midnight followed the other horses around the back of the caravan and into the forest.

Chapter 12

"They're following us!" Eve said, at the distant clamour of voices as they left the gypsy camp and followed a moon-lit path that led deep into the forest.

"I thought you said they wouldn't come into the forest after us," Seethan said to Eve, wary of increasing speed with his limited knowledge of horsemanship, and the low branches hanging like traps in the darkness. Thankfully, Midnight no longer tried using them to knock him from his saddle.

"Okay, so I was wrong," she retorted sweetly.

"They must be desperate," Chris said loudly, over the drum of hooves. "They wouldn't have risked coming so far in the dark otherwise."

A short while later all sounds of pursuit had faded away and all they could hear was their hoofbeats pounding below them, accompanied now and then by the eerie hoots from owls, along with rustling and scurrying in the undergrowth, as unseen things fled from their approach. Sometime later, it was apparent that the villagers had indeed given up pursuit, and the group settled down to a more sedate pace. When Seethan asked what time it was, they looked at him in confusion.

"It's early morning," Jon replied, despite the fact it was still incredibly dark.

"Yes, but…" Seethan suddenly wondered whether his new friends understood the concept of time.

"There's a sundial outside the village hall but obviously it doesn't work at night," Chris said, with a hint of humour. "Look, we just don't keep track of the time. Why would we? Alan told us about your culture's fascination with it but I don't think any of us really understand why, nor wanted to emulate it. Oddly, he always seemed to know the hour. No idea how, or whether he was bullshitting."

"Androids always know what time it is," Seethan replied. "They're machines, but I do take your point."

When they entered a clearing, Jon, who was leading, reined in his horse and held up one hand, saying, "I think we should stop and rest. It'll be a long day tomorrow, and there's quite a journey ahead of us."

They dismounted and hobbled their horses, allowing them to roam but not far from the campfire Jon was building. They all set out their bedrolls amidst the grass, not far from the crackling flames. Chris offered to take the first watch, to be followed by Eve. The routine was strange to Seethan. Without clocks they stayed on watch until they felt tired, and that's when they shook their relief.

As they settled in for the night, Seethan called for their attention. "Listen," he said, "you heard what the old woman said, that some of us might not return. I'll understand if that makes you uncomfortable, and you want to stop here and go back."

"Don't be daft," Eve replied. "We've made up our minds. You're our friend now, and you asked for our help. It's not in our blood to let people down. Besides, to be totally honest we've always had an odd – but strong – feeling that there's something off about Alan. Call it a gut feeling, and now we feel that what's going on is going to affect all of us too. We want to help. Try and get some sleep, you look exhausted."

Seethan stifled a groan as he struggled to get his bedding comfortable. His whole body ached. He was grateful that they'd stopped for a rest, and very much so that they'd agreed to continue with their journey. When he lay down, he tossed and turned striving to find one position that didn't hurt.

For a while he found himself looking up at the stars, wondering at mankind's expansion in the long years since the disaster the *Mako* had caused, and whether it had affected the colonies. Was there anything he could have done differently; some way he could have averted the destruction he'd caused? With this going over and over in his mind he finally fell into a troubled sleep.

*****

Seethan woke several times, as always unable to remember the nightmares that caused the palpitations and the sweat that streamed from him. Sometimes he was boiling, other times cold. Occasionally he woke to see one or more of the others looking at him, and he knew that he must have been calling out in his sleep. He was finally woken with a gentle shake from Eve, who handed him a bowl of a hot creamy mush. He looked at it in surprise and asked what it was.

"Oats, a little salt, hot water, dried apple and a few blackberries that I picked."

"Oh." Seethan said, jabbing at the mash with the small wooden spoon in it.

Eve's amusement quickly turned to annoyance. "It's not poisonous!"

Seethan took a tentative taste and then smiled, taking a mouthful. "Hey, this isn't bad!"

Eve snorted and stomped away to pack up her bedroll, muttering under her breath.

Chris chuckled and said, "You've managed to offend my sister, that's quite a feat. You may not know it but she's renowned for her cooking skills. Great job, fella."

"Well, I've never had porridge before. Sure, it's used as a staple throughout the colonies. I've had shore leave on many of them, but I tend to aim for a fully cooked breakfast whenever possible. Besides, I did say it was nice," Seethan added, defensively.

"It's rolled oats, not porridge. There's a difference. Don't worry, you've just wounded her pride," Chris said, saddling the horses. "She'll get over it."

As they mounted and rode off, Chris travelled besides Seethan for a while, and he could see that Chris wanted to say something. Finally, he broached the subject Seethan had been dreading.

"I didn't mean to eavesdrop but you were talking in your sleep and quite clear. I was going to rouse you at first but decided against it. There's no-one around to hear you anyway, except for us of course. You blame yourself for what happened to your friends."

"Something like that," Seethan responded sourly.

Chris nodded, the muscles in his jaw bunching as he chewed it over. "Want my opinion?"

"Feel free."

"Bad things happen. Carrying guilt weighs you down, so try to be kind to yourself. What happened in the past is exactly that, in the past. My mother used to have an old saying, *don't look back, you're not going that way*."

Seethan looked away from the twin, his eyes focusing on their path, and after a moment or two Chris gave up and rode on ahead to take point.

*****

Around midday they entered another clearing. This one was more lawn than the jumble of grass that had until now made up such areas. What's more, in the dead-centre stood a cloverleaf-shaped water fountain. Its three matching tiers were of pure-white marble that shone in the bright sunlight. To Seethan's surprise, crystal-clear water jetted from the lip-like spout that was at least four times his own height, cascading around in a musical cacophony to the deep, pool-like base.

"What the hell is that?" Chris asked, leading the way forward until they dismounted and stood looking down at the cool, clear waters.

"It's a fountain, a water-feature we had way back before The Sundering," Seethan said, noting with surprise the solar panels that blended in along the full length of the pool's lip, dating it early 21st century. "I thought you said that most of mankind's works had been obliterated?"

"A few of them are still around but they're rare. Over the years I've heard of people coming across such things, but this is the first that I've seen myself," Jon said, his sentiments quickly echoed by the twins. "And this is, well, beautiful."

"It's also still working and there are no leaves or dead insects in it," Seethan replied. "Nor algae. It should have been overgrown and discoloured by now, the water filters blocked and maybe the water supply dried up. This fountain, and this well-mown lawn surrounding it, suggests someone's looking after this place."

"Elves probably," Eve said. "After The Sundering the Spooks broke the barriers hindering the return of the old races from the hidden lands – ones that run parallel to ours. The elves keep mostly to themselves but, in return for being brought here, they were tasked by the Spooks with tending the forests and looking after the animals."

Seethan sat on the side of the fountain, listening to the sound of splashing and relishing the cold spray that the gentle wind blew against his face. He moved closer and swished his hands back and forth in the chill water, before raising double handfuls of it to his face to refresh himself. He turned to look at the others, wiping his face dry with his sleeve. "All of this is hard for me to take in. First, we get werewolves. Now there's elves and witches. I've been visited in the night by a friend of mine who's been dead for a long time and, to be honest, I'd like to know where the hell all of this is going to end. I feel like I'm in the middle of a nightmare I can't wake up from."

"Things are what they are," Jon replied. "One of the mistakes people of your generation made was to believe the old races were just stories. I've no doubt that some were, but many were based on reality; on things that really existed in bygone ages. Your people needed proof rather than faith, and usually provided that by your technology. But there's much more to life than you know."

"So I'm discovering," Seethan replied, wiping at his face. "But I'm still trying to figure out how this fountain replenishes itself. I can tell that it gets its power from the sun, the technology that runs it was old even in my own time. Surely there's a lot of water wastage with it spilling over the sides, so what's filling it back up?"

"Perhaps it's fed by an underground river," Jon replied with a shrug.

"Who the hell cares?" Eve snapped. "It's about time we were on our way. We can't afford to spend our time being distracted, if you're intent on killing Alan."

"I'm not intent on killing him, more like stopping him hurting my friend. I've no idea if we can even wound him, let alone kill him. Androids are almost impossible to stop, which is one of the reasons we were reluctant to teach them combat skills. But you're right, we had better get going. How long is it until we get to this witches' village?"

"On a flat road, we could be there by nightfall," Jon said. "But with the slow going in this forest I'd say probably sometime tomorrow, possibly later. I doubt that the old gypsy told our pursuers where we're headed, and it's unlikely they'll follow us all the way through the forest. Only an insane person would want to travel through it by day, let alone by night," he added pointedly, looking at Seethan.

"Well, then that's me, officially mad then," Seethan said with a grin. That faded however, as he added, "Something's bothering me. You must have known Alan a long time, why would you suddenly take sides with me?"

Jon locked eyes with Seethan. "Because we don't trust him. There's something odd about that man that we can't explain. Many of us are uneasy around him, and we three believe what you're saying is true. As Eve told you earlier, it's a gut feeling."

Seethan fed Midnight a handful of oats given to him by Chris, rubbing the horse's nose while talking to him in low tones. The recalcitrant beast responded by nuzzling his face and pushing at him. To his surprise Seethan found himself warming to it. When he mounted the horse, he patted the creature's neck and received a snort of pleasure. Although that was followed by what he could only describe as a raspberry blown between its rubbery lips.

*****

They stopped before dark that evening in the largest clearing they'd yet come across and it appeared an ideal place to make camp. It must have been half a kilometre from one side to the other at the widest part. There were occasional bushes and a few trees and the forest proper surrounded them at a distance, like a thick impenetrable border filled with shadow.

By the time their staple diet of a spicy stewed meat and vegetables was ready, the stars were already glimmering. Seethan had struggled to keep his eyes open throughout the meal, and it felt like an effort to lift the spoon to his mouth. He ached all over from riding, and felt like he'd lost a fight with six dockies armed with baseball bats. His back pressed to a tree, Seethan tossed a piece of stale bread he'd been using to mop up the gravy towards a large black bird that was hopping back and forth a few steps away, watching him. It cawed loudly, as if in thanks. Hopping over to the bread, it hacked away with a finger-length beak.

Seethan watched it for a while and groaned involuntarily. The others noticed his winces and stiff movements and teased him good humouredly.

Eventually Eve came to sit next to him.

Seethan gestured towards the bird. "That crow must be the size of a chicken."

She glanced at the bird and snorted. "It's a raven. Now take your clothes off."

"Come again?" He looked at her askance.

"Don't be shy, a big man like you. That thing you're wearing, remove it."

Confused, he looked where she was pointing. "My flight suit?"

"Whatever, take it off. I have some medication that I can rub into your muscles. It'll help ease your aches."

Spreading her blanket on the ground, she told him to lie on it, vigorously shaking a dark green bottle as he complied. Seethan heard the pop of a cork and then she smeared a foul-smelling, oily lotion all across his back, shoulders, and thighs. He groaned as her fingers dug deeply, kneading his complaining muscles.

"You don't talk about her much, this Rose we're looking for."

"It's the way I am. I'm constantly thinking about her, I just don't say much about it."

"Tell me about her, how you first met."

Seethan groaned as her fingers dug into him. "I was recovering from an accident and, while healing, I was sent to an establishment to help with a classified project and met her there."

"There has to be more to it than that."

"I was looking over the ship, it was a new class and I'd not seen one before. I'd heard from my boss that a synthetic – an artificial person – had been assigned but when she stepped from around the far side of the craft it was as if someone had slapped me across the face. For a moment I couldn't breathe, I could only stare at her. She has the most incredible green eyes and I felt that I was falling into them."

"Are you bonded, physically?" she asked, and when Seethan looked up at her embarrassed, she added, "I only ask because it's natural in our society to talk about such things, to know how people interact."

For some reason Seethan trusted her and found he could talk about it. "Yes, we are bonded, as you put it. She is a part of me that's missing, and I'll do anything to get her back."

"Don't worry, we'll find your Rose. Now, relax and let me work."

Soon he was lost in a mixture of pleasure and pain. Eventually, Eve told him to turn over, and again she worked him over. Seethan forcibly blanked his mind and closed his eyes, relishing the moment her fingers became featherlike, almost tickling him after the previous torture she'd put him through. Slapping his stomach with a loud 'thwack', she signalled she was finished.

He gasped as the playful blow took him by surprise.

"That'll help," she said, climbing to her feet and picking up the blanket. "You'll soon get used to riding, but in the meantime get some rest. The three of us will sort out anything that needs doing."

Seethan felt confused. He knew it was Rose that he cared for, so why had he felt himself starting to react to Eve's ministrations? He was only human, sure, but he was also a one-woman man and this was against his principles. The worst thing was that, although he hadn't done anything, he felt as if in some way he'd betrayed her. After pulling his flight suit back on, he went to check Midnight. As he did so, Chris approached him.

"I know you're tired but I wondered if I might have a word," his friend said.

"Sure, what's bothering you?"

"Eve's had a rough time. Her fiancé, Joel, disappeared several years ago and no-one has any idea what happened to him."

"I'm sorry to hear that. Must have been hard for her," Seethan said.

"It has been, and she's still not over it. I think she still hopes he'll come back but I think he would have by now if it were possible. All we know for certain is that he went hunting with one of his friends and they both disappeared. We've urged her to move on, but she's not interested. A couple of guys have been hinting they'd like a relationship, but that only made her worse. It's only in the last year that she's begun to accept that he's never coming back. Even so, she says she's not ready to start again and I know she's too easily hurt."

"Never knowing what happened to him must be hard,"

Seethan said honestly. "There's no closure."

Chris nodded and continued. "They were to be married a few months after he vanished. Life can be cruel sometimes. The reason I'm mentioning this is because she seems to have taken a shine to you. Please, be gentle with her."

Midnight nickered as Seethan stroked his nose. "I wasn't aware of that, but thanks for telling me. Rose and I are close but we were just starting out. I'd like to see where it leads, and find her before Alan does."

Chris switched his eyes from the horse to Seethan's, as he too stroked him. "You need to be upfront with her, tell her that you really care for Rose."

"I have, and I do," Seethan said, returning to his bedding and moving it about.

"She'll understand and appreciate that, rather than feel that she's being rejected."

Seethan sat down on the bedding and patted it to indicate that Chris sit beside him. As his friend did so, Seethan said, "Listen, even in our enlightened society there's a stigma about artificial people. Some liken them to sex dolls. It's a difficult situation and there's a lot of prejudice and not many speak about it."

"Sex dolls?" Chris looked confused.

"Yeah, well, I think that's a subject for another time. But the long and short of it is that artificial people can look extremely realistic and it's led to a lot of abuse of them over the years. Eventually, through a rights activist group, they won their freedom. The result of that is they became so lifelike it's hard to tell them from real people, but by law they have to declare what they are to potential suitors. As for a long-term relationship, it's usually a no-go for several reasons. The first and foremost being that they don't grow old as humans do. They live for centuries without aging physically. Imagine being in your nineties and your partner still looks like she's twenty something. Worst still, she wants to party."

"You live until you're ninety?"

"Longer in most cases; war, disease, and disaster depending."

"I'm having a hard time believing all of this," Chris said. "Sounds kind of wrong to me."

"It did to a lot of people."

Having said their goodnights, Seethan laid down on his bedroll. He tried not to think of Rose, as he looked up at the stars glittering in the heavens and the ghostly glare of the moon as it rose over the trees.

*****

Seethan was on watch, staring into the flames of their fire, when deep in the forest came a long-drawn-out groan of a horn. His eyes snapped towards the direction of the noise. When it came a second time he went to rouse the others, but found them already climbing to their feet. A stiff wind sprang up and blew hotly against their skin, much like the draft from an opened oven. Overhead, dark shadows of treetops whipped this way and that against the backdrop of stars, as if huge plants were on the march. The wind brought with it a rushing sound, as though something were charging towards them. He'd never known a wind like it in such a clear sky.

The gale dropped suddenly, as if they were in the eye of a storm, and then they heard the moan of the horn once again. It was closer, the sound unearthly, and like that of a mortally wounded beast. It got louder and the sheer eeriness of it made Seethan shudder and swallow, despite the fact that his mouth had suddenly gone dry.

"What the hell is that?" he called to the others, catching himself reaching for his useless pistol. He grimaced and swore softly in frustration.

By now they'd taken defensive positions. They knelt with their weapons ready, faces a blend of fear and determination as they stared into the darkness. Bravery, Seethan noted, is being desperately afraid of something but doing it anyway, and a grim admiration for his new friends filled him.

"It's the Wild Hunt," Jon said, as if he were choking the words out. He gestured Seethan closer, to kneel besides him. "We told you earlier that the elves guarded the forests, and that includes against human incursion. There are tales of abductions, and of the atrocities and torture the hunt bestows on trespassers."

They were interrupted by a sudden, deafening clamour made up of dull painful horns and shrill trumpets. Seethan clapped his hands over his ears to keep out the noise, but even so the racket made him want to scream. It was as if the denizens of hell had decided to get together and form a band, their thunderous music hideously out of tune. The pain in his ears was akin to that of a demented dentist drilling into cavities in his teeth without anaesthetic, the fist-clenching agony of the cacophony driving all thought from his mind.

There was such a sudden hush that for a moment Seethan thought he'd gone deaf. All noise ceased. There was no rustling in the undergrowth nor trills from unknown birds. Such was the silence that he could hear the pounding of own heart. Seethan had to break the quiet, he had to. But his voice sounded loud and strange to his own ears, as if someone else was speaking for him.

"Jesus, I'd rather be back in a battle than listen to that again," he said lamely. He was still kneeling beside Jon, when a large band of men on an array of wild animals rode into the starlit clearing. Most were on horses, but there were also bears and deer, moose and wolves.

The newcomers wore metal armour that glittered like burnished silver against the stars and moonlight. The riders stopped, reining in their mounts, as they faced Seethan and the others. Their horses reared and whinnied, the bears reared and bellowed, while the wolves howled, yammered, and snapped at them. The eldritch riders lined up in long rows across the furthest side of the clearing, glimmering long-tipped spears pointed skyward but were threatening nonetheless.

A solitary, helmetless figure on a huge white stag strode forward, stopping a few feet in front of the other riders. The stag's antlers, splayed out like the branches of an ancient tree, bobbed and swept from side to side as it pawed at the ground. Atop the rider's head, a thick circlet of gold held his long flowing locks back from a frost-white face filled with cruelty.

Seethan glimpsed the lavender furnaces of their eyes, as their visors were thrown up to display their snowy faces. A moment later, their leader raised his spear as high as he could and then lowered it to point straight at Seethan and the others. The horn blared again, a deafening two-tone warble, the second note much higher and longer than the first.

At first nothing happened: it was as if the forest itself held its breath. Throughout the woodland, denizens large and small, natural and unnatural, froze in mid-step, afraid to move in case they too were discovered or caught up in what was to come.

Chapter 13

The clang of the elves' visors snapping shut rang through the clearing. As one, they began to move forward, followed by the thunder of hooves as the riders gathered pace and rolled towards them.

By now Seethan had picked up his spear, realising the futility of the heavy weapon against so many. But if this was to be where he would die, he'd go out fighting and meet his fate head-on. The wind sprang up again, howling as it whipped the treetops back and forth, blowing so harshly into Seethan's face he had to cover his eyes and peep through his fingers.

A loud croaking cry came from overhead and a large bird exploded from the trees and took to the skies, where it circled them from a safe distance. It flew as if unaffected by the tempest, which to Seethan didn't make sense. And then, just as the riders were gathering an unstoppable momentum, a dark oval shape suddenly grew between Seethan's group and the oncoming horsemen.

It quickly grew in size and then popped like a bubble, leaving a caped shadow in its wake. The figure raised the staff that was clenched tightly in its right hand and slammed it into the ground. Blue bolts of energy cackled and swirled around the stranger, growing quickly into a light so blinding that Seethan and the others had to shield their eyes and turn their faces away.

When the light dimmed, he managed to look back at the horsemen. They had stopped and were now milling about, as if unsure. They calmed down and the leader of the horsemen rode forward at a slow trot towards the solitary figure, the other mounts huffing and snorting behind him. As they met, the great stag stopped and lowered its head, as if in acknowledgement. The small figure reached upwards with its left hand and stroked the creature's nose. The two people conversed, whatever they said muted by distance and the dying wind. At length, the leader of the elves turned and rode back to re-join his fellows. They wheeled after him, back towards the forest at the far side of the clearing, and there quickly vanished into the darkness beneath the trees.

The Wild Hunt had gone.

With sighs of relief Jon, Eve and Chris came to stand beside Seethan, watching as the figure turned to face them. A hood was drawn over the stranger's face and, in the night, they were unable to make out any discernible features. As they started forwards to thank their benefactor, the shadowy bubble reappeared and engulfed the figure. When it burst a few seconds later, their saviour had gone.

"There you go," Seethan said loudly. "Just when I'm beginning to get used to things, a new kind of weird happens."

"I've never heard of anything like that before," Jon replied. "Was that a friend of yours, Seethan? It has to be something to do with you."

"Why me? I don't know anyone here apart from Alan, Rose, and you guys. Maybe the fortune teller or the Spooks had something to do with it."

Chapter 14

Jon suggested the next morning that Seethan change out of his uniform and into some of the spare clothes they carried between them. They'd brought a few things that should fit him, and so hopefully he'd be able to blend in more fully when they came to the village, or met others on their journey. They left the forest proper early that morning and entered a long sweeping moor that extended towards a plain in which horses and even cows could be seen munching silently on grass, raising their heads as they watched the group pass.

It wasn't even midday when they entered a small village, outside which a garish hand-painted sign declared in red 'Welcome to Burley'. Buildings ran parallel both sides of the curved dirt road, and dogs ran up to greet them, barking furiously. With the canines creating a ruckus around their feet, they began to pass numerous shops and hovels. Ducks squabbled in woven-reed baskets, placed carefully outside some of the buildings. There was the whinnying of horses and commotion from pigs in the background, in loud competition with the dogs. Villagers stopped to stare in open-mouthed curiosity, some muttering quietly to their neighbours while giving the travellers dark looks.

Most of the houses were thatched and similar to the ones in his friends' village. A few of the others had grey-slated roofs, the first Seethan had since his arrival. The town itself looked like something from an old movie set, and he quite expected actors to leap forth from alleyways and hidden doorways with pistols blazing.

One of the first things that struck Seethan was how much the place stank. It was a horrible mixture of raw sewage and rot, which he quickly mitigated by breathing through his mouth. Eventually they stopped at a two-storey building that had a swinging, white-painted sign hanging outside well above head height. The sign was so amateurish Seethan couldn't help wondering whether a child had created it. Upon it was an image he took to be a horse, along with the barely readable words 'Burley Inn', which made Seethan chuckle.

Leaving their horses tied up at the stables behind the inn,

they entered the bar through a low pitch-black door at the front of the building. The mouth-watering smell of cooking washed over them as they went in, masking the stench from outside. Dumping their bags on the sawdust-covered floor, Seethan and the twins took seats while Jon ordered them the dish of the day from the menu above the counter. They sat at one of the rough-hewn, lozenge-shaped tables and looked around, trying to ignore the silence and stares from the few other patrons. Jon soon joined them, handing each mugs filled with foaming dark ale from a tray, as he eased onto his seat.

"Enjoy," Jon said. "It's Witches' Brew."

"You're kidding, right?" Seethan asked, peering into the dark foam-capped liquid as if expecting to see frogs and newts.

"Relax," Eve said. "It's the name of the local beer, nothing more."

Embarrassed, Seethan took a sip of the strong dark ale and coughed. "Holy shit! That's like drinking a hand grenade."

"A what?" Jon asked.

"Hand grenade. Things that go – ah, never mind," Seethan hid his embarrassment by looking up the timber-beamed ceiling and whitewashed walls. He leant forward and said, "You know, this being a witch's village and all, you'd think there would be pictures hanging up there on the wall of people standing proudly besides their broomsticks."

"What on Earth are you talking about?" Eve asked, her eyes wide.

"Broomsticks. You know, witches' transport. In my era we have images of pilots next to their aircraft, particularly on the walls of the bars they frequent. Erm, I can see that I'm losing you. Never mind, it's an old marine-pilot thing." He changed the subject. "Anyway, now we're here who, or what, are we looking for?"

"I thought you'd have been able to help with that," Eve replied. "After all, the fortune teller sent us here after reading your cards, not ours. Does anyone have any ideas?"

"The only thing I can suggest," Jon said, "is that we see if there are any rooms available. If so, we can dump our kit in them and take a look around. Which brings me to ask, how are we going to pay for all of this? Normally we'd have brought items to trade, but we left home at the rush and without anything of value. Seethan, I'm sorry to say that we're probably going to have to use some more of that gold of yours. Unless someone has a better idea."

"Well, that's what it's for," Seethan said. "It's dead weight otherwise. But although the gypsy gave me her coin back, I don't have that many of them. We need to be careful."

"I'll go and talk to the owner of this place and see what he has to say," Jon replied. "You'll probably end up with a balance of small coin and a credit note for future stays."

"Nice," Seethan commented. "Just what I need. A return ticket to Pigsville."

"You'd better come to the bar with me," Jon added to Seethan. "After all, it is your money."

The two of them approached the beer-stained wooden counter, where a rotund, middle-aged, balding man greeted them with a bland smile. "Hi, I'm Mathew," he said. "Some people call me Matt. How can I help you?"

"I used to have a friend called Matt," Seethan said, his tongue taking charge of his brains. "People use to walk all over him."

The man's eyes narrowed and he looked Seethan up and down, but before he could say anything, Jon spoke quickly.

"Excuse my friend, he's not used to your ale and that Witches' Brew is pretty strong stuff. Tastes nice but sneaks up and hits you like a brick. My friends and I are looking for rooms for tonight, a hot meal or two, stabling for our horses, and a few drinks." He shrugged melodramatically. "But I'm afraid we don't have much in the way of trade."

The barman's eyes narrowed. "No coin, no room no food."

"We have a little gold."

As if by magic the man's expression changed from a scowl to that of a generous host. He gave Jon a beatific smile. "Ah, 'tis strong stuff right enough. You need to take it easy," he cast Seethan a meaningful look and Seethan produced a gold sovereign with a flourish and placed it on the table. The man's eyes widened, his mouth shaping an 'O' of delight.

As the barman reached for the coin, Jon smoothly palmed it and undertook the bartering, while Seethan meekly went back to their table with a second round of drinks. After a few more of the strong ales, the patron brought them plates brimming with thick steaming slabs of venison, wild mushrooms, chunks of garden vegetables, and mashed potatoes; all topped with a thick, rich-smelling gravy. They were ravenous after their journey and demolished the fare with aplomb. It was followed immediately afterwards by servings of blackberry and apple pie with clotted cream. All told, it was probably the best meal that Seethan had ever had. When they'd finished, the barman led the way upstairs to their rooms. Jon and Chris, it turned out, were sharing, while Seethan and Eve had a room each.

Seethan's was fairly small, with a single wooden-framed bed and a mattress made of stuffed straw, covered with rough sheets, blankets, and a couple of pillows. The walls were bare brick and mortar, and there was a large, deep-green rug in the centre of the room over the floorboards. After agreeing to meet downstairs after a rest, Seethan washed using the water-filled jug and bowl supplied, refilling as needed from a bucket on the floor. The barman told them the waste water was to be thrown from the window to the garden below, while night-soil would be collected by maids in the morning.

Seethan was out for the count from the moment his head touched the pillow and it was only a furious knocking on his door from Jon, who then entered and shook him, that finally roused him. Quickly dashing his face with more cold water, Seethan made his way downstairs to meet the others who were waiting in the bar.

It was late afternoon as they strolled through the streets looking for ideas, with Seethan pausing briefly to study a warning sign posted by the lake opposite the inn. While there were shops, many of the houses had open front doors through which people came and went willy-nilly. These houses-*cum*-shops bore all matter of local crafts – from home-made pastries, clothing, and horse-riding equipment to kitchen implements, tools, and bedding in the form of hand-woven blankets. There was even the occasional feather-stuffed pillow and duvets. One place bore a variety of basic weaponry and hand-drawn maps, mostly on paper but a few were on animal skin.

As they passed one building, a loud, repetitive clanging sound drew Seethan's attention and he couldn't help but look in. He stopped dead, looking in horror at the man working within.

"What's he doing to that horse?" Seethan asked loudly, wincing as the man cut away at the creature's feet with a knife of some sort, while holding the hoof between his knees and selecting a handful of crude iron nails.

"He's a farrier," Eve said. "He's re-shoeing the horses, so don't worry about it."

The farrier raised his eyes, clearly having heard, and gave Seethan a speculative look that he obviously reserved for idiots.

"It looked downright cruel to me," Seethan muttered as they walked on and meandered down the main street. "I don't know much about horses. Only that they still use them in the far colonies, genetically modified to suit the environments of course. Always seems bizarre to me just how far we've come, and yet we still resort to animals for transport and labour in outlying areas."

"Why would they do that?" Eve asked.

"Because animals don't take much looking after, and they're cheap. Fuel is difficult to produce to begin with, as are the vehicles that use it. All the colonists have is the little they're allowed take with them, due to cargo constraints. Naturally the initial colonies start off with advanced tech but, as settlers arrive and spread out, the tech-level drops. At least until local industry catches up. It's a method that works well, though obviously the spaceports take priority and are often state-of-the-art. The whole process usually takes anything from fifty to two-hundred years, depending."

They came to a building that stood out from the others. Its red-framed windows displayed wares such as statues and carvings of woodland and mythological creatures, including fairies and elves. Seethan couldn't help but grin and point triumphantly to the paintings of witches with broomsticks or pentagrams – and green-painted plaster casts with a common theme of the head of a green man surrounded by leaves. Dream-catchers made of white feathers moved languorously in the draught from the open door, above hand-painted cards and other pagan crafts on counters and tables.

Eve peeked into a small, carved wooden box by the door. In it was a musty-smelling dried cat. She gasped and stepped back, before saying, "I think this place is probably what we're looking for. If not, I'm sure they can point us in the right direction."

There were shelves lining the wall and a wide table in the middle of the shop, crammed with all kinds of wares. Each of them perused the dried herbs and crafts on display, and couldn't help picking up a few for closer inspection.

"If you break 'em, you pay for 'em," a husky-voiced, blonde-haired woman behind the counter said.

There was a loud fluttering of wings and a large black bird shot across the room from outside the door, relieving itself on Seethan's shoulder as it went. The bird then alighted on a stand that stood alone in one corner, from where it regarded them and made loud harsh 'croaking' noises.

"Seriously?" Seethan said, looking at his shoulder. There was something familiar about that creature but he couldn't put his finger on what it was.

Ignoring the bird, Chris stepped forward, and said, "Your eyes are strange. They remind me of sky-blue topaz. Our mother had a pendant like that…" He blushed suddenly and mumbled an apology.

The woman favoured him with a smile that seemed honest and full of kindness. "Oh, you like them. How about these?" As she spoke her eyes turned to a jade-green, which sparkled with amusement.

"You're an android!" Seethan exclaimed, quickly stepping backwards and reaching for his knife.

"I am not!" the woman declared, as if offended, and then looked puzzled. "I don't even know what that is."

"Then explain what you just did?" Seethan demanded, hand hovering at the hilt of his knife. "Where I'm from, only androids can do that, and I suspect things aren't much different here."

Her voice was rough, like that of a singer with a smoking habit, as she replied. "Tell me, can your…androids do this?"

Seethan jumped as the sheath snapped open and the knife flipped over the counter towards the woman's hand, where she deftly caught it. Unsure what to say, he simply eyed the weapon in her hand, as she tossed the blade in the air end over end and caught it easily each time.

"The craft has many gifts," she said huskily. Her eyes turned to discs of spinning gold before reverting to their original blue. "Now, is there something I can help you with?"

Eve spoke boldly, unfazed by the display. "A fortune teller advised us to come here, but not who to contact. She said–"

"Ah, you mean the old gypsy woman. You might as well come around the back, for I've been expecting you." She lifted a blanket serving as a curtain to one side and ushered them into the sitting room beyond, while they listened to her shutting up shop behind them.

"I'm Shona," she said, rejoining them. Inviting her guests to sit on rough wooden chairs scattered around a matching coffee table, she added, "I have to say that you've taken your time getting here." She looked at Seethan, who remained standing. "I received a message from the old woman, telling me that you were on your way. I can see that you're still unsure of me. Let me assure you that I've been watching over you, and if I'd wished to harm you would have by now."

"When you say 'the craft has many gifts', I take it you mean witchcraft?" Seethan said.

"Of course, foolish boy. Take a bit of convincing, don't you!" She held out her right hand, palm up. As she did so, a small ball of blue plasma appeared and rotated slowly above her open hand. With a deft flick she sent it flashing towards him.

Seethan gasped, but before he could step back it stopped an inch or so in front of his nose. He could feel the searing heat and stared at it, unsure what to say or do. And then, in an instant, the plasma snuffed out of existence. Dumbly, he sat down with the others. She took a seat opposite him and spoke.

"Despite what you may think, witches have existed in all societies. In the one you came from, they were limited in their abilities, mainly by their faltering belief in themselves and the limits that were imposed on them in ancient times. When the Spooks arrived on Earth, they gave us back the powers we lost long ago – along with others we're still learning about. Many can learn the craft, if they are called and take the time needed to study it.

"Some use their gifts wisely, some not. But rest assured that those who misuse it pay the price. Now; I will help you, for all of this has been written and I've been waiting many years to do so." She held up a hand to forestall him. "There is no question of cost, this is the price I must pay for my gift."

"Um, are you sure about that?" When she didn't reply, he added, "That's very kind of you. We're looking for–"

"The woman who isn't." Shona said. "I see these things. She's far from here and we need to move quickly. While she's well-hidden, I fear someone else is on her trail. This person is an enemy of yours, and he means her great harm." She unrolled an animal skin map onto the table and smoothed it out with both hands, jabbing a black-painted fingernail at it.

"There are two routes we can take. This way leads us through The Big Wild, which is full of danger. I strongly suggest we take the other, much safer, route. It will add to the journey but not by long, and at least we'll get where we are going in one piece. Hopefully. We'll set off at sunrise, once you're rested."

"The Big Wild, huh?" Seethan said, studying the map before them. "Why do they call it that; because of big wild animals, or because it's just big and, uh, wild?"

Shona peered at him quizzically. "Both. Are you playing with me? There are things there that could rip the soul right out of you, if you're lucky. Like I said, it's best avoided. The other way is mostly forest, but at least it's safe. I'll be waiting for you here in the morning. Make sure you're well provisioned. Our shops are still open, but the barkeep at the inn will help with any problems." She smiled at the look on Seethan's face. "Yes, I know where you're staying. It's a small town, word spreads quickly. Besides, there's nowhere else for you to stay, so where else would you be?"

"Much appreciated," Seethan replied. "But before you decide to help us, there's something you should know." He told her about the old woman's warning, adding, "I don't know whether what she says is true or not, but it would be remiss of me if I didn't mention it."

"The tarot is a form of witchcraft in its own right," Shona said. "And the lady you speak of is highly regarded. She's also a kitchen witch, most traveller groups have them you know. Their knowledge helps keep their groups safe. As for her warning, it's so noted but it doesn't change anything."

Seethan made to stand, but the witch held up a hand.

"Before you go," she said, looking him straight in the eye,

"Do you have any item belonging to this person who wishes your friend harm; perhaps something he might have touched?"

"Well, no. He and I aren't exactly friends. I didn't even know he was still alive, if you can call it that. Oh, wait a moment," Seethan handed her his knife, "He touched this."

She took the blade thoughtfully. "I may be able to use it to hinder, but not hurt him. You must understand that whatever energy we put out into the world, will come back to us thrice-fold. And, as they've not taken sides against the Spooks, I cannot harm them."

"Well I can." Seethan said, biting his lip, "To be honest, even a little hindering would be appreciated."

"So be it," she replied.

"See you first thing in the morning then," Seethan said, leaning forward to shake her hand. With the others following suit, he rose to leave.

As they arrived back at their lodgings Seethan asked his friends about the more dangerous route, having noted their looks of dismay on their faces at its mere mention.

"Only fools risk going there," Jon said. "Or the desperate. We tend to stay away from it and all mention is best avoided. Few of those who explore ever return, which speaks for itself. It's said to be haunted and filled with mysteries. Farmers once tried living on the outskirts, but they abandoned it after a while. Their sheep and cattle kept disappearing, along with members of their families."

"Then I'm glad we're going the other way," Seethan mused.

As they entered the bar the first thing that Seethan noticed was the deathly hush, and his combat awareness instantly kicked in. The second thing was how the barman's eyes flicked in warning, from him to the door. Seethan span and stepped backwards into the room, so that he stood facing the entrance. There were four men standing behind the door; one of them pushed it closed as Jon and the twins joined Seethan.

"Well, well, look who we've got here," a thickset man, obviously the leader, said.

One of his four companions stepped forward to tap Seethan on his shoulder with a small hand-axe, while the others all held knives threateningly. They were fairly nondescript, although their leader looked like he'd been badly beaten in years past, and Seethan felt himself commiserating with whoever had done it. The man's features were twisted into a permanent leer, and his nose was out of alignment. Adding to it, his jaw looked like it had been broken and then healed by a drunken doctor. All that, combined with his limited height, made him look like a misshapen villain from a very bad movie.

"Can we help you gentlemen with something?" Seethan asked, his voice crisp and cutting.

"Samuel," Jon said, speaking above Seethan. "You've known us since we were kids, we grew up together. What's the problem?"

"The *problem*," Samuel echoed with a sneer, "is the elders said that you couldn't leave the village, but you ignored them. We were sent to bring you back, in one piece or not. Personally, I prefer the latter." He stepped towards Eve, a crooked smile on his face as he ran his fingers down her face and patted her cheek with a light slapping sound. "Hello, gorgeous. Miss me?"

"Leave her alone!" Chris demanded. "What's got into you? You never used to be like this."

"Tie their hands behind their backs!" Samuel snapped at his comrades. "And take them outside, while Eve and I have a little...chat." The man's eyes bugged and he raised his eyebrows, at the same time swallowing and licking his lips suggestively.

As his men produced ropes from the leather satchels around their waists, Seethan grabbed the back of the axeman's hand in a wrist lock. Stepping backwards and away from him, he threw the man several feet while keeping hold of his weapon. In a fluid motion he threw the axe with deadly accuracy and it hit a second man in the forehead, knocking him over backwards as the blade buried itself in his skull.

The third member of the group lunged towards him with a knife but Seethan inward-blocked the weapon away with his right forearm and chopped the man hard in the throat with the edge of his hand, once, twice, and then a third time, before stepping clear. The assailant he'd thrown across the room hit the wall headfirst with a single but horrible 'thunk'. He fell to the floor and lay still, even as the third man fell to his knees holding his throat, choking.

Mouth falling open, Samuel stared at his fallen men as if he couldn't believe his eyes. Seethan had dropped them in less than a minute. Quickly, he grabbed Eve and swung her in front of him, a knife appeared in his hand and he held it to her throat. Eve gasped in fright, even as Seethan held up his hands in a placating motion and stood still.

"Stop!" Samuel snapped. "You don't want anything unpleasant to happen to this lovely lady, now do you."

A single bead of sweat trickled down the man's forehead and he licked his lips nervously. Holding Eve in front of him he moved slowly backwards towards the door, opening it he stepped through while still facing them. The others, including the barman, kept pace with him.

"Sam, you care about Eve too much to hurt her," Jon said softly. "Think about what you're doing."

As Samuel continued crossed the road away from them his face contorted in a snarl. "You ain't human, no-one can do what you just did!" He nodded back to the hotel, adding, "Stay back. I'm warning you!"

Seethan heard the barman behind him begin to say something and he held up a hand to stop him. "Let me do the talking." He wanted the man to focus on him alone. "Samuel, is it? Let her go, take me instead."

"You think I trust you, after what I've just seen you do? Eve's mine and always will be. Joel got in the way once but I made sure he disappeared. If you hadn't turned up and taken her away when you did, she would have eventually come to me. It was just a matter of time!"

"You killed Joel?" Eve shouted, squirming in the hefty man's grip. "Bastard! The Spooks should have –"

"Maybe they aren't watching so much these days. Besides, they probably know the scumbag deserved it," Sam snapped. He chortled, saying in a loud voice, "Your wedding is off, bitch!"

Seethan heard the intake of breath from the others at the admission, willing them not to move or say anything, but Jon broke the silence.

"Everyone here heard what you said. Joel was a good man; he didn't deserve to die and you're going to pay for it." Jon made as if to step forward, but Seethan stopped him with a hand gesture.

As Samuel continued to retreat, Seethan moved with him, saying calmly, "I know Alan Wrong sent you. I'm the one you're really after, and he won't be happy if all you take back is the girl. Let her go."

"Sod off. You'll turn on me the moment she's free and, having seen you move, I won't stand a chance. You're after that Rose woman, but you're going to be too late. Alan knows where she is and he'll be there soon to get her."

"Look, let me get the others to tie my hands, just like you wanted," Seethan said, ignoring the man's claim and focusing on the moment. "Here, I'll show you. Chris, grab some of that rope back in the tavern and tie my hands behind me."

Chris ran off and hurried back with the rope that had been dropped by ′ the other hoods, and followed Seethan's instructions. Seethan turned to one side and held his hands away from his body, so that Samuel could easily see exactly what was going on.

"More tightly, Chris," Seethan said, keeping his eyes on Samuel and his hostage.

Samuel squinted. "You give me your word that you won't try anything?"

"What can I do? My hands are tied. Test them if you want. The rest of you move back, give him some room." Seethan struggled with the rope to show how tight the knots were. "See, I can't get free. The others will let you go if you exchange Eve for me. You have my word, are you guys listening?"

The others muttered unhappy agreements.

Samuel nuzzled Eve's ear, licking her lobe and then sucking it into his mouth, keeping his eyes on the others. "I'll be back for you soon, girlie, you'll see." He pushed her forward so suddenly that Eve staggered. Her brother, Chris, pulled her to safety.

Eve's eyes were beseeching. "Seethan."

"I've given him my word, so don't do anything stupid."

Seethan stepped forward and past Eve, hearing her join the others behind him. Samuel's face split into a pie-eating grin. They were three arms' length apart now and Sam reached for Seethan's shoulder with one hand as he stepped forward, the other holding the long serrated blade pointing towards the others.

Seethan half hopped forward, kicking with his right foot and catching the man full in the stomach. Samuel's breath whooshed out of him and he was propelled backwards towards the lake, which was by now only a metre or so away. He fell into the shallows with a huge splash, legs in the air, and came back up spluttering with rage.

"You son of a bitch, you gave me your word!" Samuel bellowed.

"And I've not broken it. Here I am, yours for the taking," Seethan replied with a laugh, "Sorry for getting you wet, I couldn't help myself."

"Sorry? You will be!" Samuel regained his feet, water running from him in a constant stream. A look of maniacal rage filled his twisted features. "I'm going to cut –"

Samuel's words were cut off with an eruption of water behind him, and a leathery shape shot forward. A long dark-grey snout grabbed him and twisted sideways, and he disappeared in a flurry of spray. Eve screamed and scrambled backwards while the others shouted horrified curses.

Seethan retreated rapidly, tripping over his own feet as he did so. Unable to get to his feet he wormed his way backwards as a gigantic alligator half-lifted Samuel. It turned its huge head with the man in its jaws, and began to swim back into deep water. Seethan knew he'd never forget Samuel's horror-filled eyes staring back at him from the monster's jaws. Arms trapped at his side, his mouth opened and closed silently, as if he were trying to speak but was unable. The gator leisurely swam away and after only a few moments disappeared back into the depths, taking the man with him. There were a few swirls of water and then, apart from occasional ripples, the surface of the lake lay still.

The others grabbed Seethan's arms and dragged him backwards towards the inn. As one, they stared at the water, now calm and unbroken. For a few moments, no-one said anything, and the silence was only broken by ducks on the far side.

"That gator's been hanging around for ages, everyone knew about it," Mathew spluttered, his words tripping over themselves. "I was trying to warn you."

"I saw the signs earlier, before we went into town. Never seen a gator in England before, but these guys warned me about them. When we followed Samuel out, I saw movement in the water, and suspected that's what caused it. Made my blood run cold, but I knew it was our only chance."

Seethan sat upright in the dirt as they finished dragging him, and then someone pushed him forwards and cut the ropes from his wrists. In a few moments he was back on his feet, dusting himself off and staring with the others at the water. He shuddered, knowing it could so easily have been him.

"That man may have been a killer," Mathew said, "but I don't think he deserved to go that way."

"Talking of going, I think we'd best be on our way. There are probably other groups looking for us, and the longer we're here, the more at risk we are," Seethan looked straight at Mathew.

The barman gave a wry look. "You're right, it's best you go before any of the neighbours get here. They're bound to have been roused by the commotion. I'll go get some victuals for you and saddle your horses. But, just so that you know, you're welcome back here anytime. That was a brave thing you did." With a respectful look at Seethan, he turned and walked to the inn ahead of them.

Seethan dusted himself off before they trudged back to the inn. As they entered, they saw that the thug Seethan had thrown across the room was now conscious. He was sitting in a chair, watching Mathew fearfully as the barman tapped a stout-looking club into one hand while glowering menacingly at him.

"I forgot all about him," Mathew said apologetically. "Came back here and saw that he was awake. Thought I'd better watch over him until you got here."

"Thanks," Seethan said, and addressed the seated man. "People like you shouldn't be allowed sharp sticks, let alone knives and axes. Your friends are all dead, but I suspect you know that. Now, unless you want to join them, I suggest you sit there all nice and quiet."

The barman brought their horses around to the front of the building, while they took it in turns to collect their kit from their rooms. With one look at Chris, who was now guarding their prisoner, Mathew quickly reclaimed his club, obviously concerned the brother meant the man harm.

"There's some victuals on the counter, least I could do. Best you be on your way, quick like," Mathew said. "I saw some townsfolk approaching and they'll be here in a few minutes. I won't be able to hold this guy here for long, unfortunately. All the killing's been done by you and that gator, so they'll insist I release him. I've no doubt that the village sheriff will want you held in jail, while they debate what to do with you all."

"We appreciate your help, thanks for everything," Seethan said, shaking the man's hand before they all trooped outside and mounted up.

When they reached Shona's place, she quickly responded to Jon's insistent pounding on her door. While the rest remained mounted, Jon explained what had happened. He followed her into the shop, where Seethan and the others could hear them talking loudly. A short while later, Jon came back out and remounted his horse. Seethan patted Midnight to calm him as they waited, able to tell that the horse had picked up on the tense atmosphere as it shuffled its feet and huffed nervously.

"It's okay fella," Seethan said. "Everything's fine. We'll be on our way in a bit."

When Shona appeared from behind the building, she was wearing a purple, hooded cape and trailing a pale pony behind her. The first thing she did was hand Seethan the blade he'd given her earlier. "Here, you might need this. I've done all I can with it."

"Thanks."

Shona mounted quickly, and said, "Follow me. We don't have long before others get here, and they'll try to delay us until the sheriff arrives."

As they cantered down the streets, there was shouting behind them and lights were flickering to life in many of the buildings. Seethan spoke loudly over the drum of their hoofbeats.

"We have a problem. Samuel said Alan knows where Rose is. I doubt he told us the truth, but it is possible and we have to consider it. That means we're running out of time and can't afford to take the long way around, not anymore. We need to take that shortcut, Shona."

"You mean through The Big Wild?" Eve said, her eyes

widening. "But it's supposed to be teeming with monsters, and God knows what else. Have you ever seen a troll?"

"I've been out with a few, metaphorically speaking. But we don't have a choice. We have to get there as quickly as we can, and if that means going through the gates of Hell then I'll happily lead the way. I'm not leaving her to the mercy of Alan Wrong, God knows what he'll do to her. We also need to figure out a way to stop him. Androids have what you'd consider super-human strength, speed and agility, so just getting there isn't going to be enough. If you have any ideas, speak, because I'm all ears."

"The gods will provide, they always do," Shona said.

Seethan knew that none of his friends had the slightest idea how powerful and dangerous the android was, nor what they were getting themselves into. Back where he came from people were afraid of their strength, intelligence, and sense of purpose. Mankind knew that if the machines ever turned against humanity then they'd be in serious trouble. Hence why the Laws of Robotics had been embedded into their programming.

Chapter 15

As they rode into the night a crescent moon rose over the forest, allowing Seethan to see the cape that the witch was wearing more easily. Something pricked at his memory, and then it came back in a flash.

"Hey, Shona," he called. "Tell me something. What did you mean when you said earlier that you were watching out for us? We had a confrontation a short while ago with what the others tell me was the Wild Hunt, and I can't help wondering whether it was you who helped us out."

The witch chuckled. "I wondered if you'd catch on. Yes, that was me. There are several paths ahead of us, each of which lead to different outcomes; not all of them are good. They couldn't be allowed to interfere at this stage."

"I don't understand what you mean."

A shadow swooped out of the darkness and Seethan snatched at his knife before suddenly relaxing. There were a flutter of wings and a loud two-toned 'croak', as the bird from the shop landed on her left shoulder and squawked several times in greeting.

"The crow's coming?"

"Raven, and yes."

Seethan rolled his eyes, surreptitiously checking his shoulder.

"I can see through his eyes, and he has a name: Peter."

Seethan grunted and mulled it over, unsure if he'd heard right. Peter. Pete? It couldn't be, but everything here was too damned weird for it not to be true. He shrugged aside the use of his dead friend's name. "Okay, so tell me about the elves. I read as a kid that they're supposed to have magic too. How come they didn't know we'd be there on that night?"

"Their magic is more about nature and the wilderness around us. They only know what they need to, anything more can be dangerous. We all tread a very narrow path. But they won't try to stop you again."

"I'm glad about that, they look a handful."

"Do remember they're only doing their job and to them, you were intruders."

The bird took off suddenly, and deposited a large patch of white on Seethan's shoulder. He clenched his fists and bit his lip, unable to stop himself wondering how Raven tasted when roasted over a fire.

They rode all night and into the morning, passing huge, lichen-covered, greyish boulders scattered here and there, as if they'd been tossed absentmindedly aside by a giant. Gorse bushes, with small spiny leaves and yellow trumpet flowers, grew sporadically, and they came across a large clump of brilliant-purple, thumb-sized blooms. Attracted to the dazzling flowers, some of which were at least three-metres in height, Eve was about to reach down and pick some when Shona gave a sharp warning.

"Don't touch them, that's Devil's Helmet! It'll kill you, and trust me when I say it's not an easy death." Shona explained what she knew of the plants through her studies. "In times past, the most poisonous part was the roots but since The Sundering, it's mutated for the worse. It's a poison allegedly used by assassins, who taint their weapons with it and often grind it into a powder for administering to food or drink. Even touching it could make you ill. If you're lucky."

After that, whenever they came across clusters of the plant, they gave them a wide berth. There were numerous adders and grass snakes, which thankfully fled as they were disturbed. About halfway through the morning they finally reached the other side of the forest that encircled Burley at a distance. At the line of trees they paused briefly, scanning the way they had come to see if there was any sign of pursuit. Thankfully there wasn't, and they continued until they came to a chuckling stream of fresh, chill water.

Shona reined her horse in, and said cheerfully, "We're at the outer rim. We should be safe here and this is an ideal spot for a rest."

Relieved, Seethan slid to the ground. Stretching stiffly, he set about gathering wood for the fire.

Shona gave a strange tooting noise, and Peter took to the skies from his perch on her shoulder. "We should all get some rest while we can. Peter will alert us of any danger."

Rather than get some sleep straight away, Seethan took the opportunity to wash both sets of his uniform and his smalls, draping them loosely on the vegetation around them. He'd be glad to get shot of the scratchy, rough, and tight garments the others had given him to wear while in Burley. For the time being though, he knew better than to take the risk of putting on clothes that were wet. Sure, the outside of the flight suits were dirt and water repellent but they still stank of sweat. He finished off with a shave and dip in the cold stream. Clean and refreshed, he dried himself off and took some sleep. On awaking, he decided to dress in one of his still slightly damp uniforms.

Despite Samuel's proclamation, he now felt a lot more optimistic about finding Rose.

*****

"So, this is The Big Wild," Seethan said, as they set off again several hours later.

"No," Shona replied tartly, "this is a forest. We should pass into The Wild sometime this afternoon, given there are no distractions."

Seethan looked up at the circling Raven high overhead and looked at her questioningly. "You named your raven Peter?"

Shona frowned at him. "What's wrong with that? Did you expect something dark and mysterious – how about Spellbinder or Eye Scratcher?"

"Erm, okay, Peter's fine. Guess I'll shut the hell up," Seethan replied, taken aback. "Look, I'm sorry. I know that I can be a dick at times. It just seemed an unusual name for a bird. Huh, now that I come to think of it, a friend of mine had a budgie called Peter when we were kids. Not quite the same thing as that big black chicken of yours though."

"Chicken?" Her unusual blue eyes twinkled with amusement. "All witches have familiars, Peter's mine. Ravens are rare and can live for well over twenty years. I've had him for about ten now. For a male he doesn't have much to say, unlike so many of his human counterparts."

Somewhere behind them, Eve snorted.

Jon rode up beside them and paced Seethan for a moment, before saying, "Something that Samuel said back at the inn has been playing on my mind. You killed those men without a thought, and so quickly that I still doubt what I saw with my own eyes. How did you do that? I've never seen anyone move so fast, or known anyone so deadly."

"All marines are taught to kill, when it's needed. I also studied various old styles of fighting that were developed over the centuries. Unarmed combat became a speciality of mine, one that I taught to my unit. Our military code demands we protect the weak and those that cannot fend for themselves. I was only doing what I was trained to do, and what my honour dictated."

"Well, perhaps you'll teach me to do what you can do. But in the meantime, remind me not to annoy you." Jon offered a half grin before falling silent.

"No disrespect intended, Jon, but it takes time; a lot of hard work, dedication, and self-discipline. That being said, I'd be happy to teach you as much as I can. It's not just a knowledge thing but muscle memory. Conditioning, knowing how and exactly where to hit people, so that you can knock them out with one punch when needed as I did that fellow Frank back in your village."

Jon just nodded as if he'd expected that answer. He smiled as he glanced towards his cousins, saying, "I think you'd probably have a couple more students as well."

Seethan didn't have the heart to tell him that, once he'd found Rose, he was probably going to try and find them a way off world and back to civilisation. As lovely as Earth was, it was his duty to do so.

They rode until late afternoon. As fit as he was, Seethan could hardly stand by this time. None of his previous training had helped when it came to riding, and he knew that it would take time for his body to adjust. He still ached terribly but he was starting to get used to his new daily regime, although stretching out after each ride was a bitch. On the bright side, he and Midnight had become friends, the horse often nuzzling him in signs of affection. As they rested, Eve came and sat down next to him. She searched his face as if looking for something, and then looked away. When she spoke, she was gazing at the forest around them.

"Thank you for what you did back there in the village, it was very brave of you." She paused, as if lost for words. "I still can't believe that Samuel killed Joel. I've known both of them my entire life and they were good friends. I'd always hoped that my Joel would come back some day, although I realised something terrible must have happened to him. I knew that, as time passed, the chance of him returning was becoming more unlikely."

She turned to look boldly straight into Seethan's eyes. "You're a dangerous man, Seethan Bodell. I hadn't truly appreciated that before, but to watch you casually kill those men, well, it was frightening." She moved behind him and worked on the muscles of his shoulders.

"It's not something I'm proud of," Seethan said, grunting as her fingers dug deeply. "But sometimes people just need killing, and it's often a soldier like me that ends up doing it. If not, worlds become crime-ridden and ruled by horrible people. In the long run, someone has to stand up and be counted."

"How can you move so fast?"

"Combat training and hyper-arousal, that's all."

Jon obviously heard what Seethan had said, for he coughed and looked at him with a half-smile before Seethan caught on.

"Not that kind of arousal, Jon." Seethan said, feeling his own lips twitching in response. "It means a heightened state of awareness, where you can snap into action at a moment's notice."

Eve finished what she was doing and sat where she had been before, her dark-brown ponytail bouncing back and forth as she moved. "I can understand that. There are stories about long-ago wars, but there's been no conflict here for a very long time. Armies are a thing of the past. I guess there's simply too few of us left to go on fighting each other."

Somewhere in the distance a bird called in a shrill, drawn-out cry, interrupting the chorus of other bird song. They watched as squirrels scampered across the ground a short distance away, then up and down tree trunks in a constant search for food. While staying close to them, the horses browsed the foliage, pausing to munch quietly.

Shona's gravelly tones cut in. "You all need to have faith. The Spooks have guided and protected what's left of us for many years. Perhaps Seethan was brought here for a reason, or reasons, one of them being to protect you from that fiend Samuel. Who knows?"

"Faith, you mean as in religion?" Seethan said, addressing

the witch. "That's a joke. Sure, some of my friends found comfort in it. For me, the loss of close ones made me lose what little I had."

There was no malice in Shona's smile. "Faith and religion aren't necessarily the same thing. Faith often compliments fate. For instance, if you hadn't been there in Burley with your friends here, some of them would probably have been killed. And before you say it, I know that Jon and the twins might never have been there in the first place. But think about it. That man had already killed her fiancé. Don't you find it strange how fate caught up with him through you, and that Eve was there when it happened? Consider that the Spooks might have used you to balance things. After all, I've no doubt that he'd have caused more death and unrest in due course. So, you see, sometimes faith sustains us when fate deals its hand."

With a loud cry, Peter broke the mood and leapt to the skies. They watched as he flew up and above the trees, until he was lost from sight.

"Problem?" he asked.

"Ravens sense things. I think perhaps we'd better get moving," Shona said. "I suspect the sheriff of Burley will have sent riders to try and track us. I'm sure Mathew will put in a good word for you, but I've no doubt that information will be sent back to your village about what happened, and of course the route we're taking. We can expect your enemies to try to intercept us."

*****

Several days later they had finished traversing the moors and were once again deep in woodland. As they progressed, they noted a rich, damp autumnal smell. Summer was ending. The leaves were turning brown and many had already fallen. Those dry, papery leaves stirred as they passed, rustling across the ground as if in deep conversation, before joining their fellows as they whirled up in little eddies like mini typhoons.

Eventually they came across a wide, grassy path that stretched into the distance both to their left and right. There was also a strange watery look to it stretching from the ground upwards, as if there was a barrier they couldn't quite see. Seethan's hackles rose at the image and even Midnight shied back until they were urged on by Shona. The instant they crossed the threshold they found themselves in a jungle-like environment; heat and humidity, and noise from insects and birds, hitting Seethan like a blow. Midnight danced and blew raspberries, as if venting his displeasure. Looking behind them, they could see no sign of the way they had come, while all around lay the jungle. He turned to say something, only to see that the others had ridden on ahead.

Hurrying after them, he was astonished to see the thick boles with incredibly wide trunks and buttress roots at their base. Their countless branches blended in with the plethora of vegetation overhead, so that it was difficult to tell where one began and another ended. Other trees sprouted more thinly, shooting upwards like poles – some wrist thin – with few branches at their uppermost levels.

Something splattered against his arm, and when he looked there lay another white patch. Damn that bird!

The springy ground around them was now mostly of deep shadow. It was made up of loam, he was told – dead foliage such as fallen pine needles and leaves. Plants with wide, deep green leathery leaves the length of Seethan's forearm sprung from the ground here and there, while others had wispy, finger-like fronds. Many of the trees had fallen and lay rotting on the ground with patches of lichen and mushrooms sprouting from their decaying boles. Others trees leaned against their neighbours like drunks, or powered-down conveyor walkways. Seethan was struck by the constant sound that assaulted them, from unknown creatures munching at a never-ending crispy treat to odd, intermittent, bird calls.

He became aware of something unknown leaping from tree to tree at a height, keeping pace with them but at a respectful distance. Try as he could, Seethan couldn't make out what it was, only that it was man-shaped, small and apparently shy. He suspected that there was more than one of the *whatever's* and it worried him. He was relieved as Peter landed again on Shona's right shoulder, apparently undisturbed by their presence.

"It's hotter now. Or is it me?" Seethan said, when he

171

finally caught up with the others and wiped the sweat from his forehead with a sleeve.

"It is," Chris said shortly, as if unwilling to discuss it further. Then, in a more considerate tone, he added, "Look at you in all that get up. I'm surprised you haven't taken it off, it must be stifling."

"This flying suit allows my body temperature to be regulated. It warms me when I'm cold, and keeps me cool when it's hot. Not technology, just reactive fabric. Guess I'm kinda lucky there, huh."

Shona had taken off her cape and now wore a simple, thin, white cotton shift that may well have kept her cool, but without doubt played on the men's imaginations. With two such good-looking women around, Seethan was glad that he had Rose to keep him focused. Already aware that Chris had a bit of a soft spot for Shona, he smiled as he watched his friend's eyes constantly follow her and found himself hoping things between them would develop favourably.

"We're in The Big Wild, now," the witch said. "It'll get hotter still, the further we go."

"Reminds me of South America," Seethan said, wiping the sweat from his brown again. "I was at Buenos Aires before coming back to the UK. I'd been disembarked for sick leave, and spent a few days in the Baritu National Park while resting up. Nice place. Very much like this, but that doesn't make sense because we're in England."

Shona said nothing.

"Come on Shona, fess up," Seethan pressed. "What is this place? And don't just say *The Big Wild*."

"You have to remember that The Sundering left Earth's reality torn," she replied. "In some places there are hidden doorways, where one step will take you instantly to somewhere else on the planet. Which explains how animals that don't belong to certain areas suddenly appear in them, the gators for example, or even creatures that are legendary. We've just travelled through one of those gateways.

"Others lead to places that no-one really understands and where, trust me, you don't want to go. They are like this world but we suspect they're not of it. I've only been in this place once before, so it's all relatively new to me too. Wonderful though, isn't it," she enthused.

"Blinding. Perhaps you should have warned us," Seethan replied.

"Your mind was made up to go this way. Pointless worrying you needlessly, don't you think?"

Their horses reared back suddenly and Seethan reassured his mount with pats and soothing words, leaning forward he stroked the long neck calmly, as somewhere ahead there was a series of horrendous hisses and gargling sounds. It was like water rushing down a drain, crossed with the sawing of wood. It was the most unearthly sound Seethan had ever heard. To make matters worse, thunderous crashes added to the furore. It sounded like something was ripping up trees and smashing them to kindling.

"What the hell is that?" Seethan asked, muttering reassurances and leaning forward to pat Midnight on his neck to calm him as he pranced away from the ruckus.

"Who knows," Shona replied. "Gorillas, trolls, hydras, could be anything. What does it matter?"

"Gorillas in South America? I give up," Seethan muttered, licking the taste of salt from his lips. "No idea why *that* bothers me, when we now have trolls and other beasties stomping about looking for a fight." He shook himself, and strode on.

The terrain around them worsened as time wore on, getting denser and boggier in places, yet more easily passable in others. From time to time they heard all kinds of animals, from the threatening roars of big cats to a chorus of monkeys, the symphony of bird song broken as they exploded from the trees in an eruption of colour. There were spine-chilling calls from raptors swirling high above on the air currents, others flittering between the trees and branches. There were squeaks, whistles, and hoots from other, less visible creatures in an apparent effort not to be outdone. Occasionally a roar shook the jungle and the chorus around them fell silent, only to resume a short while later.

All around them was a muggy verdant green interspersed with outrageous colours of the rainbow, as if nature had been inspired by a gifted painter. Spiny bulbs of bright orange grew from thick, leathery leaves. Poisonous rose-coloured chunks lay temptingly in a sage salad dressing, while small black and white leaves sprouted timidly from unassuming vegetation as they passed. Puffs of red, blue, pink, and yellow erupted in fragrance if they touched them, the spores adhering to their clothing and the horses' flanks. Seethan was worried about it at first but relaxed when Shona told them it was simply part of their pollination process.

Light feathery fronds brushed lightly at their faces, and spiky appendages stirred as they passed as if waiting in ambush for the unwary. Their noses were assailed by a delicious aromatic menu, pungent perfumes that entrepreneurs of his time would have spent fortunes and lifetimes emulating.

They ate snatches of food, little and often. Each day, they pitched camp as twilight threatened, rather than risk mishap in the oppressive darkness that fell so suddenly. They posted guards to share the watch with the raven, while the rest of them sought sleep, all the while plagued by ants and multitudes of other biting insects.

Monkey and bird cries greeted each dawn and woke those still resting, while squadrons of leathery-skinned, bright yellow butterflies the size of their heads took to the air, flying gracefully with their wings making slight 'whopping' sounds. Dragonflies as long as Seethan's arms buzzed about like military drones as they snatched the butterflies in mid-air. The monkeys bounced from tree to tree chattering and gesticulating, as if constantly discussing their progress. All the while the apes used them for target practice; by throwing pieces of bracken, half-eaten fruit, or rough-shelled nuts at them.

And still the unseen *somethings* kept pace.

On their third day in the sweltering wilderness they came across a monstrous snake battling a moose. Olive green with dark circular blotches, the snake was much thicker than Seethan's thigh and was at least eight metres long. It was wrapped securely around the animal's middle, tightening each time it breathed out. The trapped creature struggled, bellowed, and swung ponderous antlers at the snake's head, which kept darting just out of reach. The moose, large as it was, struggled futilely in the deadly embrace and, as they passed, finally ceased moving and fell silent. They watched with morbid fascination as the reptile's jaws stretched wide and it swallowed its prey whole.

"Nature can be cruel sometimes," Seethan said.

"Yet, it's a necessity of life," Shona replied. "The moose was already injured during the encounter. If we'd freed it the poor creature would have died anyway and the snake would have to find other prey."

"Well, there is that. But it's a shame, and that was one huge goddamn snake. They were on the brink of extinction in my time."

"They were?" Chris asked.

"Yeah, mostly due to people hunting them for their skins, and sometimes for food. And, of course, there was persecution by the local population who were afraid for their livestock and understandably their children."

"You hunted them for their skins?" Jon asked, his eyes wide with shock. "I can understand if it's necessary to kill them for food or protection, but for ornament? That's barbaric."

"I didn't personally," Seethan replied. "And yes, I agree, but that's enlightened society for you."

The snake seemed unwilling or unable to move after its incredible meal, and it just lay there. They were about to skirt the creature when a mottled grey lizard at least twelve metres in length slipped into the scene. The lizard's eyes were dark red, apart from coal-pit centres, and it squinted at the snake while a long, forked tongue flicked back and forth.

Without warning, the lizard rushed the snake, inflicting a few speedy bites before retreating a short way, where it turned and hissed as if observing the results. Similar lizards quickly appeared from the undergrowth and followed suit, their alligator-like jaws inflicting savage wounds before they too withdrew, as if to stand back and watch. By now the snake was regurgitating its meal and, once free of encumbrance, it sought to escape. But each way it went the lizards headed it off, although they kept at a respectful distance. Four of the remaining lizards seized their chance and leapt at the discarded moose, pulling at the dead creature while snapping at their fellows.

Shona gestured for Seethan and the others to follow her. "Quick this way, before they see us!"

The knobbly-skinned lizards moved in sinuous plodding movements; occasionally showing a turn of speed that was awesome to behold. Their group wasn't noticed until Shona spoke in whispered tones. As they followed her instructions, and the horses burst into a gallop, the lizards nearest them spun around. They made deep whirring noises that Seethan likened to a badly-tuned vehicle. Several of the creatures immediately thudded after them, crushing everything in their path. As the lizards pursued them, their calls changed to throaty growls and low hisses, as if high-pressure steam were escaping through a very thin pipe.

"Faster!" Eve shouted and, as if understanding her, the horses increased speed.

Seethan saw that a few of the lizards were trying to head them off, as they had repeatedly done to the snake, but he saw an opening and immediately shouted, "Quick, this way!"

With prompts from their riders, the horses instantly raced towards the opening, avoiding the now rearing snake as they did so while the lizards pursued them with surprising speed and grace for such huge creatures. One of the lizards appeared from behind the bole of a tree directly in their path. Jon lowered his spear and ran the beast through with one thrust. As the creature uttered a keen of agony it jerked away, ripping the spear from his grasp. Unwilling to leave the weapon behind, but knowing there was no choice, Jon followed the rest of them as they sped through the jungle.

Their horses needing no urging as they ran for their lives, jigging this way and that, avoiding trees and bushes while leaping over obstacles, spurred on by the creatures hissing and bulldozing after them. One of the huge lizards almost caught up and it ran parallel for a while, looking as if it were searching for a suitable place where it could launch itself at them.

As it edged nearer, the battleship-grey creature's thunderous steps got louder and louder. It went ahead for a moment and before they could swerve onto another course the creature took its chance and leapt straight at them.

To Seethan's astonishment the lizard stopped in mid-jump and hung in the air, while making odd jerking movements. With horror he saw that the animal had been caught by a monstrous spider's web that was spun between the trees. The lizard struggled and after a moment, its heavy bulk ripped it free and the beast fell. That freedom was short-lived, however, as it landed in a sea of further webbing that cuffed its legs, effectively hobbling it. The last thing Seethan saw, as he glanced backwards, was a wide carpet of cat-sized spiders scuttling towards it. The dark-brown legs and creamy body with the rough outline of a skull made him shudder. The spiders had been easily camouflaged by the vegetation, and he thanked the heavens it wasn't them that had been caught. He was astonished to see the spiders working collectively, as they swarmed over the struggling creature, biting as they gift-wrapped it in silky web.

"Did you see that?" Eve asked over the pounding of hooves.

"I'm not going to forget it. We were damn lucky not to be caught in that lot ourselves," Seethan said.

No one else replied, all probably imagining the fate that they'd so narrowly missed and Seethan noted their pace reduced somewhat as they peered more closely at the path ahead.

Behind them, Peter swooped at their pursuers with harsh cries. Concerned he too would be caught in the web, Shona shouted at him repeatedly, enforcing her commands with hand gestures. As they sped through the jungle, they could hear the enraged hisses fading, and it appeared their pursuers had given up on the chase. Seethan caught sight of a milky haze just ahead of them and then, quite suddenly, they plunged through yet another gateway and found themselves riding through a cool English forest once more.

The constant low wind blew coolly against their skin, bringing with it the damp, musty scent of autumn. Peter flew low overhead with loud victorious cries and, relieved, they slowed their flight to a canter. They stopped briefly to look back at the glimmering water-like barrier of The Big Wild. Seethan's uniform allowed him to quickly adjust to the temperature change, and he watched as the others took the opportunity to don extra items of clothing from their packs.

"What were those things, dragons?" Chris asked, horror still evident on his face.

"Kind of," Seethan replied. "If I remember correctly from history lessons, they were called Komodo Dragons. Long extinct in my time, they might not breathe fire but you wouldn't want to piss them off."

"It seems to me that a lot of things were extinct in your time," Chris replied. "I'm surprised we humans survived at all."

"We had a few close calls believe me—"

A loud crashing from the far side of the barrier interrupted them and they took the hint and moved on wordlessly, Shona taking the lead. Their speed rose to a canter and then to a gallop, as they raced through the landscape, their hoofbeats drumming until finally common sense prevailed and they slowed once more. Eventually the strange land of The Big Wild was lost far behind them. All around now lay an autumn English woodland. Still concerned about pursuit, however, they continued on without rest though at a far more leisurely pace.

Chapter 16

"How much farther have we got to go?" Seethan asked as they made camp that night, the moon rising high in the star-filled sky.

"It depends," Shona replied.

Seethan stared at her. "What the hell does that mean? Surely, you know how far we have to go, or are you saying that we're lost?"

"Not at all," she said patiently. "Look Seethan, you have to understand just how much The Sundering changed things. This isn't the Earth you knew. The places we want to travel to may remain in the same location on a map, but it's the reaching them that proves elusive. You see, the gateways come and go. They'll often disappear and reappear somewhere else, and they might not lead where you think. That said, some gateways remain constant. It's as though the very fabric of our universe has been torn and the wounds are still fresh. Thankfully at the moment the craft tells me we're on the right track, we just have to keep going in this direction. Remember what I said, and have a little faith."

Seethan noticed Jon looking anxious. "Hey, are you okay?"

"Seriously? It's a full moon, and it's not safe out here in the open. I'd feel better if we were indoors somewhere with a big fire going, but I guess we'll have to make do. Best we post a guard again tonight, even with Peter looking out for us."

"Okay, that makes sense," Seethan agreed, by now accepting he might as well be on a different planet to the Earth that he left.

"I'll take first watch," Jon said. "Seethan, I'll wake you around midnight. If Chris takes over from you, that'll leave Eve to take the morning watch."

They quickly agreed and set about collecting wood for the fire, making up their bedrolls and eating a cold evening meal washed down with water from their bags.

"I'll set wards around the camp," Shona said, as she finished eating and tossed a chunk of the stale bread to her patiently watching bird. "They should keep anything unsavoury away from us while we sleep." She drew a wand from her sleeve and invisibly painted a five-pointed star in the air before producing a bag from her satchel. Sprinkling the contents sparingly around the camp she muttered gutturally under her breath. She'd finished off and said more loudly, "Remember to stay inside the circle. Whatever you do, don't break it. We're back in the land we started from and we can't afford to take risks. It could be that our pursuers are also using the craft, and their power will grow as night falls."

Seethan woke as Jon was reaching down to wake him, knocking his wrist aside in a reflex action. He blinked and sat up, shaking his head in an attempt to focus himself. Jon stood back and eyed him curiously, as Seethan breathed slowly; conscious of each breath.

Giving his friend a twist of the lips as way of apology, Seethan went through his routine of five senses. He'd had a disturbing dream but as usual couldn't remember anything about it. His chest ached as if someone were sitting on it, and he felt as if he were falling into a deep hole. Thankfully, he was well used to the symptoms of PTSD by now and used his strategies to deal with them. He wished he had a sharp scent to help break the spell; somewhere along the way he'd lost his eucalyptus oil.

"I've made some tea," Jon said, his eyes flickering to a pan in which hot water and leaves of some kind bubbled above the glowing embers. When Seethan joined him, Jon handed over a spear and a hunk of stale bread. "This needs eating up before it goes mouldy, and there's a little honey left for the tea too, if you want it."

Seethan took a bite of the stale bread and mumbled a thanks as Jon wished him goodnight. He chewed gratefully, keeping his eyes away from the flames to enable his night vision. Looking up at the sky he watched a shooting star blaze in brief fiery glory. He finished the bread and mug of tea, and picked up the spear before slowly patrolling the camp.

The spear was a relatively light but cumbersome weapon, and one he was still trying to get used to. Between patrols he practiced strikes and parries with it, which the others had been showing him during their breaks. He much preferred his pistol and still carried it, hoping one day it would come in useful. Archery was something he enjoyed immensely but needed improving at, and he determined to get himself a bow and quiver of arrows at the next opportunity.

Seethan was adding logs to the fire when a loud 'crack' sounded in the darkness. He whirled to point his spear in the direction of the noise and scanned the gloom carefully. There was nothing to see and, after a while, he made another circuit of the camp. By now he was carefully attuned to every sound and the slightest movement, but even with the brightness of the moon he could see little in the night beneath the branches.

A fox appeared suddenly in his path, meandering back and forth as if it were drunk. He swore and then grinned at a mental image of himself, poised with the spear and ready to do battle. He waited, watchful, but nothing else stirred in the darkness. After a rummage in the undergrowth the fox disappeared, and Seethan continued on his rounds. He was on his way back, intent on another cup of tea, when something leapt at him out of the darkness.

Seethan saw it coming from the corner of his eye, but as he swivelled to face it there was a sudden brilliant flash that semi-blinded him and he staggered to one side. Holding one hand up to his eyes, his ankles caught on something and he tripped, dropping the spear. Hitting the ground hard, Seethan gave a shout of alarm, rolling and scrambling back up into a crouch. Still dazed by the flash, he fumbled around for the spear.

Where the hell was it?

He could hear the answering calls of alarm from the others as they clawed awake. His fingers closed around the spear's shaft and he used it to push himself to his feet. "I'm fine," he said loudly, in reply to their calls to see if he was all right. He was confused at what had happened but thankful his night sight was quickly returning.

"Seethan, you've broken the circle! Get back inside, now!" Shona shouted suddenly, running towards him.

But she was too late. Even as Shona began to chant and reinforce the magical barricade, Seethan had turned his back on the darkness to speak to her, and something came for him. The force of the impact smashed him from his feet. Losing hold of the spear once again, he hit the ground hard, and then it was upon him.

His vision still wasn't one-hundred-per cent, but it was

enough to see a large, dark-furred shape leaping for his throat. The creature snarled as it leapt and Seethan grabbed it around the neck with both hands, desperately holding snapping teeth away from his face. His right fist clenched thick fur as he reached across his body with his free hand for his commando knife, but no matter how he tried he just couldn't reach it. The creature's claws scrabbled at his chest and the weight of it held him down. The image of the silver knife Eve had given him flashed into his mind and he reached down into his left leg side-pocket and pulled the weapon free.

He caught glimpses of white, thumb-length teeth in the firelight as he plunged the knife into the heaving struggling creature; once, twice, and then again. The dog-like creature yammered in agony and tried to wrench itself free but Seethan held on tightly, continuing to stab as he buried his face in its fur in the hope it couldn't get at him. He knew he had to finish the beast off, and this could be his only chance. He stabbed again and again, screaming in rage as he slammed the blade home. Its jaws suddenly closed around his left arm in a crushing grip, wrenching it from side to side. Despite himself, Seethan bellowed in pain and frustration, and dropped the knife.

Seethan suddenly heard the thrum of arrows and the dull thwack of impact as they hit home. The creature gave repeated, high-pitched yelps as Seethan thrust it away and rolled free. As he did so the creature staggered and then slumped to the ground. Panting, Seethan could see the body of an enormous grey-black, shaggy-coated dog lying in the firelight close to where he himself had fallen. Shocked, he reached down to pick up the knife with his good hand, from where it lay glinting in the moonlight at his feet. The creature hadn't moved and, holding the blade, he clutched his injured forearm to him and stared at the dog.

"Are you okay?" Eve asked, rushing to his side. Her eyes widened as she saw him cradling his arm. "Shona, it's bitten him!"

The witch came running over and hissed frantically when she saw the blood running from his arm. "Quick, get him to the fire. I need to treat this, now!"

Sitting him down, Shona knelt beside him and rolled up his sleeve, to reveal a large bite. She poured cold water over it from her canteen and dried the wound with a grubby cloth.

Noticing his look as she draped the cloth over his wound, Shona said, "You've more important things to worry about than cleanliness."

Telling Eve to hold the makeshift dressing in place and apply pressure to the wound, Shona mashed a mixture of herbs and water into a paste. Then, ushering Eve aside, she wiped clear the free-flowing blood and uttered a guttural incantation, slathering the wound with the mixture before binding it tightly with a fresh and this time clean cloth. Despite his best efforts Seethan winced as she knotted it tightly, the blood already seeping through the material.

"Do you think–" Eve began, but Shona stopped her with a glance and furrowed brow.

"Pray that we're lucky, but we'll just have to wait and see," the witch said.

"It's just a bite," Seethan said with a grin. "I've had worse, believe me."

"I suspect not, Seethan Bodell. There's nothing worse than a bite like this," Shona replied.

"Hey a bite's a bite. I'm sure it'll heal."

"Perhaps," the witch replied, eyes on his. "But you need to be aware, not every bite is the same and this is one of the worst."

"It's just a dog bite for heaven's sake."

Shona pointed to where the animal had fallen, and when Seethan followed her gaze he was shocked to see a young man lying there, two arrows protruding from his back and several deep wounds in his chest. Seethan hissed with a sharp intake of breath. *No, it couldn't be.* "It was a dog! I saw it!".

"It was a wolf," she replied. "And no ordinary one at that. You've been bitten by a lycanthrope, my friend. Let's just hope the poison hadn't entered your system before I got to it. That wound is deep, and we'll just have to wait and see."

The next morning his arm was aching badly, and the others told him that was a good sign. Heartened, Seethan mounted Midnight and rode with his injured arm strapped to his chest to avoid jostling it. By midday, however, he was feeling unwell and within a few hours had developed a fever, forcing them to stop and make camp before he fell from his horse. His friends watched him anxiously as Seethan slipped into a deep sleep. He remained unconscious for the next twenty-four hours and, no matter what they did, they couldn't wake him. By the third day his fever had worsened and he was rambling in his sweat-drenched slumber. The others took turns bathing his forehead while Shona muttered incantations over him and changed his dressings.

When Seethan finally awoke his arm was throbbing abysmally. He felt drained of all energy but at least the fever was lessening. Still weak, he found himself with a raging thirst. Idly, he wondered whether the wolf had carried rabies. The shots the marines gave him when he'd joined should have eased his worries, but he knew such diseases tend to mutate over time, and that added to his concerns.

His fever lessened however, and Seethan gradually improved. The wound wasn't as bad as they'd first feared. To his surprise, by the fifth day he could flex his fingers, although he still kept the injured limb strapped tightly to his chest. He was washing one-handed in the water of a stream when he realised that he'd begun putting on weight, and from what he could see, it was all muscle. He tried not to see the watchful and worried glances his friends threw his way and told them with a wry grin that he was doing fine whenever they asked.

Over the next three weeks as they made halting progress across the countryside, he almost began to forget he'd been wounded at all – though the looks from the others never went away. When, at the end of the fourth week, the full moon rose again, Seethan sat upright and screamed a long, hoarse cry of pain and began to flail about.

"Shona, do something!" Eve shouted, rushing to his side to help her brother hold him down.

"There's nothing I can do. If the poison's taken him then it's the will of the gods."

They watched silently as Seethan twitched, and then shook all over. His eyes rolled and his lips pulled back, splitting until they ran with blood. He arched his back and screamed in agony as a burning sensation seared his chest, increasing until it felt like he'd been stabbed with a branding iron. It was the silver cross Eve had given him. It was red-hot and he burnt his hand tearing it away, before tossing both it and the silver-edged knife towards her.

Eve picked both up and held the weapon out in front of her, eyes intent on his.

Throat sore from his cries, Seethan fell to his knees and ripped his clothes free with a strength he didn't know he possessed. He knelt there, naked, changing physically in front of them. Hair sprouted all over his body, his flesh bubbling as it rippled and warped until he looked far from human.

Seethan stared at his fists as they extended into paws. His fingernails were torn away as dagger-like claws grew underneath them, and they dug gullies in the dirt as he tried to clench fists that were no longer there. His jaw lengthened and bayonet teeth protruded, running red from the metamorphosis. Continuing to scream, his lips pulled back, leaving him with a razor-blade smile. Finally, he raised a shaggy head and his screams turned into a long, drawn-out howl.

"Fight it, Seethan," Shona insisted. "You can do it, you know how. Remember who you are, focus on rescuing Rose. She needs you and you need her." She watched his eyes turn to swirls of burnished gold with coal-pit centres, his nose a broad, fur-covered muzzle.

Shona watched his change complete, until in Seethan's place stood a huge wolf, his fur dark-grey with blond streaks. He shook his bucket-sized head as if to clear it, jowls making a rapid-fire rattling sound as he did so. "Fight it Seethan," she insisted. "You can do it. Rose needs you, and so do we. Fight it, fight!"

At the sound of her voice, the wolf-Seethan locked his furnace eyes onto hers and a low rumbling growl escaped him. He seemed to swell in size, those powerfully muscled shoulders bunching as he gathered himself to spring. For a wolf, he was huge – at least breast height – but unmoved, Shona stood facing him down. His lips curled back and his head lowered, the deep bass rumble rising in volume. Still Shona remained steadfast. His massive jaws snapped inches from her and just before he leapt, Eve stepped into his view and he paused, recognition dawning, as she slowly put the knife into the bag around her neck and held out her hands to show they were empty.

Shona saw the sudden hesitation, the glint of memory in those sun-bright eyes. "That's it!" she crowed. "It's Eve.

Look around you, we're your friends!"

The brown-haired woman stepping into Seethan's vision struck a chord with him. He knew her. Eve! He looked from her to the others. A dim memory came back and he recognised them; friends who were now looking at him in undisguised horror. What was happening to him? He fought back the rage threatening to spill like an overfilled glass. There was a bloodlust there he'd never known. It was his all, demanding that he rip them to shreds and feed on their flesh.

But they were his friends!

Feed?

A few moments ago, his entire body had been racked with agony. Now he felt reborn, filled with a vitality he'd never known before. In the near distance, an owl hooted. The drone of flying insects increased and he could track the flight of each and every one of them. His hearing improved, as did his sense of smell. Somewhere close by there was magnolia in full bloom. Ah, the romantic pull of wild honeysuckle, the enticing scent of grass, and the acrid tang of his companions' sweat.

He could sense their terror. See it in their eyes. But, why were they so afraid and looking down at him like that? He'd been much taller than all of them before, so...?

Eve walked towards him and he felt himself calming under her warm chocolate gaze. She knelt and reached towards him but hesitated. He sniffed at her and stretched out a hand in turn, desperate to understand what was happening and seeking solace. But his hands were now paws. He'd seen that before, but somehow forgotten it.

What's happening to me, what's going on?

A long eerie howl rose in the distance: a siren's call so compelling in its loneliness that he automatically sniffed at the air, catching that faint whiff of femininity carried by the warm breeze. Seethan padded towards the call but there was the vague memory of an invisible wall. Confused, he looked back at Eve and Shona as that distant song came again, compelling him on. This time he answered.

Raising his muzzle, he gave a long, blood-curdling howl that echoed through the forest. Padding back and forth around their camp he growled and snapped in frustration at the barrier, the dim memory of that brilliant flash from before preventing him from throwing himself at it bodily. He heard a deep intake of breath from Shona, as she stepped forward and scuffed out part of the circle with her shoe. And, just like that, he was free and bounding through the forest to meet his moon maiden.

"It's okay," he heard Shona say to the shouts of alarm from the others. "He needs to be free. Don't worry, he'll come back when he's ready."

"Well I hope so," Jon's voice came in distant reply. "If he doesn't, then we're well and truly fucked."

*****

Seethan sped through the forest like a grey-black blur. Everything felt so fresh, so vibrant! He could hear rabbits bounding in panic towards safety as he passed, their warning thumps causing pulses of hot blood to thrum in his ears. To his left, one of them squealed in pain, the sound a cross between a cough and a baby crying. There were deer nearby too. He could smell them and knew instantly how close they were. They sensed him in turn and he could hear them run away to safety, with short, sharp bleats of alarm to warn their fellows.

He padded to a stop and raised his head to the moon, as another howl built inside him. He let it loose in a climbing, mournful song that reverberated through the night-shrouded forest. The deep woodland had fallen silent, apart from the drum of his paws as he raced through the trees. Answering howls stopped him in his tracks and his ears pricked up. There were so many of them out there, far more than he would have imagined. The closest ones told him that they were coming to greet their new brother, and he sprinted joyfully to meet them.

A barn owl swept like a ghost through the night sky, watching him but keeping a respectful distance. How far Seethan had run he had no idea, and then suddenly a grey-black she-wolf appeared in front of him and he stopped to stare at her. Black ears flicked above the shadowy muzzle, and stunning green-blue eyes were locked on his. She dropped her head slightly as she approached and they sniffed at each other. Others slipped out of the darkness and they too greeted him.

This female was in season, her musk driving him to the point of insanity. What's more, she wanted him. He knew it. Lust built up in his loins and pounded through his veins, but before he could mount her a warning growl alerted him to the alpha male that had only now joined them.

This wolf was far bigger than any other, including him. Blacker than the night itself, it blended in beautifully. While Seethan had been aware of the male's scent, he'd been distracted by the female and hadn't realised the owner of it had been missing.

Threat, conflict.

Seethan's instincts kicked in, as they faced off. *Think, Seethan. Remember your strategies!*

Five: what could he see? The blazing eyes of the alpha in its broad, dustbin-like head. Other members of the pack, the glow of the goddess high overhead as she looked down at her children and bathed them in light. The dark silhouettes of trees all around them, and the dew-damp grass beneath his feet.

Four: what could he hear? The warning snarls from this sudden opponent, panting from the other pack members as they moved back in anticipation while watching the scene unfold. Bats chittering as they flickered through the night sky in search of panicking insects.

Three: what smells were there? The female's musk was strongest. It built a lust in him he'd never known before. There lay the dreamy scent of honeysuckle, in sharp contrast to the bitter urine of the alpha's marker.

Two: he could feel the rage building inside him at the impertinence of this beast who thought to deny him the female. The tension of his body, as muscles rippled and bulged, his ears lying back as his body prepared for battle.

One: The salty, bitter-sweet taste of blood in his mouth, flowing freely from the wounds of his first transformation.

Seethan's scream of defiant challenge roared through the woods as they leapt at each other. Huge jaws dripping with saliva went for his snout but he turned aside instinctively, locking his maw around the collar of thick, dark fur. He tore at the other wolf, even as he felt his opponent doing likewise, and his body twisted and clenched in response to sudden pain. They landed and whirled back to face each other, snarling. Growls and yips as they danced in and out, feigning, defending, biting, rending. Looking for openings that could lead to the other's defeat.

The alpha leapt at him with slathering jaws, trying to use his superior bulk and strength to end the battle. They clashed with a cacophony of snarls, barks, and snapping jaws, as they tore bloodied clumps of fur and flesh from each other before moving away to circle time and again, eyes blazing with cunning.

Think Seethan, he's bigger than you.

He had but a moment as the black male charged him again, tail confidently high, and Seethan leapt towards him in response. At the last moment, Seethan rolled to one side, snatching at the paw of his opponent as it sailed past. He wrenched at it with all his might, causing the larger animal to twist in mid-air and land heavily on the limb in an untidy heap. But Seethan's jaws had torn through flesh and skittered off bone, ripping the joints and ligaments.

Don't hurt him too much. He can't help what he is any more than I can.

The alpha gave a gibbering yelp as it scrambled to its feet and limped backwards, raising the injured paw to its chest protectively. There was wariness in those luminescent blue eyes, and the sudden spark of fear. Without pause Seethan attacked again, slashing and biting, while the other yammered and shied away. Seethan stopped and then approached the other more slowly, threateningly. A deep bass growl was building within him, promising to overflow like an avalanche. Lips curled back from his dagger teeth and his eyes blazed like raging forest fires.

Cowed, the other wolf bowed its head and hunched its shoulders, backing away further as Seethan advanced. But before he could attack, the other wolf rolled on its back in submission. Seethan approached cautiously and stood over his foe, snapping at the other as he yelped and yammered in distress. Slowly, Seethan leaned down and closed his jaws around the other's bared throat, feeling the hot pulse of blood beneath the thick shaggy hide. It was as if he had a tasteless bunch of cotton wool in his mouth. Urine spurted from the other in submission, but Seethan left his jaws there for a few more moments. Finally releasing him, Seethan remaining there, glaring downwards. The other wolf remained on his back; eyes glued to his as if frozen. Turning away, Seethan trotted back towards the waiting and willing female. But not before he saw the tongue-lolling gratitude in the black wolf's eyes.

Seethan raised his muzzle and gave a long, haunting howl that echoed and re-echoed through the forest. The female submitted to him; all his thoughts of Rose had fled. His animalistic urges took over and he mounted her quickly. Once finished, he turned his muzzle towards the moon and howled yet again, the others joining in with the triumphant echoing battle cry.

*****

The next morning Seethan stepped naked into the clearing to find the others there waiting for him. Eve called out his name and ran towards him, bending to snatch up his pack, which she quickly handed him.

"Are...are you okay; how do you feel?" she asked. Her eyes were round with fearful curiosity, and beneath it lay a look of dread.

"I'm fine, thanks." Pulling a uniform from his pack Seethan put it on. "I'm not really sure what happened. One moment everything was normal and then–"

"You were different," Shona said, interrupting him. "I'm afraid that the bite from the wolf turned you. You're no longer human, Seethan Bodell. You're a lycanthrope; a werewolf."

"We need to leave him and go home. Screw helping him find his friend now," Chris said, his words dripping with anger. "He's dangerous, a beast who's unable to control himself. You know he can't be allowed to live. He'll turn on us sooner or later and rip us to shreds." His glare from one to the other demanded support.

"He could have done that last night," Shona said, noticing the fresh bite marks on Seethan's body and a new grace to his movements as he dressed. A strange smile came over her face as he zipped up his uniform and put on his boots. She was beside him in a few short steps, reaching forward to touch the 660-Squadron badge on his left breast.

"I told you, remember?" she said with a beaming smile. "I said that the gods would supply, and they have. What has happened here was meant to be."

The others were staring in silent astonishment and, for a moment or two, Seethan was confused. But then he looked at what they were staring at.

It was the wolf's head patch of his squadron.

Chapter 17

Unlike normal wolfpacks, which are usually made up of family members based around a mated pair, werewolves consisted of those who in normal life had usually been strangers to each other. There had been five members originally in the pack.

Dan, the one who'd been killed attacking Seethan, had been young and inexperienced. He had only recently turned, and had been chased from his village once his family and friends discovered what he'd become. That, and the fact he was unable to control his maniacal urge to kill. While the other pack members preyed only on wildlife, Dan had slain humans. Those included his own brother, and he'd left clues to his identity in the process. Now there only remained Fae, Angry Andy, Simon and Michael.

Fae was a young woman of twenty-five, with luxurious black hair that had one vivid white streak on her right side. She wore her hair swept back, and kept her breasts strapped down in human form, giving her a lithe and somewhat boyish appearance. For reasons unknown to Seethan, she always wore blue. As wolves, she and Seethan copulated constantly, a means he'd found to control the insane bloodlust. It was only when he came back to human form that he fully realised what he'd done, and tears of guilt trickled down his face.

Rose, oh my God Rose. I'm so sorry!

Time and again he mounted Fae, despite all his determination and effort not to. It was as if the wolf in him was a different person, and that he had to be with her to cement his position in the pack. He felt unable to control himself but, while in human form, it never once crossed their minds to have sex. Mating was a wolf thing but it didn't help assuage the guilt he felt when he returned to normal. He loved Rose with all of his heart. How would she take what he'd done, and kept doing?

Simon had lank blond hair, which he brushed over his bald spot in an attempt to conceal it, a trait for which the others teased him mercilessly. He was a quiet man of average size, but when he transformed into an almost pure-white wolf he became a formidable foe. He was close friends with Michael, who had a tousle of blond hair above hooded eyes, giving him a shrewd look. Both Simon and Michael were about the same height, while Fae was a little shorter.

Angry Andy, however, was completely the opposite. He was a genial black giant of a man, much taller than Seethan. Although often first daunted, people soon warmed to him, as his dreadlocks danced around his well-trimmed beard when he laughed. The others called him Angry because of how he changed so dramatically when the pull of the moon was upon him. Then, the gentle giant – who so often snorted with humour, strummed his guitar and sang songs around the campfire – vanished in an instant. In his stead there was a ravening monster, who had sometimes to be held back from the kill. Thanks to Seethan, Andy's leg had a gaping tear through which bone showed. Luckily, the werewolf in him meant he recovered quickly and already the wound was starting to heal. Strangely, he bore no malice towards Seethan and the two of them quickly became friends.

Seethan had told the pack about his mission to find Rose and prevent her murder. They had been understanding and quickly joined in with the quest. Their new alpha's wishes were orders as far as they were concerned, even while in human form. Well used to the change, they'd not left their clothes far away and had dressed quickly, leaving Seethan to walk back to his friends naked. Although they supported the project to rescue Rose, the pack set up their own camp outside that of the humans and the two rarely mingled.

Michael, with his shoulder-length brown hair and clipped beard, missed the presence of normal humans more than the others. Outcast, his sad hazel eyes often dwelled on Jon and the others, as they warmed themselves around their own campfire. Out of the pack, he was the one who concerned Seethan the most. He had the feeling that Michael was biding his time, waiting patiently for an opportunity to seek the position of Alpha Male, and always kept a half-eye on what could easily be a potential rival.

On Seethan's return to Jon and the others after his first change, he'd felt surprisingly well enough for them to continue their journey. However, for the next few days he noticed that they kept their distance. Only Shona rode beside him or really spoke during their rest periods. Sure, the others replied when he addressed them directly, and they even chuckled occasionally at his weak jokes but nonetheless, he felt ostracised and punished for things that were beyond his control. Thankfully, as the days went on, the tension between them eased and the group seemed to regain some of its old camaraderie. But when it came to the pack it was a different matter: the two groups simply didn't mix.

One evening, while other members of the pack were on guard duty, Andy and Simon approached their fire and tried to make conversation. Eve, however, soon put them in their place, telling them that werewolves were considered a menace in her society and she'd rather they kept their distance. While it was nothing the two pack members didn't already know, they were obviously wounded by her words and solemnly retreated back to their own fire. They'd made an effort and, to Seethan, that meant a lot.

"Eve," Seethan said, knowing the pack could easily hear him with their vastly improved senses. "Firstly, there was no need for that. Secondly, what wrong have these guys actually done you? The only member of the pack group who's ever taken a human life was Dan. He was the one who attacked me, and we killed him for it. Compared to those thugs from your village back in Burley, the pack are angels, so what gives you the right to speak to them like that?"

Eve's eyes narrowed to slits. "I've known people who've been taken by these creatures, and have seen the effects it's had on their families. I told you before how I feel about werewolves, and you becoming one hasn't changed my mind."

Seeing the look on his face, her tone softened. "Look, I know that it's not your fault, nor is it the others'. I'll even admit that your badge being a wolf is…well, a bit weird. Perhaps Shona is right when she says some things are meant to be, but that doesn't change things. I can't make one rule for one and another for you and your gang of mutts. When this is all over, I suggest that you and those other animal fiends stay out of our way."

"I get what you're saying Eve, but think on this. We need the pack on our side, pure and simple. They're protecting us, and by 'us' I mean all of our group. In my opinion you're out of order, and I'd like you treat them with more consideration." That said, Seethan turned and walked away, leaving Eve staring after him.

Later that day, when they took a break by a brook, he was approached by Chris.

"Eve told me what you said earlier and for what it's worth I agree with you – both of you actually. Yes, I get that how we feel is unfair on the pack, but you have to see our side of it too. Just because the Spooks were pissed and made werewolves a reality, doesn't mean we have to be happy about it. Particularly when some of them have killed our friends."

As he spoke, the others joined them and so he raised his voice and spoke to them all.

"Look," Seethan said," I know that the wolves are a major issue for all of you. But I need to know that we've got each other's back, that both I and the rest of the pack can trust you. We have to work as a cohesive unit. There *cannot* be any dissension, particularly if it comes to a fight. That the pack have agreed to help us makes our group stronger, so please show them some respect. I'd hate to lose people now, but it's up to you. Make your choices, and leave if you feel you have to."

They looked at each other for a moment or two and it was Eve who finally spoke.

"You can be an idiot at times. That we're still here should tell you our decision was made some time back. You're right, we're not happy with the mutts, but we won't abandon you now. We are with you, and intend staying that way."

"Thanks," Seethan said, hearing the relief in his own voice. "I'd ask you be a little more understanding of the pack. Please?"

"We can do that," Chris said.

"Thank you. And another thing, don't call them mutts."

*****

The full moon always forced Seethan's werewolf's change. He'd see the moon climbing above the trees, bringing with it waves of want. His eyes were drawn to its warm romantic glow and he felt the urge to hunt, to rut, and rend with his teeth. To give vent to the song rising within him. No matter how he fought it, in the end there was no choice. He'd strip naked and lay down in the musty moistness of the long grass, savouring the myriad scents the night air brought with it. But as the time dragged on, Seethan learned to harness that power. He might be helpless in the glow of the moon, but his control was growing. Before long he found he was able to force the change at will, even during the day, although changing back to human form took longer.

The horses were travelling about thirteen kilometres each day. During full moon the wolves laid low until sunset, catching them up some time after that. When Seethan passed on to the pack how he'd learned to control the changes, so that he could become a wolf at any time, it didn't take them long to catch on. Taking it in turns – a few of them were soon padding alongside the group of riders during the daylight hours. But those extra hours in wolf form soon took a toll on their vitality. The wolves became more volatile and anxious as time went on. Thankfully when Seethan explained what was happening to the others, they took it on board and said nothing if any of the pack were overly curt with them.

Since his induction into the pack, Seethan's skills and powers had increased. The other wolves now came when he called them, either mentally or by song. They became adept at focusing breathing and calming their hearts' rhythms. To be in the moment with nature. He was surprised at how quickly they took to his five senses strategy, and knew from personal experience how this cleared the mind – he sensed that this was in part key to their being able to control the change.

Their animal senses increased exponentially while in wolf form, their remembrance of mankind's society dimming until they were human again. His strategies helped him remember when he was in wolf form, and he watched as their awareness increased when he taught them that too.

Now they could change at will and most evenings they would come to the camp but wait out in the shadows, unable to enter due to the protective circle Shona cast around the camp. There they stayed. Silent and watchful silhouettes, until Seethan rose to join them and they melted into the night as one.

The wolves were always there, one or two of them on guard day or night. Some mornings they left small game as breakfast for the humans, as close to the camp as they could get. Those gifts had a positive effect on the humans' acceptance of them. Seethan had heard many times that a full belly often heals rifts and it certainly proved to be the case here. Not only did his friends' temperament improve but also their attitude towards the pack itself, eventually becoming one of grudging acceptance.

"I was able to change several times today, and back again shortly after," Fae said as they sat around a campfire at dusk, watching the humans practicing archery from a safe distance. "You were right, it's exhausting but achievable and practice makes perfect. Where did you learn those mind tricks of yours? I've not come across them before."

"In the military."

Quick to pick up on Seethan's defensiveness, Andy butted in. "On the subject of practice making perfect, I think that you and I did pretty well until Spaceman here arrived." As he spoke, he added an exaggerated lecherous smile and poked at Fae with a thick finger.

She laughed, and said, "Admit it, you never could really handle me. Seethan's shown me a lot of new tricks since then."

"Really?" Michael sneered, white teeth gleaming white as he threw a stick into the forest. "Then here, go fetch,"

"Sometimes you're not funny, Michael," Fae's green-blue eyes narrowed dangerously.

Michael snorted but otherwise ignored her.

Saying nothing, Simon watched the byplay. Of average build and slender with it, he never had much to say and spent a lot of his time in contemplation. He wore a moustache, and had a long, blond beard that came to a point just above his breastbone. Revealing a bald crown, his hair was tied back and hung in a ponytail between his shoulder blades. Seethan found it strange how all the male members had beards, except him. But when he thought about it, he realised that he had to shave more often these days, and decided their trend was due to frustration.

"Time to go," Seethan said.

He watched as his friends changed and spread out in a wide

protective formation around the humans. He much preferred to ride, to keep his bond with Jon and the others strong. Rejoining them, he mounted up and they set off once again.

*****

That night they came to an inlet. Seethan's keen sense of smell had scented the sea some time back, but when they finally came across it the scene was spectacular and they made camp there that night. For once werewolves and humans sat in a communal group together on the beach, watching the vivid sunset. It was an unworldly vision, the sea aglow like burnished bronze as the sun sank towards the horizon. As they watched silently, the sky darkened until stars peeped brightly over the horizon; the sun disappeared and the sky filled with stars. Seethan looked up as Angry Andy settled his bulk on a log next to him.

"Want to tell me what's up?" Seethan asked quietly. "It's unlike the pack and humans to mix like this, you're making a special effort. There's a change in the air, everyone can sense it."

Angry looked at him without flinching. "The pack's unwilling to go forward. We're getting close to a land that's forbidden to us, and is well-guarded against our intrusion. I'd ask that you rethink our path, so that we can travel together."

"We have to go where the witch leads. I have no choice, only she knows the path."

"Then we'll be gone in the morning," Angry's words carried above the gentle shush of the waves on the shore. "On your own you may sneak through, but with us it's highly unlikely anyone will survive."

Hearing him, Eve's head snapped around and her eyes widened in surprise. "You agreed to stay with us, until the end!"

"We never said that."

"You implied it."

Both Jon and Chris were listening in now, all other conversation had died and only the rush of the sea on the shore punctuated the discussion.

"That path is forbidden," Angry insisted. "We can't break the law, just for you."

"I understand," Seethan said, shushing all protest from the others with a gesture. "Go then, Andy. I'm sure that the pack will be safe in your hands. After all, you have far more experience at it than I do. Take care of them, and we'll see you on the other side."

"Is that it, you're just going to let them go?" Eve demanded hotly, hands on her hips.

"If I remember correctly," Seethan replied, "you didn't want them with us in the first place."

"And it seems to me that at the slightest threat, your so-called wolves turn into puppies." Eve turned on her heels and stamped off to her bedroll.

And, just like that, their strength had halved.

Chapter 18

It was mid-afternoon, and they were riding through a section of the forest where the trees bore hand-sized, blood-red flowers that somehow reminded Seethan of pursed lips. The blossom fell around them like crimson snow, only to be kicked up into clouds by the horses' hooves. Amidst the foliage there were bursts of the deadly Devil's Helmet, smaller individual canary-yellow flowers, and surprisingly a multitude of fuchsia-like blooms.

"We're getting close now," Shona said.

"Are you sure?" Seethan asked, and added, "No, don't answer that. I've had my fill of magic and mysticism."

"Have you thought on how you'll combat this enemy, when you meet him?"

Shona was right, he realised. Being an android, Alan Wrong had incredible strength and agility. How could a human fight against something like that? But then, he was no longer human, was he. He was a werewolf and Alan wouldn't be expecting that, even if he was aware that such creatures existed.

"I don't understand much about these androids of yours, Seethan," Shona said, "But from what you've said I can understand your trepidation."

"He intends killing Rose and we have to stop him. That's it. But it's not going to be easy and we have to find her first."

Shona was still dressed in her white cotton shift and multi-layered purple cape. Those strange topaz eyes studied him. "What will you do if your friend Rose doesn't want to know you, have you considered that?"

"Why wouldn't she?"

"Because things happen. People who have been friends all their lives suddenly become bitter enemies. I want you to be prepared, just in case."

"If she doesn't want my help then there's nothing I can do," he replied. "But I'll not abandon her. We don't leave people behind. She's my co-pilot and friend, and she'd do the same for me. I know she would."

"Are you sure you're ready for this?" She waited for his

nod and then stopped her horse.

"Look, Shona, what do you want from me?" he asked in frustration.

"To believe. What you call mythology walks a fine line with reality. All it takes is a little faith; or one misstep."

One of the many things Seethan had learned lately was that what he'd known as reality was false. The paranormal existed. It always had. The Spooks' arrival had simply rekindled the magic that had once been abundant, but had lain dormant in recent centuries. When he could eventually leave this world and return to whatever remained of mankind's space-bound empire, he'd have a lot of explaining to do. Much of which would, no doubt, be followed by a visit to a military psychiatrist. He already knew that society in the colonies would have changed from what he knew. Whether he'd fit in, and what he'd do out there, was beyond him. And what would happen if he ended up somewhere with more than one moon? He thrust the thoughts aside, for the time being he needed to concentrate on the present. The here, the now.

"I've seen things that can't be, but are. Look at me, I'm no longer just a man. I'm human sure, but I'm also much more. Given all that, when you ask whether I believe in magic the answer has to be yes, so let's get on with it."

Shona resumed riding alongside him and pointed across the meadow they were travelling through. "I needed to be sure, because we're here now and once we enter there's no going back."

Seethan looked ahead and he pulled Midnight to a halt, the others stopping with him. The forest had cleared into blossom-covered grassland and in the centre of it he could see two elm trees. Their branches, profusion of dark-green leaves, and reddish flowers sprang from the boles only a short distance from the ground. Several of those branches met and joined in an arch, forming a green shroud in which a purple-painted door stood closed. It looked wooden, with a simple old-fashioned colour-matched handle with a thumb catch, and with a circular lattice-work square design towards the top.

Together they set off towards it, but some hours later they appeared to get no nearer.

"What's going on?" he asked Shona finally. "We've been riding for ages and yet that damned doorway isn't getting any closer."

"That's because until you fully accept magic exists you won't be able to go through it."

"But I do believe," Seethan said, his words tempered with frustration. "I've told you that. I'm a werewolf: if that doesn't make me believe, what will?"

"There's a difference between magic and the paranormal. You're focusing on the latter, which is something that happens outside normal existence. Lycanthropy and ghosts for instance. Magic, however, is using the forces of nature to make the things you want happen. You can't use magic to make someone into a werewolf for instance, they have to be bitten by one for that to happen."

Seethan reigned Midnight in and the group stopped as one, all of them listening to the discussion.

"I didn't think there was a difference," Seethan said thoughtfully. "So...how do I believe in magic?"

"You just believe."

"And how do I do that?"

Shona produced a wand from her sleeve and he listened to the guttural chants she began making. Try as he might Seethan couldn't make out the words. They seemed elusive. To ebb and flow on the soft autumn wind, bringing with it the floral scent of the meadow around them.

Seethan relaxed into his newly-sharpened senses. He could see a hawk rising on air currents far in the distance, and smell the sea when it was still miles away. There was a constant drone of flying insects, of bees buzzing in and out of pollen-laden flowers, a fox slinking through the grassland toward rabbits munching away and unaware of their threat. He could taste salt on the air, almost matching the sweat on his lips, and the sweet richness of honeysuckle that the still-warm breeze brought with it. Sounds were more noticeable, scents enriched, and colours vibrant. Maybe it had something to do with Shona's spell, he thought.

Shona made circular motions with her wand and her chant stopped, as something like a soap bubble at least ten metres across suddenly appeared in front of them. A milky luminescence swirled like wind-swept clouds. Gradually the bubble cleared and he could see the soul-sucking darkness of space. He recognised the dull rusty surface of Mars, with its cities glittering like jewels beneath a pea-sized sun. He could see the lights of dwellings on the lumpy grey potato shape of Phobos, and the dark ball-bearing of what could only be Ganymede as it sped against a backdrop of Jupiter. Those visions came and went, flickering before him like photographs. Places he'd seen and others he hadn't. Majestic kilometre-long ships overtook asteroids that had been hollowed out into generation ships and sent on their way in times long past. There were cities on Venus – there hadn't been in his time. He knew in his heart that what he saw was real.

"How..."

His words trailed away as the scene changed to show a large spaceship with two escorts approaching the Earth. It was unlike anything he'd seen before, bristling with hidden armaments that he could only sense. Gone were the multiple auxiliary drives mounted externally on the craft's main body, and the blaze of the fusion engines aft in the vehicles of his time.

"That doesn't look like any kind of ship I've seen before. I'd say it's not human, but I suspect it is. As far as I'm aware, apart from the Spooks we've not come across other lifeforms; their ships look more like ghostly plants."

"It is human, Seethan. It's been a long time, remember?"

"Is it coming here?" Jon asked, his voice anxious. "Why now, when they've left Earth alone all these years?"

With a quick wave of the wand, the images vanished. Another wave of Shona's hand and an apple appeared in mid-air. Seethan caught it as it fell. At a pointed look from Shona he took a bite. It was delicious and he smiled with pleasure as the juices ran down his chin.

Shona looked at him pointedly. "If you can't explain what you've just seen, now do you believe in magic?"

Seethan wiped away the juice with the back of his hand, reaching out to give the half-eaten fruit to Midnight. Yes, he believed. She was right: nothing else could explain what he'd seen, but it was the apple that did it. The belief coursed through him like a heartbeat, bringing with it a calm feeling of acceptance.

"What happens now?" he asked.

For an answer, Shona urged her pale pony forward and before long they found themselves finally approaching the purple door. To Seethan's surprise the frame was half his height again, tapered at the top like a church door. Paint peeled away in places, and the door furniture looked old and worn. When they dismounted, Jon asked Chris to stay behind and look after the horses.

"I think not," Chris replied tartly. "I didn't come all this way just to wait here while the rest of you see this through."

Jon and Eve gave rueful smiles, as they joined Chris in attaching the horses' reins to the trees, and – as one – the group approached the door. They gave each other trepidatious smiles to show they were ready. Eve put her arms around her brother and then Jon, kissing them each on the cheek, before blowing at a wisp of hair that had escaped her ponytail.

On their right side the two purple hinges almost but not quite melded into the overall picture. The door itself was framed by foliage, leaves from the branches poking over it at the edges, while ivy disappeared into cracks and crevices. Seethan reached forward and grabbed the door handle. He pressed his thumb down on the latch.

The mechanism lifted, and he pushed.

*****

They stepped through the door and found themselves in a field filled with countless pink flowers. At the fringes of the clearing the trees had skirts of it that washed up against their stern sides like waves against cliffs. Here and there were bursts of snow-white, yellow, and blue; blooms that fought back the pink and stood out like scattered islands. Behind them the door closed and vanished. To their left, a narrow river rushed madly, running a few paces from where they stood to the far side of the clearing. Clouds of mist drifted and swirled solemnly across the ground and between the distant trees, looking like wandering ghosts. Everything felt muted somehow, the only sound the rhythm of the river as it chuckled along beside them.

The damp, eldritch mist left water beading on their bare

skin. It swirled and drew apart to reveal a hooded figure waiting patiently in front of them. The figure held a tall, thin staff that ended in a tangled knot of wood at head-height and looked intricately carved. Wordlessly, they followed the path of the river to the solitary figure. As they approached a hand rose and drew back the hood, revealing an old man with long sparse white hair and a beard that hung down to a point at his wide, black leather belt. His hooded cloak was made of a deep-blue velvety material, and in his weathered face his startling gold-coloured eyes looked both knowing and joyful.

"You are Seethan Bodell," the old man said in a gentle, pleased voice.

"Yes. Who are you?"

"I am Nadons, one of those you call the Spooks. Some call me a mage, I'm here to help you."

"I came here looking for a colleague of mine, Rose Mills. Have you seen her?" His left arm had begun to itch terribly and he scratched at it while scrutinising the old man.

"I have. She's been waiting for you."

"Where is she? Come on, I need to see her! Don't keep me waiting. We've been through all kinds of hell and an android, Alan Wrong, is on his way to kill her. I have to find Rose before he does, and warn her."

Shona put her hand on Seethan's shoulder, as if to calm him down. His left forearm was driving him mad and he scratched at it furiously, shrugging Shona off as he did so. Just then he heard a burst of static. Realisation dawned on him and he pulled back his sleeve, staring incredulously at his Smart-Arm. It was powered up and countless messages were showing on flashing icons, above an image of Earth from space.

"What?" Seethan gasped. "My Smart-Arm...look, it's working!"

"You've arrived just in time," the old man said. "A contingent from your colonies have arrived in orbit. They are here to hold talks with us in hope of establishing a lasting peace. Since your mission tore this planet apart, Seethan Bodell, it's somehow fitting that you be here, don't you think? There's been little contact between our races in all these years. None since the last of your evacuation ships took most of the survivors to the other worlds."

"Why now?" Seethan asked. "This is too much of a coincidence. But I'm more worried about Rose, to be honest. Where is she?"

"All in good time," the old man said. "There's no such thing as coincidence."

"In good time my arse," Seethan growled. "Who the fuck do you think you are?"

"I've already told you, call me Nadons. Your Augury Witch, Shona, can tell you much about me and my kind in time."

"Bodell. Commander Seethan Bodell!" A voice squawked from his Smart-Arm.

"And now my Smarts are working again," Seethan said, ignoring the demand to speak. "None of this makes sense, you'd better start talking."

"Oh, but it does make sense," Nadons said. "A long time has passed since your little adventure ruined this planet. During that time this world and your colonies have changed. Humanity has tried to copy our powers, in an effort to combat us with our own abilities."

"Surely," Seethan said, "it would take more than a couple of hundred years for that trait to breed true."

The old man raised his gnarled white eyebrows. "You're right, it would. But who said it was a few hundred years? You've been gone for well over a thousand."

Seethan stared at him, for once in his life speechless. He found himself mouthing the old man's words.

Jon spoke up. "Alan Wrong told us that it was a few hundred years. And from what Seethan's said about him, this artificial person knows all about time. But why would he lie?"

"Never mind all that," Seethan said dismissively, glaring at Nadons. "Where's Rose? I've asked you several times and I want an answer now. She's done nothing to you, and none of this was her fault."

The old man's enigmatic smile infuriated Seethan beyond words. He felt the rage building within him and the wolf flooding his body with adrenalin. He remembered what his counsellor said to him: that he didn't do anger, but PTSD did. That memory allowed him to force back the feeling. But before he could say or do anything, Nadons stepped back and gestured behind him with his left hand. The mist swirled aside to reveal a mahogany, coffin-like structure lying on the ground amidst the flowers and fallen blossom.

Seethan's rage vanished instantly. "What?" he gasped. Running the few steps, he grasped the coffin's side and stared down into the smooth white marble-like inner, to see Rose's unmoving face pillowed in red velvet inside it. "Is she...?"

"Dead? No, but she was very badly damaged when your ship crashed. Your technology is outside of our magic. We don't understand it or know how to repair her, or even if she could be."

Seethan realised that tears were coursing down his face and he gripped the silky-smooth side of the coffin with one hand, while turning aside from the others to surreptitiously wipe the tracks clear of his face with his free hand. Unsure what to do, he leant forward and down, kissing Rose on the cheek. Immediately her emerald eyes flickered open and the scent of apple-blossom wafted over him, a warm welcoming smell that made his heart surge.

"Seethan?" her voice was low and weak.

"Rose! My God, I've been so worried about you. Here, let me help you up." He reached down into the coffin but Nadons, who'd appeared beside him, laid a warning hand on his arm.

Rose gazed up at him with a longing that matched his own, and Seethan felt his love for her suffuse his whole being. He had an urgent need to take her in his arms, to pull her close and protect her from all the bad things that life brings, and to tell her he'd never let her go again. He'd be by her side, forever.

"She's injured, be gentle with her," Nadons said.

Seethan looked from Rose to the old man, and back again. His hand had slipped behind her head, and it felt wet and sticky. He saw it was covered in blood, but the colour was wrong somehow, as if her body were failing to generate the fluid correctly. It was too light a red to be true.

"We tried using one of your medical pods from within your craft but it didn't appear to do anything. So instead we put her in a pod of our own construction and were able to make her sleep, knowing that you were here and sooner or later you'd come for her."

"Those pods weren't designed for androids," Seethan said. "That's why it didn't work. She needs specialist care. You could have brought me here earlier!"

The old man shook his head, his beard flicking from side to side. "No. We knew your nemesis was stalking her, and we didn't dare give you any clues in case he intercepted them. It was better that you found your own way here, with a little guidance along the way.

"That ship you saw through your smart-arm is bringing other humans back to this world. It will be able to land safely, despite our null field. We hope you can help in the negotiations and I'm sure those people will be able to help Rose in return for your efforts. In the meantime, I suggest you let her sleep."

"Commander Bodell!" an insistent voice demanded from Seethan's arm.

Seethan kissed Rose gently on her velvet lips. Her eyes fluttered and closed. "I'll be back for you soon," he said. "Don't worry, a ship's on the way. They'll be able to repair you." A single tear rolled from her right eye and down her cheek, as he lowered her back down into the coffin.

"Bloody Ruperts," she murmured, before consciousness left her.

A half-choked chuckle slipped from Seethan, as he looked down at her for a long moment. It seemed cruel that now he had found her he might lose her again. He laid a hand on her cheek and it was as cool as the marble-lined coffin, like touching a jug of milk fresh from the refrigerator. She lay still, her chest neither rising or falling in its usual imitation of life, a sign that she was critically damaged and that her systems were running on emergency power.

"Who's Rupert?" Eve asked, watching from a short distance way.

"It's a nickname given to military officers. She was trying to make me smile."

A shout from his Smart-Arm demanded his attention. "Bodell!" It was a command he could no longer ignore.

Seethan stepped away and tapped at his Smarts. Instantly the image of a short, middle-aged, white-bearded man in a blue uniform appeared in front of him. "Who are you?" Seethan demanded.

"Ah, Commander Bodell. I'm Admiral Jeffries, senior officer here. I'm pleased to meet you at last. We picked up the signal from your Smart-Arm as we approached. Your details are still in our data banks and you're quite the celebrity. How you got where you are is a discussion for another time. For now, let's talk about the present.

"As I suspect you're aware, we now have the ability to land on Earth and we're currently in orbit. I've been despatched to see if our differences with the Spooks can be settled amicably. Oddly," he held up a small white card and peered at it, a surprised expression on his face, "a printed invitation to do so appeared on my desk a few moments ago. I take it that was from the aliens, and genuine?"

Distrust, some things never change in the military, Seethan mused. "It's no trick, Sir. The Spooks," he glanced suddenly at Nadons, wondering whether he should rephrase, but the old man simply nodded in reassurance, "are happy to meet with you." He put his Smarts on privacy and said to Nadons, "The card's impressive. Does that mean you can put things on our ships at a distance, unlike before?"

"Only small things at the moment," Nadons replied. "It's a work in progress. Your technology and our magic don't mix well."

"Conference mode," the admiral commanded loudly.

Seethan untapped his privacy and was instantly surrounded by a hologram bubble of security measures projected from the ship. Ones that apparently isolated him from the others because despite his efforts he couldn't see them through it, as he could back in his own time. He was, to all effects, in the admiral's cabin on board the ship. Jeffries was sitting behind a chocolate-coloured desk, the kind easily extruded on board ship at need and designed to suit the specific user's requirements. He glanced around quickly, to see the walls were painted white and the carpet was a deep red.

"Don't worry, Bodell, they can't hear or see us. To them you've suddenly been enclosed in a grey ball. Amazing what our paranaturals can do now," Jeffries said. "Tell me, Commandeer, do the aliens really want to meet with us or are they playing for time? More importantly, are they to be trusted?"

"You have to bear in mind that I've only just met them, Sir.

They're aliens, so who the hell knows what their thought processes and motives are. If your question is 'would I put my life on the line' then the answer is yes. That's because they could have killed me at any time, but chose not to. That says a lot."

The admiral pushed himself back into his chair and harrumphed. "Good. Then you will help represent us at this meeting. We need this to go our way, Bodell. Earth belongs to mankind and it will stay that way. It's our intent that these proceedings allow us to get our planet back. Humans should rule here, not aliens."

"Sir," Seethan said, "I signed up for twenty-five years. I'm no longer a member of Earth's military, nor any offshoot of it. You can't command me to do this if I don't want to."

The admiral's eyes glittered. "Your twenty-five years haven't expired. The fact you somehow jumped through time means that you still have the balance of your service contract to address. However, I'll consider releasing you on completion of these talks; in appreciation for your help, you understand. You'd not be any real use to our military anyway – things have changed far too much for that."

Seethan felt himself redden and he bit his lip to stop himself from snapping a terse reply. Instead he chose his words carefully. "I signed on for a term of duty, but that was until a date fixed on my contract. That date has passed, and we both know it. Any court of law would agree that I'm no longer a serving member."

"In which case I'll simply reactivate your contract," Jeffries said with a cold smile. "I have that authority. Welcome back to the military, Commander."

Seethan said nothing. He knew he was caught and there was nothing he could do about it. Instead he stood and bit back his anger. It wouldn't help.

Jeffries didn't even blink as he continued. "You will do everything necessary to swing the talks our way, is that understood?" He waited until Seethan nodded before continuing. "Excellent. You don't need to worry, I'm hoping there won't be any need for nastiness and, be assured, my promise stands that you will be released from service on completion."

"I'll do this on one condition," Seethan replied. "My co-pilot, an android named Rose Mills, was damaged during the crash landing. I'd like her repaired and likewise released from service."

"I have her details here, linked to yours. That android's outdated, I can easily arrange for you to get you a more modern one. In the end they're all the same, you know."

"I don't want a new one, I want Rose!"

"Well, I'll see what I can do – on the understanding that you do as I ask. Our instruments have tracked your…Rose, and the fact she's still semi-active is quite remarkable. If you play nice, I'll ensure our technicians take a look at her and do their best when this is all over."

"Thank you."

"You're very welcome, Commander. We're not animals, you know. Now then, believe me when I tell you that we have a unit with enhanced paranormal abilities, much like the Spooks. Which means, in layman's terms, that you don't need to worry about them anymore. We can land in force at any time, if needed; but the last thing we seek is further hostility. Our governments are hoping that eventually we can work with the Spooks for the betterment of all."

The older man glanced at a beige wall to one side, and the image of a large, circular, dark-wood clock appeared at head height, and then it merged with the wall again and disappeared. "We'll be landing within the hour. The fact we only sent this ship and two escorts ahead of our Task Unit should demonstrate our sincerity and desire for peace. We just want them off the Earth. Where they go afterwards is up to them, as long as it's not anywhere occupied by us. Now, do tell them what I've said: and I look forward to seeing you in person shortly."

The scene around Seethan disappeared and he was suddenly back in the glade with the others. There were looks of alarm in all but Nadons' eyes, as his friends obviously didn't understand what had just happened. Seethan breathed in deeply, relieved to be back, and then expelled his breath as if he were blowing up a balloon.

"What the hell?" Eve demanded. "You disappeared and there was this big ball thing right where you used to be. Our knives didn't even scratch it. Are you okay?"

"Don't worry," Seethan said, "I'm fine."

"That was a bit like our null-fields," Nadons said calmly but with a raised eyebrow, "similar to the one we surrounded this planet with. It prevented us from seeing or touching you, but you were still physically here on this world. Look, your admiral's ship is approaching."

They all looked up to see a pastel-blue-coloured but featureless lozenge shape growing in size as it dropped towards them. In moments, the craft, the size of a football pitch, was hovering about thirty metres above the mist-shrouded ground and within walking distance. It was a small landing ship. Seethan felt positive that it would be armed but he could see no weapon emplacements.

Overhead, several much smaller aircraft zipped back and forth without sound. Seethan didn't recognise the type but realised immediately that they were fighters, possibly from the landing ship itself. They'd be flying Combat Air Patrols to protect the Admiral's ship and its personnel in case of trouble. He watched curiously for a moment or two. The teardrop-shaped craft were like drops of rain flittering through the sky overhead. That he could even see them had to be deliberate, Seethan thought, convinced that advanced camo would have concealed their presence had they so wished. Perhaps it was as reassurance to the landing party below, or a visual deterrent to any possible aggression.

A door grew from a small hole that appeared on the seamless side of the ship. One moment it wasn't there, the next it was. They watched silently as a silver platform with several people aboard slid out, and slowly lowered to the ground to form a stairway, the mist swirling around its base as it kissed the grass.

Admiral Jeffries and another man marched down it and then towards them, with two un-visored guards bearing holstered side arms. The man besides Jeffries was dressed in what appeared to be a grey all-in-one outfit that covered him from his matching shoes to his buttoned-up collar. From his haughty demeanour, Seethan suspected immediately that he was a diplomat.

Seethan noted colour-coded bumps on the shoulders of the guards' blue armour. Something about them made him uneasy but he was unable to put his finger on what it was. The guards' tight haircuts made him wonder about their sex, but the swell at their chests and their slim hands gave it away. As the four approached them, the mist eddied around their feet.

"Commander Bodell," the admiral said, "I'm Admiral Jeffries, we spoke earlier and I have to say that I'm delighted to meet you in person. This gentleman beside me is First Minister Haden, who's here to represent Earth's government in exile. Is this a member of the Spook delegation?" He bathed Nadons in his smile and held out his hand, dropping it with barely concealed irritation when the old man didn't respond.

Seethan eyed the white-bearded admiral. "Yes, Sir. This is Nadons, a representative of those we call the Spooks. These are local representatives, Jon, Chris, Eve, and Shona; descendants of the survivors." He realised as he introduced them that he didn't actually know their last names, or if they had any.

"Well Mr Nadons," Haden said, with curt nods to Seethan's friends, "It's a fine morning to—"

"Nadons will do," the old man said curtly.

"Very well, then. Perhaps we could continue this in comfort aboard our ship, the *Rosalon Redemption*. It's in orbit but we'd be delighted if you could join us for lunch. We can take this landing craft, and my chefs can prepare anything you might like."

Haden wore a constant smile, as if it was stuck there. In fact, the man looked as if someone had just got him out of a box. Manicured to the extreme, his well-trimmed lightly-peppered grey hair showed an age beyond the man's youthful manner. Seethan wondered whether the hair colouring was a deliberate ploy to help convey an air of experience.

"We can speak here," the Spook said, as the aircraft again shot noiselessly overhead.

The admiral flinched but Haden continued smoothly.

"Very well, Nadons. As the admiral says, I represent the colonies and he our armed forces. I bring greetings to you from the colonies. We're here to seek a formal ending to the hostilities between our two races. I'm sure that we have much in common and I would like to deeply apologise for the misunderstandings that caused this conflict in the first place."

Nadons waved a hand and a large wooden conference table,

with matching chairs, appeared close by. The group of visitors hid their surprise and they all sat and looked at each other silently for a moment, while bowls of fruit materialised on the table in front of them.

"There was no misunderstanding, as you put it," Nadons replied at length. "If you recall, your people invaded our world, and attacked us by polluting our atmosphere. When we resisted, you bombed us with nuclear and chemical weapons, killing a great many of us in the process. We are, however, a peaceful people and are willing to move forward. While we don't forget, it is, as they say, all in the past. We have lived here on Earth undisturbed since coming to this world, and your consequent abandonment of it. You have your worlds and we have this one. I suggest that you be content with what you have."

Seethan was watching the admiral's face and he saw him flinch at the alien's words.

"We didn't abandon the Earth, we were driven from it," Jeffries snapped.

Haden held up the fingers on his right hand and shifted his entire body to face the admiral. He didn't say a word; his gaze was stern enough and the older man had the good grace to blush, drop his eyes, and fall silent. Only then did Haden turn back and continue.

"It appears from these colleagues of yours that some of humanity remained here after most left. How many survivors there are we do not know, but it gives us the premise that humanity has continued to occupy Earth and, perhaps even to a degree, control it. The colonies would like to cement a lasting peace between our races. All we only ask that you return this planet to colonial control."

"Mankind doesn't control this world," said Nadons. "We allow humans to live here, there's a difference. Humanity destroyed our planet and we took this one as reparation. The people of both worlds were diminished as a result. You occupy many other planets; if you truly desire peace then leave us this one. It's all we ask."

Haden stood up straighter, a defiant glint in his eyes. He pushed back the chair and stood, as did the admiral, while the two guards took several steps back. Despite the slight breeze, not a hair on the diplomat's head moved.

"This is the cradle of our civilisation," Haden said, "Our home. We want it back. We're reluctant to take it by force but we will if we have to."

Seethan looked from one to the other, wishing he were anywhere but here. The admiral and diplomat ignored him, staring intently at Nadons. Seethan eyed the faces of the armed guards standing behind the colonial representatives, but their stoic expressions gave nothing away as their hands remained by their sides.

Nadons retained his cool, benign look as he spoke again. "Consider what you did to this world. Earth was dying when we arrived. It was choked by pollution and so overcrowded it was a mass of seething flesh. In the long years of your absence we have healed it. Look around you: Earth is now the garden it once was.

"All here know that if you return in large numbers, and no doubt you would, all of this work of ours would be undone. It's the way humans are. You use and destroy everything around you, and without thought to any other life."

Nadons paused and gestured to Jon and the others.

"But you're right in one thing, humans did remain here although in limited numbers and we came to accept it. These occupy Earth as do we. We share it and live together in harmony. This will continue as is, and thus bring the peace between us."

The admiral's cheeks and nose had reddened perceptibly. Fists clenching, his eyes burned into Seethan's, willing him to intercede. His jaw worked, as if words were fighting to get out.

Seethan appeared to notice suddenly. "Um, First Minister, Admiral," Seethan said. "You've told me that you want the Earth to belong to humans and have insisted that I represent you in this."

The senior officer scowled and said in a warning tone, "Bodell–"

Seethan ignored him and turned to face Nadons. "The Colonial representative's point of view is that the Earth should belong to the race that was born here. It is their price for the peace process. I ask that you accept this as a starting point and, if you do, I'm sure that we can move forward with the negotiations."

Nadons turned to look at him, his golden eyes bright in the sunlight. It was as if he peering deep into Seethan's soul. The wind dropped and only the 'caw' from Peter flying high overhead broke the silence. He gave a slight nod, and said, "We accept that this world reverts back to Earth People."

Seethan gave a smile of relief. "Gentlemen, he's accepted your offer. The peace deal is agreed."

Haden's smile never slipped as he stepped towards Nadons and held out his hand. Solemnly the Spook looked down in confusion, but then reached forward and shook it.

"Good," Jeffries said as he too shook hands. "We will give you a year to leave this world. That includes you, your ships, and anything else you brought along for the ride, or have deposited here since. Of course, you're free to take any other planet out there; apart from any in this system or those housing our colonies. We're more than happy to provide ships to help, if you need them. Perhaps once all this is settled, we can look towards a trade agreement. One I'm sure would be beneficial to both races."

"Sir," Seethan said, holding up a hand and interrupting him. "The aliens aren't going anywhere."

The colonial representatives whirled to face him, Jeffries eyes narrowing as he demanded. "What do you mean, Bodell? The Earth belongs to humans. We were born here; the agreement was that we'd have it back."

"But you weren't born here, were you?" Seethan said casually. "The only Earth people now are those descended from the survivors that you abandoned all those years ago; namely my friends you see with us and the others scattered far and wide around the planet. You are the outsiders now, Admiral. The Earth belongs to humans, yes, that's been agreed. But those born here, the true Earth People. To be blunt, Sir, you are the aliens here."

"Semantics!" Jeffries thundered. "You've broken your word; you were supposed to represent humanity. That was our agreement!"

"I did fulfil my word, Admiral. I've done the very thing you asked. You heard the Spooks cede control to the descendants, but it doesn't mean that the aliens have to leave. You see, my friends here, who are part of this process, told me prior to this meeting that those we call the Spooks are welcome to remain. After all, this planet's large enough for both races, particularly since The Sundering left us somewhat depleted. In return, they will protect the planet and its inhabitants, as they have since the fighting stopped."

"You treacherous dog!" Jeffries bellowed, as he and Haden backed away towards the guards. "You've betrayed your own people, wave goodbye to any help for your android friend!"

Seethan felt his eyes narrow. "Now, wait a minute. You got exactly what you asked for. In return you promised me that–"

Everyone jumped as a figure rose from the river bed and strode towards them.

"Did someone mention androids?" Alan Wrong said, water cascading from him as he sloshed from the river to the shore. He strode confidently towards them, a smug look on his face as he left a trail of water behind him. He wiped at the duckweed adhering to his face, and his clothes made a wet swishing sound as he approached.

"What the–" Seethan gasped. "How the hell did you get here?"

"Oh Seethan, please. Do you honestly think that the admiral hadn't noticed my digital signature on his arrival, as well as yours? He contacted me before he did you and said that he might need my help. Oh, and he also agreed to my terms of payment." Alan stood beside the coffin and looked down at Rose, reaching down to touch her face and say, "Hello, my pretty."

"That's enough, Wrong. Move out of the way. We have issues to discuss," the admiral growled, his eyes furious.

"Very well, Sir," Alan said graciously, reaching down one last time into the coffin with a gloating look, before glancing back and saying, "We'll catch up soon, Seethan."

The android turned and walked towards the ship and everything seemed to happen at once, although in Seethan's eye it was like a series of camera stills. A thought flashed into his mind that if his Smart-Arm was working and these ships were flying, maybe other technology might work too. He heard the admiral shout for his guards, even as he himself snatched at his side arm and pulled it free, snapping off a shot and seeing the beam sizzle straight through Alan's right shoulder. As Alan was thrown to the ground the limb fell away, leaving a gaping hole tinged by glowing embers, that flickered and brightened in the light wind dispersing the mist.

The guards ran forward and past Alan to stand in front of the admiral and Haden, ushering them backwards as they drew their weapons. Split seconds later, the bumps on their armoured shoulders shot off in all directions like a small swarm of birds, quickly forming a swirling shield of devices around the delegation.

The guards' armour had colour changed too. No longer blue, their camo blended into the background, making them look like moving mirrors. At the same time, the drones fired needle-thin beams straight at Seethan. Nadons raised his staff to the full reach of his arm and then slammed the base of it into the ground. There was a brilliant white flash, and the weapon in Seethan's hand died. The beams from the drones splashed against Seethan like harmless torchlight, and at the same instant he felt the tingle from his Smart-Arm vanish. Their camouflage failing, the two guards reappeared. As they did so, their miniature drones fell to the ground like mechanical rain.

Two loud explosions sounded behind Seethan and his instincts kicked in, making him hit the deck. He knew even as he did so that it was the sound of the patrolling aircraft crashing. The guards had pulled their side arms free as he rolled to his feet. They were waving them from one person to the other, covering their retreat, as the admiral and Haden scuttled away from what was a now dangerous situation. The guards' remit would have been to protect their charges at all cost, but at a terse command from the admiral both aimed their weapons and tried to fire at Nadons.

Only then did they discover those weapons no longer worked.

*****

Monitoring the situation from the bridge of the Colonial Ship *Rosalon Redemption*, Captain Samson immediately brought his ship from a relaxed state to condition Zulu, where all airtight and Z-marked doors and hatches were closed. In high orbit, their weapons could incinerate anything from a single person to a whole continent if needed, but as he waited for instructions from the admiral, his data feed suddenly vanished. He glanced anxiously at the display on the grey bulkhead in front of him, which showed the two destroyers keeping station in a protective screen had followed suit.

He'd always been a confident fellow, even under fire, but ever since the landing ship had departed from their hangar he'd been unexplainably nervous. For some reason a terrible and unreasonable dread filled him. For the first time in his life, he could actually smell fear on himself. It was a grim perfume, and he hated himself for it.

"What the hell's going on?" he bellowed. "Why have we lost comms with the ground?"

"Sir," his sensor officer said, shock evident in his voice, "the null-field, it's…. it's back up again! We've lost all contact with the landing ship and are getting no readings at all from the surface."

"Don't talk rubbish, our psi-corps took that field down. There has to be another reason. Find it and fix it, don't argue!"

"Sir," the sensor officer turned to face him, his eyes wide with shock. "I'm sorry but that field is definitely back up. I don't know how or why, but nothing's getting through."

Samson keyed his intercom. "Psi, this is the Captain. What's going on down there? Report."

In the stunned silence a shaky voice replied. "Captain this is Psi Ellis, we've been locked out."

"What do you mean, locked out? Speak up man!" Samson roared.

"My men suppressing the field suddenly collapsed and I've no idea why. They're out cold, in fact I think that they're dead. First aid teams are on their way. Scrub that, Sir, they've just arrived. Others on watch took over their posts and report that the equipment boosting our signal *is* still working but it's having no effect on the null-field. Looks to me like the aliens fooled us. Sir, from what I can see, they let us think we'd taken the field down but they were controlling it all along. I don't know what happened down there, but the Spooks have just definitely brought the field back up again and…there's nothing we can do. We can't penetrate it."

"Comms," Samson said loudly, thanking his lucky stars they were outside the range of the alien field, "send a flash message to the Task Unit in the Kuiper belt." The T.U.

consisted of three carriers, five heavy cruisers and numerous escorts. The admiral's second-in-command, Commodore Andrews, was in charge of it. He was from a long line of distinguished military officers; a good man to have on your side, he was also an excellent tactician. Hopefully between them they'd be able to do something. "Inform the Commodore about what's happened, and request that he get here at best speed."

"Message sent, Captain." Lieutenant Emily Jenkins, his comms officer, said.

"Good. Now—"

"Enemy ships inbound," Ops said, his voice frantic. "Six Spook vessels, all frigate-sized."

Samson's eyes snapped to the full-length display across the bridge's forward bulkhead. He could already see the ghostly, lilac-coloured flower-ships, growing in size as they sped towards them.

"Hands to action stations!" he said, trying to be calm; but his voice sounded shaky even to him. What the hell was the matter? This wasn't like him at all. "All ships, engage those enemy vessels. Weapons free." He could hear his X.O. shouting the command to action stations over the ship's tannoy. The sound of running footsteps and curses came between the on-off blare of the ship's klaxon, accompanied by the red flashing band along the walls and overheads.

As the alarm died away, the bridge crew held their breath, watching the forward display as their beam weapons sliced towards, and then through, the enemy ships. The beams were like a spotlight through fog, leaving them completely unharmed. Mere seconds later, the deck beneath the captain juddered, as they fired a full salvo of torpedoes. Then came the unmistakable '*blam...blam...blam...*', the deck jerking again as their three heavy rail guns fired. Their torpedoes and rail gun rounds passed straight through the spectral ships and on down towards Earth's atmosphere. Suddenly the torpedoes' safeties kicked in and they flared briefly into a fiery death, while the railgun rounds turned to dust.

Captain Samson stared at the displays incredulously. With a flick of a finger, he changed the display, already knowing what he'd see. He was right, the Commodore's Task Unit had paused in its flight towards them, no doubt stopping to watch developments before committing his units. It was the right thing to do, and in the Commodore's place he'd have done the same thing. They were all well aware of what had happened to the ships caught in previous battles with the Spooks, and were no doubt understandably nervous about getting involved in similar engagements. The fact that the null field had come back up again, and the fate of the projectile and beam weapons, didn't bode well.

Damn them, damn them all to hell.

"Prepare to repel boarders!" he bellowed over the intercom, knowing in his heart that it was already too late. He watched on the wall screen as the enemy craft grew in size before merging with his ships.

There was no sound of impact, nothing. Just a long, eerie silence as the ghostly ships slipped aboard. Like everyone else, he found himself holding his breath as he waited to see what would happen. That brief peace was broken as bulkhead doors were suddenly ripped from their mounts and crashed to the decks here and there throughout the ship. Those doors weren't armoured – they were light and simply designed to seal off sections in case of atmosphere breach or fire. Green lights on the damage control board, showing section integrity, changed in places to red. Whatever was coming had free passage, with only his security teams barring the way. Even as the lights changed and information updated, marines reported in from their stations. He knew each and every one of them. They were all good soldiers, as tough as they came and armed to the teeth. They'd been taught what to expect in such a situation and, with luck, perhaps they could stop whatever was coming their way.

Somehow, however, he doubted it.

"Psi, report!"

Nothing.

"Psi Ellis, this is the Captain. What the hell's going on down there?"

No answer.

He sniffed. What the devil was that smell? A putrid odour rose to Samson's nose. No, it couldn't be. He knew that odour, it was the stench of rotting corpses. He'd witnessed first-hand the thousands of dead when plague had struck Shiloh. He'd been one of the few lucky to escape the colony world and the experience still haunted him. He'd been visiting friends and returned home just as people began dying. It was a stench you never forgot, nor ever wanted to experience again. He swallowed repeatedly, forcing back the bile that rose in his throat. Others on the bridge held their hands to their noses, some cursing while others retched, perhaps unaware quite what the smell was and what it brought with it.

His head jerked sharply towards the bridge hatch, as the screaming in the passageways began.

*****

"Did you think we'd really trust you?" Nadons called to the diplomat, as the guards checked their weapons with stunned expressions on their faces. "We gave you a chance to make peace and you have broken your word. You are a fool to think that you could force a development of powers that we hold naturally, and then try to overcome us.

"We allowed you to come here in the hope that humanity had changed, matured into something we could deal with. But apparently not. The null field is back operating again at full capacity, your technology will not work. You wanted this world, Admiral, and now you have it. You're stuck here, just like everyone else. You can never leave."

Even as he heard Nadons, Seethan was still desperately pulling at the trigger of his handgun, but nothing was happening. Something was tugging at the back of his mind. He stopped with a jolt, registering suddenly that there had been a series of clunks from the ship just before he'd fired. When he looked towards the craft, he saw that numerous doorways had opened in its side. Like seeds on the wind, countless black-armoured and helmeted soldiers on anti-gravs had started dropping towards the ground, clouds of drones launching from their shoulders before the troops landed.

But even as some of the soldiers touched down, the anti-gravs cut out. Many troops fell the remaining distance, while the landing ship hit the grass with an earth-shaking crash. Some of the soldiers disappeared beneath the bulk of the craft, while others were ensnared by their legs. Several were trapped from the waist down, their helmets rolling or tossed free.

Seethan and the others could see their eyes bulging with agony, as they vomited up their insides. The craft lay with a tilt to one side, doors open, with soldiers and crew staggering and falling through the exits. Here and there, a few of them dragged their comrades to safety. Many collapsed once they were safely outside the ship; others simply sat on the ground as if to gather their senses. One man could be seen on the floor with a comrade in his arms, rocking backwards and forwards repeatedly. The drones they'd launched still pitter-pattered to the grass. A few of the less injured ignored their pain and joined the yelling ranks charging towards Seethan and the others. The columns washed over the fallen android and Alan disappeared beneath the mass of troops. They faltered then, suddenly realising their weapons weren't working.

"Halt, fix bayonets!" An officer at the front barked, in a voice that could be heard from where Seethan and the others stood waiting.

As one, the soldiers dropped to their right knees and drew long serrated blades from sheaths on their right thighs. Fitting them quickly to their rifle-like weapons they rose and, on order, resumed their charge with long drawn-out screams of defiance.

"Holy shit," Jon gasped, snatching his bow from his shoulder and firing arrow after arrow at the charging troops. His sister followed suit, putting one through the diplomat's chest, the bloodied projectile passing straight through him and burying itself in the ground behind him. Haden simply stared at the blood pouring down his chest. Reaching towards the wound with both hands he suddenly toppled face first into the mist swirling lightly around his feet. The second arrow lodged in the admiral's neck and he too fell, clutching at his throat and coughing up blood.

To their dismay the arrows bounced off the soldiers' armour and, realising the weapons were useless, they threw them aside and readied their spears.

The two guards stood undecided, looking from the fallen admiral to the diplomat, as if wondering what to do now. Meanwhile, Nadons stood still, watching the chaos erupt around him with disapproval and growing anger.

As the troops rushed towards them, Seethan's own rage grew and, suddenly, he transformed. One moment he was an ordinary man, the next a dark-grey wolf that, while on all fours, easily came level to the average man's chest.

Seethan leapt towards them, his jaws dripping with saliva, and he plunged into the massed ranks. Snapping at their limbs and faces, his jaws easily crushed the armour, flesh, and bone. From above came Peter's shrieks of rage and frustration, as he plunged towards the ground from up on high. Behind him, Seethan he could hear Shona begin to chant. Her sing-song voice turned into guttural words that, no matter how loud, eluded his ears. Her voice rose in volume, somehow echoing until it ended in a sudden clash of thunder. As it did so, Peter gave a loud strangled '*caw*' that turned into a mind-numbing '*skree*' and he changed form in mid-air.

In Peter's place was suddenly a huge bird of prey, easily double Seethan's height. The back of this monster was as dark as night, its breast and beneath its wings a pale cream with dark brown speckles. Narrow, evil-looking orange eyes with large black centres locked onto the enemy with cruel intent, and a long, serrated beak matching the orange of his legs opened in a high-pitched scream. His legs stretched out, the claws of which held black scythe-like talons opened, and he swooped down.

Seethan felt the pack's answer to his mental summons, as he tore into the massed ranks. He'd known the wolves weren't far away, despite their fears of the forest and the threat it held. He felt them rush to his aid, bursting through the reappearing purple door and scrabbling towards the boggling troops. The regimented lines faltered as they stared, gasping in disbelief at the horrors attacking them.

From the corner of his eye, he saw the wolves savage the bodies of Jeffries and the diplomat, while bolts of searing plasma shot from Shona's hands and cut swathes through the infantry like a brilliant knife. Even a touch of the searing energy left the soldiers screaming in agony, while those caught fully simply burst into flame. Their comrades, desperate to hold rank, fought back against the wolves, using their bayoneted rifles like spears as best they could. Peter tore into them from above, ripping them to shreds with beak and claw while deafening them with his shrieks of rage.

Here and there, stretcher parties could be seen trying desperately to ferry the wounded soldiers back towards the relative safety of the crashed ship. Peter screeched as he dropped again and again from the sky, biting one of the enemy in half while tearing others limb from limb with his talons, scattering torn flesh far and wide. The wolves leaped into the fray, brushing the enemy aside as if they were mere toys and crushing bone and armour alike with their terrifying jaws.

A new sound rose. It was a drawn-out groan, akin to the lonely call of a ship weaving cautiously through the sea on a cold, foggy night. It came again, louder and louder. The wind gathered force around them, whipping at the mist and seasoning it with the crimson petals.

Hell's orchestra began. That nightmare melody of dull horns and out of tune trumpeting. It rose in volume and as far as Seethan could see, people were clutching at their ears, trying to muffle the dread sound. His own ears, more sensitive than ever, sang with pain but also with the joy of recognition. Many of the soldiers were rolling on the ground, pulling off their helmets and clutching at their heads.

There was a sudden silence, as if everyone had gone deaf. Bewildered, the soldiers looked around them and drew a deep breath. That silence was broken by the rising drum of hoofbeats, as massed ranks of The Wild Hunt exploded from the forest's edge and rushed across the grass towards them. Shocked, and in utter despair, the colonial forces stared at the elves and backed away. Clad in gleaming armour, most of the newcomers were on horseback while others rode huge deformed moose, deer, giant cats, wolves, and towering bears.

The charge of the horsemen scattered the blossom in red waves before them, the deluge falling like drops of blood in the white swirling mist. The Wild Hunt ploughed into the soldiers in a crash of a thousand cymbals; nothing could withstand their charge. Some of the fighters were smashed backwards, others trampled underfoot, many thrown into the air like leaves on a breeze. The bears swiped the troops aside, their claws shredding armour and tearing through exposed flesh. Spears punched through armoured chests as though they were made of paper, the riders thrusting and slashing the colonial troops aside, the rearing beasts trampling others.

A stench rose that was so strong many gagged, and other nightmare creatures joined the throng. They were the undead. Among them, Seethan saw a familiar platoon of marines.

It was his own. Those killed in the crash that had severely injured him.

At the sight of the undead, many of the soldiers threw their weapons to the ground and ran, as if that would help them. Low moans from the undead joined the battle cries, screams of rage, agony, of the wounded and dying. More soldiers broke and ran for the trees, in hope of finding sanctuary.

Yet, most remained and fought on, as if realising running would do them no good at all.

*****

Captain Samson stared at the door to the bridge. Outside in the corridor, the gunfire and shrieks, yells, and pleading had stopped, but he still couldn't take his eyes off the door. That rank stench filled the room, making breathing difficult. Behind him he could hear someone sobbing. He thought at first that it was one of the women but realised it was his X.O., a veteran navy commander, his mind gone.

Well, we all have our limits, he thought, knowing the man had long since reached his.

A dull pounding began on the door and with each distinct thud, dents appeared in the metal, as if a battering ram was being fielded by a platoon of robots. The sound that really terrified Samson, though, were the dry chuckles between each of the resounding crashes. A split appeared in the alloy of the door. That couldn't be, but as he watched the next strike tore it still further. A few more thuds and a muddy-green reptilian hand forced its way through the rent and ripped part of it away as if it were tissue. From behind the door, long black claws dug grooves in the alloy, and more and more of the material fell away. Finally, in the centre lay a gaping hole. There was a pause as a blood-red eye peered through at them, accompanied by deep breathing and a blood-curdling snicker.

Keeping his eyes fixed on the nightmare that looked

directly back at him, Samson reached one hand down to open a drawer hidden in his armrest and pulled out an ancient percussion pistol. It had belonged to an ancestor and had been passed on to him by his father. He'd been shown it as a child, when his father had told him that the weapon had first been used in a distant and forgotten war, and that each serving member of his ancestor's descendants had taken it into battle. He knew for a fact that his father had used it during the Independence Wars. It was a large, chunky, heavy weapon with a six-inch barrel. The weapon had six chambers, although traditionally only five were filled. He remembered once asking his father why one always remained empty, and had been told it was to prevent accidental discharge. How he wished for that extra bullet now but, ironically, he only needed the one.

The door was suddenly torn asunder as a monster from his worst nightmare pulled itself through, the metal doing nothing but gouge cuts in the reptilian skin. Its bellow, filled with wrath, assaulted his ears and shook the bridge. The creature was so large it had to bend over to fit in the room. Its leprous skin was that of a toad, but worst were the eyes, which glittered with a fierce and terrible malevolence. Those baleful eyes said, 'no matter where you go or what you do, I will find you'.

Its forearms were shorter than the hind legs but when it shuffled in the room on all fours, and stretched sucker-tipped fingers towards him, those mottled arms and hands looked massive. The frog-like creature paused in mid-step and vomited forth a steaming stew of blood, bone and chunks of human flesh. Samson felt his sphincter give way. There was a sudden hot feeling in his trousers, as he watched an eyeball roll towards him from the bloodied mess on the floor. It stopped finally, and then lay there as if looking up at him.

Samson lost it. No way, no way! It wasn't going to get him. He turned the gun towards his chest and pulled the trigger. Even in the uproar the gunshot was deafening, a stark punctuation to the closure of the crew's story. The last thing he saw was someone else's hand stretching desperately for his handgun, while in the background his shipmates clung together and screamed.

*****

Commodore Andrews waited. Filled with dread, he watched as the *Rosalon Redemption* and her two escorts fell to the enemy via the remotes. He'd seen the old recordings of the battle over Halloween time and again, and knew full well what the enemy were capable of. His fingers lay poised above the keyboard with which he could enable the explosives hidden aboard the three ships. The last thing he wanted was to face those creatures too. He bit his lip, knowing that if he enabled the explosives, it might inflame the war further. And so, he waited. Dry mouthed. Feeling the tension mount, and the bridge crew's eyes upon him. Someone began to cry, and he thanked God it wasn't him.

Andrews swallowed the bile in his throat and waited for some sign from the enemy. If he survived and returned home, they might say he'd been indecisive, but so be it. His waiting was deliberate. For he was desperate to avoid further conflict and hoped that by not firing on the enemy, they might reciprocate and stand down. He'd deliberately turned off the screen that displayed the internal cameras aboard the three ships now facing him. It was still being recorded, and so he had that evidence if needed. He knew, deep in his heart, that there was no way he could win. And so he waited, praying to a god he didn't believe in for the first time in his life.

*****

Gradually the lessening sounds of combat reached through Seethan's rage. He paused and looked around him, as his friends fought on. There were not many of the enemy left and, with a blood-soaked growl, he turned and leapt back into their ranks. He ignored the agony of slight bayonet wounds as they jabbed at his body. Snapping, ripping and rending, he tore away chunks of flesh from screaming men and tossed the bodies aside like rag dolls. The dead were scattered around him like confetti, rising one after another from the enemies' depleted ranks to harass and kill their former comrades.

He saw one of the elven army, its visor painted as a screaming skull, standing astride one of the troopers while plunging a glittering lance down through the fallen man's chest time and again. The armour was designed to only deflect high-velocity projectile and beam weapons, not magical weapons. The soldier gasped and briefly clutched at the glimmering lance, then his hands fell away and he lay still. The elf gave a joyous battle-cry, ripped free its weapon, and turned to charge one of the few soldiers who remained on their feet. All around Seethan the dead soldiers continued to rise up and meander, arms outstretched and with low groans, towards their former comrades.

The few troops that remained threw down their weapons and ran for the woods. The werewolves and Wild Hunt pursued them, side by side for the first time. They were like the shadow of a cloud racing over the landscape, until they were lost to the woods. The screams of agony from dying men could be heard well into the evening.

"Seethan, Seethan!"

He could hear Eve calling him, and his rage ebbed as he focused once more.

"Seethan!" Eve shouted his name and slapped his face to grab his attention.

The battle finally over, Seethan found himself in human form once more. He stood shaking, naked, and unashamed on the battlefield. Shona ran towards him and handed him his spare uniform. He dressed quickly, while Eve forced her gaze away.

"Is it finished?" Eve asked eventually, her eyes flickering to his.

"I guess so." Seethan replied, looking around them. Where was Rose? Seeing the coffin, he loped over while pressing a palm over a bayonet wound in his thigh. He looked down into the coffin at her, his heart full of love. Then he gasped.

He hadn't even seen the knife that must have been in Alan Wrong's hands, the one he'd slipped into her neck, when to all appearances he'd only been touching her face. Rose's once olive flight suit was now stained a deep red, and she was either unconscious or dead.

"Oh...Rose," Seethan knelt beside the coffin and reached in to cradle her head. Half lifting her towards him, he tried to staunch the vermillion stream that had long ceased flowing from her neck. "Nadons! Quick, do something!"

"I can't," the old man said from behind him. "Our magic is

different to yours, remember? I can't help her, my friend. I'm sorry."

Rose's eyes opened and she smiled weakly. "Seethan, my systems...I can feel them shutting down. He's cut through my life lines."

Seethan knew that the life lines were the electronic conduits of body function, which passed information to the many parts and artificial muscles of her body. Without them she was doomed. "Rose I–I–."

"It's okay my love," she half whispered. "To be honest it's better this way. Seeing the man I love grow old and die, while I didn't age a day, would have been too much for me. I couldn't bear it. Nor could I have taken my own life: it's written into our code and forbidden to us. When you'd gone, there would be the living alone for hundreds, possibly thousands of years. I wouldn't wish that on anyone." She coughed and bubbles of blood formed like miniature balloons, popping and dribbling from the side of her mouth. "Do you think androids have a soul?"

"I know they do, and that yours is beautiful."

"Then I trust that we'll meet again one day, in a life that's better than this one. I truly look forward to it. I love you, Seethan."

"And I love you." He'd never said that to anyone before. Doing so brought a sense of release; he was finally able to tell her how he felt.

Her body relaxed suddenly; the emerald eyes that carried her laughter stilled as he held her. Finally, Seethan closed her eyelids before lowering her into the coffin once more. He stood staring down at her, unable to say anything as tears rolled down his face. There was a saying he'd heard as a youth, that you should never turn away a kiss or a hug because you are only allotted so many and you will never get them back again. He thought of all the missed opportunities they'd had, and the words they'd left unsaid.

Eve put her arm around him, hugged and held him before moving away. Shona appeared dumbstruck, unable to think of anything to say but she came up and clasped Seethan's shoulder for a few moments as he bit back his sobs. And then, she too, moved away. What could they say? All this time they had been looking for Rose; only for him to find her and lose her again within such a short time.

Realising that Nadons was still standing close by Seethan turned to look at him and said, "You can fix her, I know you can. Bring her back for me. Please?"

The old man slowly shook his head. "As I told you, we cannot. She is of your technology; something we have no knowledge of. Everything that lives, or does not live, has an allotted time."

"But there must be something you can do. Please, I'll do anything you ask. I've never asked anyone for anything, but this I beg of you. The Spooks can bring back the dead and extinct creatures, you must be able to bring her back also!"

"But she's not flesh, is she Seethan? Your Rose was something else entirely. Take my word, we cannot help you. If we could then we would. We feel your pain, but now you must focus yourself and finish what was started."

Seethan darted to his feet and rushed to where he'd seen the android fall when he'd shot him. "Alan Wrong, where is he?" he shouted.

There was no answer. He turned to Nadons, and said, "He's gone? You let him go?"

"I told you before, the android race has done us no harm. They stand outside our conflict."

Seethan breathed deeply to still the rage, calming himself and forcing away the bitterness he felt aching within him. He watched Eve join Shona, as they walked away through the battlefield searching, and he stood and pushed away the hurt as best he could.

"There's one thing left to be done, isn't there, Nadons?"

Chapter 19

Nadons had agreed and they waited a while, until Seethan's arm tingled once again. There it was, a single note on his Smart-Arm to denote a call from the colonial ships. He didn't need to ask. He knew that Nadons had allowed the lone signal through the null field. He tapped at his arm and found himself facing a man whose insignia declared him a Commodore. The two of them looked each other over, the Commodore eying Seethan's blood-spattered face.

"I take it that you're Commander Bodell? I'm Commodore Andrews, in charge of the Task Unit out here in the Kuiper belt. Admiral Jeffries told me about you. I'm concerned that I've not been able to raise him or any of the landing party. Can you tell me what's been going on, and where they are?"

"Well," Seethan replied tartly. "The admiral claimed that he came here to broker a peace with the Spooks. In truth, he was a dishonest piece of shit who brought troops to a peace summit and attacked when things didn't go the way he wanted. The Spooks didn't like that. In answer to your question, yes, I do know where he is. There's a piece of him here and a bit there, so I'm afraid he won't be taking any calls. He made a mistake and paid for it. Will you do the same?"

The Commodore paled and his lips thinned for a moment, but when he spoke his voice was steady. "I'm sorry to hear that, although I'm sure that the Admiral had the best of intentions. That said, he was his own man and if things got messed up because of him, then I apologise.

"Please assure the aliens that the colonies are unanimous in their desire for peace, and would point out that in all the years since The Sundering there's been no conflict between our races, which demonstrates that a peace can indeed hold." Then he added; "Commander, I take it you're speaking for the Spooks now?"

"I'm not speaking for anybody, truth be told. But the Earth's beautiful again, the garden that it should be. We both know that if you return, before long there will be cities sprouting up all over the place. The forests will be lost, wildlife will vanish, and the seas will be fished or polluted until there's nothing left. Much like it was before."

Andrews said nothing, so Seethan continued.

"Before all this kicked off it was agreed that the Earth would be returned to the control of humans. It has been, and is now in the hands of the descendants of the survivors. These are the true Earthmen. You aren't wanted here."

The Commodore stared at him. "What about the Spooks?"

"They remain as our guests."

"Your guests? I'd like to speak to them directly."

"Perhaps you would you prefer them to visit your ship?" Seethan asked.

Commodore sucked in his cheeks. "No. That won't be necessary."

"I didn't think so." Seethan reached out his arm and turned it to one side, so that the Commodore could see Nadons looking directly into the Smarts.

"I am Nadons," he said. "One of those you call the Spooks. Commander Bodell speaks the truth and we agree with all he has said. Earth is now in human hands again and, despite the fact that you initiated conflict a second time, we will adhere to this peace agreement." He nodded to Seethan and turned away, ignoring the senior officer's blustering attempts at further communication.

"There you go, Sir," Seethan said, facing his Smarts. "That's the deal. Take it or leave it. Oh, and by the way, the *Rosalon Redemption* and her two escorts will remain in Earth orbit. You can try and take them back, but you won't like what you'll get. The ships are to stay in orbit, as a reminder. Just in case you need one."

"Listen, I want to speak to this Nadons fellow again!"

"He's said all he needs to. If I were you, I'd leave it at that."

Seethan could see the Commodore chewing it over. At length he said. "I have a document here—"

"I don't believe they sign documents, Sir. Unlike us, their word is their bond. Besides, I'm sure that everything we say is being recorded. Is it not?"

"It is. What about our men down there; surely there must be survivors?" Andrews said.

"If there are, you won't want them back either. Trust me. I

suspect they'll have been changed for the worse. As for the recording, if it's working now then I'm fairly confident that it would have been during the earlier discussions between the Spooks, Haden and Admiral Jeffries. There's your evidence, if you need it."

"Is there anything else?" the Commodore asked sardonically.

"As it happens, yes there is. What about the technician for Rose, my pilot and friend. I still want her repaired."

"Sorry, if we can't have our troops back then no. That was part of the deal the admiral was working on. Didn't work, did it."

"It's not going to hurt you to give in on that! Surely–"

"The powers that be back home won't like it. The answer is no. What else?"

Bitterly, Seethan said, "The admiral told me that he'd recalled me to duty. I'd like that order rescinded. After all, you can't really enforce it. Consider it a token of good faith, and duty done."

The Commodore smiled grimly. "You can rest assured that I will get that sorted. Good luck to you, Commander…er, Mr Bodell. I take it you're remaining there?"

He felt like crying but Seethan instead managed a shrug. "I am, Sir; after all, those rules apply to me as well. Good luck to you. Bodell out." He cut the connection and watched as his Smart-Arm flickered once and then died. He looked to Nadons, who stood watching him.

"Seethan," Nadons said gently, "your determination to find Rose showed us that, despite being a human, you are a kindred spirit. As for Alan Wrong, I'm sorry we couldn't interfere. But the fact that you could love one of them shows that there is hope for humanity yet."

"But I'm right about what I said to the Commodore, aren't I? I can't ever leave?"

"Why would you want to?" The wind rose again and whipped Nadons' sparse white beard to one side. "Remember what you have become, my friend. With that in mind, do you think you would ever be welcomed in humanity's colonies?"

"No, I guess they'd see me as a monster." Seethan glanced up to see the descending flower-ships, as they floated back down to be swallowed up and hidden by the forests. He turned to look at Nadons. "What if the colonial forces come back?"

"Oh, I don't think they will; at least until they have a need to. Besides, as you pointed out, a little something of us remains aboard the ships still in orbit. Just in case."

"Until they have a need to? Is there something you're not telling me?" Seethan asked with a frown. When Nadons didn't answer he looked over the battlefield around them, and to the landing ship lying broken in the clearing. Smoke still seeped from some of the exits. "That's a big chunk of metal and a lot of dead bodies to clear up." He knew members of his pack lay amongst the dead. He'd felt them die, but at least they'd done so with a brave purpose in their hearts, knowing their curse had turned into a blessing at the end.

"Oh, I'll take care of it, don't worry. The ship will remain here. It'll serve as a testament to what happened. We'll be around, keeping an eye on things. The tenacity of humans never ceases to amaze us. Only one thing remains to be done."

Nadons made an odd gesture with one hand. A breath of air appeared from nowhere and swirled the red blossom into a cloud, funnelling it up and then down into the coffin until it covered Rose completely. As they watched, it then slowly drained away like water down a plughole. He wasn't surprised that, when it had all vanished, the coffin lay empty. Rose was nowhere to be seen. Nadons, too, was gone.

Seethan said nothing, though a sob escaped him. Through the pain of loss, he knew it was time to move on.

*****

Eve's face was set and worried-looking as she tugged at Seethan's arm. "I can't find Jon or Chris. Can you help me?"

"Of course."

Shona walked with them as Eve put both hands up in a prayer position in front of her mouth and called for her brother and Jon several times, but there was no answer.

"Jon's here!" Shona shouted suddenly.

When Eve reached her, she gave a cry of pain and fell to her knees, sobbing. Shona put her arms around her. "I'm truly sorry,"

Jon lay on his back, his face grey and still. There was a single bayonet wound through his heart. His jerkin was plastered with blood, as were his hands where he'd clutched at the wound. Seethan knew that his death must have been mercifully quick, but he felt stricken. Another friend lost; and he knew that if it were not for himself, Jon would no doubt still be alive. Biting back the blame, he buried Eve's head into his neck as she sobbed. As if coming to her senses, she suddenly thrust him aside and called out for her brother. He and Shona joined in as she frantically looked through the bodies.

Angry Andy and the rest of the pack joined them in wolf form, but there were fewer than before. His shape seeming to suck all the light from around him, Angry mentally answered the unspoken question Seethan had for him.

"They killed Simon and Michael. Fae's badly injured and the wounds won't stop bleeding. Those soldiers' blades must have contained traces of silver."

"Damn it," Seethan replied, realising that's why his injuries hurt so. *"Jon's dead as well. Can you help us find Chris? He's missing."*

Andy answered by threading his way through the scattered bodies, his head swinging one way and then the other, as he searched for Chris' scent. Seethan, Eve and Shona spread out, working through the bodies. In wolf form, Andy's senses were sharper than theirs. But, even so, with the cloying scent of blood, it took the wolf a while to find Chris.

"He's here!" Andy mind-called a short while later. *"Quickly, he's badly hurt."*

"Eve, this way!" Seethan beckoned her over and the three of them ran to where wolf-Andy waited. Within moments they were at Chris's side. He'd been stabbed with a bayonet and they could immediately tell that the wound was serious.

Eve fell to her knees and cradled her unconscious brother in her lap. She pressed her palm against the wound in an attempt to stop the bleeding. Tears streaming down her face, lips trembling, she looked up at Seethan. "Please, do something. Anything! I can't lose him as well as Jon. Shona!" she shouted. "Use your magic. Heal him with the craft. Please, I'm begging you. *Do something!*"

The witch shook her head sadly. "My powers were used for

what the Spooks intended. They're exhausted now, and what little I have left is ebbing. Chris' wounds are beyond me, I'm sorry."

"Seethan?" Eve looked to him, her eyes begging as she held her brother close. His head lolled against her, hands by his sides.

Wordlessly Seethan had already pulled his small personal first-aid pack free from a uniform pocket. It was the least he could do. He pulled off Chris' clothing and applied a large battle dressing to the gaping hole, and then bound it around Chris' body as tightly as he could. Knowing the futility of it, he tried the nano-med applicator but, as he suspected, it was dead. The only other thing he could do was wrap Chris as warmly as possible. He knew it wouldn't be enough but at least he could make his friend a little more comfortable. When the binding bled through, and he showed no signs of improvement, Eve knew the worst too.

"Eve," Seethan said, as he knelt beside her some hours later. "There's nothing anyone can do, except be here for the both of you. I'm sorry."

Eyes glistening, she reached out and grabbed him by the collar of his flight suit. "Yes, there is," she demanded fiercely as she jabbed at his squadron patch. "You know it as well as I do. You can bite him, and make him like you!"

Seethan felt his mouth gape open in surprise. "But you hate werewolves! You'd be making him into something you can't abide, something you've sworn to kill."

"I said bite him!" she roared, jerking Seethan savagely back and forth by his uniform, as if she were punching him. "Don't let him die when you can save him. Bite him, Seethan. Bite him!"

Angry Andy suddenly thrust Seethan aside, making him lose balance and fall backwards into the blood-soaked grass. Catching himself with both hands, Seethan watched, knowing it was Chris' only chance of survival. Andy's jaws opened wide and, in a swift and savage motion, the wolf bit Chris on the shoulder. His teeth embedded deeply, and he worried at the wound to ensure the curse passed. He licked at the blood seeping from the torn flesh and stepped free. With a last glance at Seethan, Angry turned and padded away to the forest, and was soon swallowed up by the trees.

"Where's he going?" Eve demanded, bandaging the new wound. "He can't go yet. Chris might need it to be bitten again. Come back!" she shouted after him.

Seethan put his hand on her arm. "He won't. Listen, Angry has done what he can. It's down to Chris now."

"And the curse," Shona added. But when Eve glared at her, she fell silent.

"He might be too badly wounded, Eve," Seethan continued. "Andy's gone because although he's done what you demanded, he knows there'll be no forgiveness for him if he saves but curses Chris."

She said nothing and turned her gaze back to her brother, cradling and crooning to him in a deep keening sound that tore at Seethan's heart. The autumn weather was moist and cold, a deathly damp chill that crept into their bones to make them achy and stiff. Seethan and Shona collected wood and built a fire, and then the witch made a brew that she gave to Eve with instructions to drink it all up. Eve stayed awake with her brother for as long as she could, but eventually exhaustion, and whatever was in the concoction, got to her and she lay next to her brother, arms around him, and held him close.

*****

When Eve woke in the morning, Chris had disappeared, as had all the bodies, blood, and weapons of the fallen. Everything had vanished in the night, except the mountainous metal of the landing ship.

Only it remained, just as Nadons had said it would.

"Where is he; where's Chris?" Eve demanded, climbing quickly to her feet and looking wildly around.

"He's gone," Seethan replied. "He'll live, Eve. In his weakened state, and with the amount of venom Andy gave him, the curse would have taken quickly. He needs to be with the pack now. Chris said he didn't want you to see him like that, until he could control it properly. Don't worry, they'll take care of him while he heals both physically and mentally. Be thankful that he lives. Even if you don't like what he's become."

"You son of a bitch, why didn't you wake me?" Eve said,

standing and pushing Seethan violently away, and then she punched him clean in the mouth.

Seethan saw it coming. He could have stopped or evaded it, but instead he let the punch connect. He rode it, tasted and smelled blood as the lip split. He hid the pain, seeing the instant flash of regret in her eyes, followed by a steely determined look. Saying nothing in way of apology, she turned away.

"You should have woken me," she insisted more softly, her shoulders shaking after she turned her back. She wiped at her face and looked over her shoulder at him. "I want him back. Please, tell Chris that it's all right. He's all I have left." She looked for Seethan's nod of agreement before she continued. "If you remember, the old fortune teller said one or more of us might not return, that all of us will be changed. Looks like she was right. Jon, Simon, Rose, and Michael are dead. Now you and Chris are…what you are."

"We've all changed," Seethan said. He thought about Rose, and turned so that Eve wouldn't see him brush away a tear; he forced his loss aside. That was something else he'd have to learn to deal with. "On top of all this Shona's lost her power, something that means a great deal to her. You have to accept your brother turning into what you consider a monster, if you still want him in your life.

"Remember when you told me that werewolves have no place in your society? What happens if you two go home and the rest of the people in your village discover what he's become? Will you stand aside while they butcher him?"

"Who's going to tell them?" she said tearfully. "Not me, and certainly not you. As far as anyone else is concerned, Chris is fine. I've lost a fiancé and a cousin, I'll have to learn to deal with that, but my brother comes with me."

"The others will find out, you know that," Seethan said. "Things have a way of being discovered, no matter what, but the choice is yours." He turned and spoke to the witch. "Shona, it's time to go back, I'll escort you two ladies as far as I can."

"I'm not coming with you," Shona said.

"What do you mean?" Seethan said, confused, and then realisation dawned. He looked up and around. "Where's Peter?"

"He's a roc now, remember? There's no return from a change such as that. He absorbed too much of my power, almost all of it. Peter will always remain what he is, and I'll stay here to help him adapt. If we tried to return to Burley the villagers would kill him on sight, afraid for their children and livestock; and who could blame them?

"He and I have been together for a long time. He's my friend, my family, and I'll not abandon him now."

"But where will you live?" Eve asked. "There's nothing left, apart from that wreck of a ship over there."

"Huh, I'm not going near that bloody thing. It's full of the dead, unless Nadons managed to clean that up too," Shona said. "Besides, the Wild Hunt won't allow us to stay. Peter and the werewolves are personae-non-grata in the forests. But don't worry, the Spooks will look after us. We'll find somewhere to live on the boundaries."

Eve looked at no-one, as she said, "Jon and Chris were the only family I had. We lived together because our parents all perished over the years. I can't risk my brother being discovered and there's no one else to go back to, but that's the only home I've ever known."

"You have to consider what's most important. You'd certainly be welcome to stay with Peter and I," Shona said, the hope evident in her voice.

Eve gave a half-smile of thanks and acceptance. She turned to Seethan. "What about you, will you come with us?"

"I need to learn more about how my PTSD strategies can be used to control the wolf in me. To be honest I wouldn't feel safe around people until then.

"Then of course I need to go and see if any of those soldiers in the forest are still alive. If there are, Andy will take pity on them and add them to the pack. Those troops were only following orders, after all. Had this been in my time, I could have been there standing shoulder to shoulder with them. I should have found another way to deal with the situation, one that didn't include so much bloodshed."

He was silent for a moment, and then said, "You know the weirdest thing? I'd swear that amongst the dead I saw my platoon. It's bizarre that Nadons called on them to help me out."

"What makes you think he did that?" Shona said. "I suspect

they came of their own accord. Remember what I told you, the Earth is different now."

Seethan thought about that and then changed the subject. "While I'm at it, I'll go find the pack and ensure your brother's all right, Eve. I'm sure that we'll swing by occasionally, and perhaps in time you'll come to accept him for what he's become."

Eve swallowed hard and ignored his last comment, "The admiral and that fellow Haden seemed pretty intent on getting control of the Earth, and that's worrying. It tells us the colonies aren't going to give up."

"We stopped them before and we can do it again," Seethan replied.

"What, with an overgrown budgie, a bunch of mutts, and a witch with no power?"

"I'm hoping that my powers will come back, actually," Shona said, with a hint of indignation. "Perhaps it'll take time, or maybe they won't come at all, but we'll see. As for the mutts, your brother's a member of that pack now and don't you forget it. Besides, they may pitch in again as and when we need them, as will the Hunt and the Spooks. Then there's Peter. He'll be all right once he settles down into his new life."

"I agree," Seethan said. "In the meantime, the ships in orbit will help deter the bad guys."

As Seethan turned away, Eve reached out as if to put a hand on his arm, and then she stepped forward and put a kiss on his cheek. Turning away from him her braided hair swung around like a weapon and slapped him lightly across the face.

He could sense the two women standing silently behind him, watching him leave. A moment or two later and they themselves departed, no doubt knowing they had a lot to do. After all, they had a camp to build before anything, and then a home.

Chapter 20

Months later, Seethan stood just inside the porch of his log cabin, looking out at the buttercup-plastered glade. He drank in the scenery, so different from the hustle and bustle of where he came from. Warm for this time of year, the deep-blue sky was cloud-free, and the air laced with the floral scent of the forest. Within walking distance lay the crisp, clear, musical river. He often spent his days fishing there, watching the weeds dancing lethargically in the slow-moving current.

Turning back inside, he moved to make a cup of mint tea. He'd spent a long time with the pack, before moving back to live a short distance from the two women. At night he would hear the wailing horns of The Wild Hunt, as they continued their patrols and pursued their prey within the forest's boundaries. He often went out to try and see them, and occasionally a few of the elves would pause at the outskirts of the trees, as if to look back at him.

He'd finally found the strength to overcome his compulsion to mate with Fae. Trouble was, it meant he could no longer be alpha male. Mating demonstrated dominance, but with his full control he couldn't bring himself to do it anymore. Yes, the urge tore at him but his strategies helped him stop. Eventually he'd taken Angry Andy to one side and told the man to challenge him. Andy hadn't wanted to, for he'd become a devoted friend and follower, but eventually the wolf complied. Allowing himself to be beaten, Seethan had slunk away, while Andy mounted Fae in front of him, their eyes filled with regret. The pack had left but they did swing by now and again.

He spoke to Rose, as if she were here beside him. He could almost taste her fragrance, hear her warm laughter. He swallowed and bit back his emotions, wondering whether he'd ever get over her, and of course the guilt of his betrayal.

Bees buzzed in the glade, as they meandered from flower to flower. The chorus of birdsong came and went, as if it too were being tossed about by the incessant breeze. With his enhanced hearing he caught the yip of a vixen, the call of a cuckoo. Along with the floral fragrance there was a hint of the distant ocean. A soft, salty fragrance that suddenly registered an alert.

Seethan dived to one side, even as a soft noise came from behind him. He knew that scent well. Hitting the floor, he rolled toward an open window on his right, coming to his feet with his fists raised in a guarding position, teeth clenched in a half snarl.

Alan Wrong stopped mid-step, just inside the door. He stared at Seethan, as if in surprise. Neither said anything for several seconds, in which Seethan noted Wrong's thick green top. It was too hot for this weather but that wouldn't matter to the android. His left sleeve lay empty and tucked back inside the shirt. Wrong drew back, his eyes wary.

"Good grief, Seethan. This fresh air seems to agree with you, for you're a lot faster than I thought you were. Been working out, have we?"

"I didn't have the opportunity to show you before; you ran away, remember? Rose told me about the pheromones you androids can put out to make yourselves more attractive to people. She smelled like an angel, whereas you adopted the scent of Mrs M's cologne and still stink like a mudflat when the tide goes out."

"That's not very nice."

"You can get fucked. I searched for you for a long time, but eventually decided to stop and wait here. You see, I knew that sooner or later you'd come looking for me."

"How could you possibly know that?"

"Well I was right, wasn't I? It's what you do. You're the Son of Man killer. Someone who murders not only other androids but any human who gets in his way. You know that I'd reveal who – and what – you really are to the villagers. Therefore, I am a threat. How's the arm, by the way? I hope that hurt. It occurred to me that had you been human, it would have been a real hindrance to your sex life."

"Have you any idea how hard it is to find parts and get repairs these days, Seethan? But yes, you're right, I have come for you. You've been a pain in my side for far too long – centuries if you think about it. That has to end."

Without warning Wrong leapt towards him but, as he did so, Seethan sprang upwards, tucked his knees into his chest and kicked out with both feet. His heels caught Wrong in the chest and sent him stumbling backwards, out of the door. The android tripped and fell, his back hitting the ground hard. Just as he was about to get to his feet, a large shadow swooped overhead. He looked up as a high-pitched *skree* came from above, and a small deer slammed into the ground besides him.

What the hell? Seethan thought.

The android prodded the carcass with his foot as if confused, and looked upwards again. It was all the diversion that Seethan needed, and he changed.

He harnessed his rage. It came in red waves that he didn't even try to stop. There was no need to use his strategies to fight it. Far from it. He drank it all in, welcoming the fury that engulfed him and the agony of his changing body. His clothes shredded. Muscles rippled, tore and reformed. Bones cracked and altered, adjusting themselves to his new shape. Once pearly teeth lengthened, tearing at his jaws so that they dribbled blood. The taste infuriated him further. But through it all he kept his control, well aware that this was it, his one chance. Seethan screamed his defiance, the cry turning into a long, drawn-out howl.

Alan Wrong's look turned to him and rapidly became one of horrified disbelief.

One moment Seethan had been a man out of his time, facing a foe that he stood no chance of defeating, an enemy who could tear a mere human to pieces with their bare hands. The next he was a ravening wolf filled with hatred.

"What the...?" Wrong gasped.

Seethan slammed into him. Dripping with saliva, his jaws stretched towards the killer's face. Alan Wrong caught him by the throat with his one hand but was hurled backwards by the wolf's weight and incredible power.

The android held Seethan as far away from his face as he could, but it didn't help. The wolf squirmed and tore with his claws, his jaws snapping at the one remaining arm that restrained him. Claws shredded the android's clothes and the artificial flesh underneath. Muscle and sinew flew away from the android, leaving gaping wounds and deep rents. The artificial blood splatted and pulsed, as Seethan switched target again and his bayonet teeth finally closed around the android's face.

The mask of flesh was pulled away with a sucking sound, and wolf Seethan spat the morsel to one side. The face gone, Seethan's jaws gripped Alan's throat. He clenched tighter and tighter. Try as Alan did, he couldn't break free. His arms and chest were shredded, as he tried desperately to force the wolf away. Soon artificial bone showed through the fabricated flesh of Alan's neck, as Seethan wrenched the android from one side to the other, worrying at him like a terrier with a rat.

Had Wrong been human he would have long succumbed to the violence of the attack, but the android was made of much sterner stuff. With a heave, Seethan tossed the killer up into the air, leaping after him again as he crashed to the ground a few metres away. Alan tried to rise but fell backwards and lay where he'd fallen. He raised the remains of his hand, as if trying to ward off the wolf. Defiance showed in the serial killer's eyes amidst the torn flesh, as Seethan padded slowly towards him, a snarl on bloodied lips.

Seethan stood astride the remains of the Son of Man killer, savouring the moment as his enemy stared up at him from the ruined face. Then, with a swift movement, Seethan's jaws seized Alan's remaining arm and wrenched it free of the body. He tossed it to one side, watching as it flopped about on its own for a moment, like a freshly caught fish on a river bank.

Wolf Seethan saw it then. The one thing he wanted. There was terror in those machine eyes, as Alan realised this was it. He was done for. The android's gaze was tinged with disbelief.

Had androids progressed so far, Seethan wondered? Were they truly able to feel fear and joy, as well as love? Savouring the moment, Seethan's jaws closed around his enemy's throat and he clenched his jaws tightly until they met in the middle. Snarling he savaged back and forth, ripping and worrying at the injury. The android screamed, as if it could feel the agony a human victim would have.

As Seethan's teeth crunched through artificial bone and tore the throat away, Alan's head tumbled free. Seethan snatched it up and tossed it into the air, watching it land with a dull thud and roll several times before settling amidst the lush green grass. As it stopped, the light in those android eyes blinked out. He watched until the body ceased twitching, and lay still.

Seethan changed back into human form and stood there naked, his breath harsh and ragged as he gazed down at his enemy. There was no pleasure in what he'd just done, but a sense of justice for Rose and Mrs M, along with the countless others that Alan Wrong had killed along the way.

The *skree* sounded again, and Seethan looked up to see the massive shape of Peter swooping down, Shona astride him. The roc screamed once more as it landed, and Shona slipped effortlessly from his back and walked over to Seethan. Peter's wings thrashed as he took off again, beating his way skyward.

"That's a huge god-damned shite-hawk," Seethan said. "I appreciate the distraction, by the way."

"It wasn't our place to do more, you had to finish it. Besides, as strong as Peter is, Alan might have killed him."

"But...a deer?"

She shrugged. "It was our dinner. Consider it a gift, Peter's decided he likes you."

"After all this time? Well, I guess it could be worse. Had it had been anything like his previous presents, I'd be well and truly in the guano." After a glance towards Peter circling high overhead, he said, "Now what?"

"Well, if you could get some clothes on, we'll wait and see. You have a place here, with us. After all, there's nowhere to go, is there? This Earth is now home for you too."

"The only thing missing is Rose."

"She would have been proud of you."

"What if she doesn't have a soul, and I was wrong?"

"What makes us human, do you think?" Shona asked. "Our bodies, humour, ability to love? Rose had all of those even though she was synthetic, so why shouldn't she have a soul too?"

"If it's true for her, what of other androids?"

"You mean Alan Wrong?" She shrugged. "The world is what it is, Seethan Bodell. But, welcome to Earth."

Acknowledgements

Editorial

My sincere thanks to my editor Geoff Nelder. I'm deeply indebted to him for his suggestions, thoughts, help, limitless knowledge, and friendship.

My thanks to

Peter Willhelmson, Rosie Oliver, David Allan, Chris Rimmell, Annette Sindall, Randall Kryzak, and Gordon Brooks, for critiquing this work throughout.

A special mention to the wonderful Kate Spencer who did a cracking job proof-reading prior to submission.

Elsewhen Press
delivering outstanding new talents in speculative fiction

Visit the Elsewhen Press website at elsewhen.press for the latest information on all of our titles, authors and events; to read our blog; find out where to buy our books and ebooks; or to place an order.

Sign up for the Elsewhen Press InFlight Newsletter at elsewhen.press/newsletter

Bloodsworn

Book 1 of the Avatars of Ruin

Tej Turner

"Classic epic fantasy. I enjoyed it enormously"
– Anna Smith Spark

Everyone from Jalard knew what a bloodoath was. Legendary characters in tales they were told as children made such pacts with the gods. By drawing one's own blood whilst making a vow, such people became 'Bloodsworn'. And in every tale where the oath was broken, the ending was always the same. The Bloodsworn died.

It has been twelve years since The War of Ashes, but animosity still lingers between the nations of Sharma and Gavendara, and only a few souls have dared to cross the border between them.

The villagers of Jalard live a simplistic life, tucked away in the hills of western Sharma and far away from the boundary which was once a warzone. To them tales of bloodshed seem no more than distant fables. They have little contact with the outside world, apart from once a year when they are visited by representatives from the Academy who choose two of them to be taken away to their institute in the capital. To be Chosen is considered a great honour… of which most of Jalard's children dream.

But this year the Academy representatives make an announcement which is so shocking it causes friction between the villagers and some of them begin to suspect that all is not what it seems. Just where are they taking the Chosen, and why? Some of them seek to find out, but what they find will change their lives forever and set them on a path seeking vengeance…

ISBN: 9781911409779 (epub, kindle) / 9781911409670 (432pp paperback)

Visit bit.ly/Bloodsworn

Coming soon

Blood Legacy
Book 2 of the Avatars of Ruin

THE MAREK SERIES BY JULIET KEMP
BOOK 1:
THE DEEP AND SHINING DARK
A Locus Recommended Read in 2018

"A rich and memorable tale of political ambition, family and magic, set in an imagined city that feels as vibrant as the characters inhabiting it." **Aliette de Bodard**
Nebula-award winning author of *The Tea Master and the Detective*

You know something's wrong when the cityangel turns up at your door
Magic within the city-state of Marek works without the need for bloodletting, unlike elsewhere in Teren, thanks to an agreement three hundred years ago between an angel and the founding fathers. It also ensures that political stability is protected from magical influence. Now, though, most sophisticates no longer even believe in magic *or* the cityangel.

But magic has suddenly stopped working, discovers Reb, one of the two sorcerers who survived a plague that wiped out virtually all of the rest. Soon she is forced to acknowledge that someone has deposed the cityangel without being able to replace it. Marcia, Heir to House Fereno, and one of the few in high society who is well-aware that magic still exists, stumbles across that same truth. But it is just one part of a much more ambitious plan to seize control of Marek.

Meanwhile, city Council members connive and conspire, unaware that they are being manipulated in a dangerous political game. A game that threatens the peace and security not just of the city, but all the states around the Oval Sea, including the shipboard traders of Salina upon whom Marek relies.

To stop the impending disaster, Reb and Marcia, despite their difference in status, must work together alongside the deposed cityangel and Jonas, a messenger from Salina. But first they must discover who is behind the plot, and each of them must try to decide who they can really trust.

ISBN: 9781911409342 (epub, kindle) / ISBN: 9781911409243 (272pp paperback)
Visit bit.ly/DeepShiningDark

BOOK 2:
SHADOW AND STORM

"never short on adventure and intrigue... the characters are real, full of depth, and richly drawn, and you'll wish you had even more time with them by book's end. A fantastic read."

Rivers Solomon
Author of *An Unkindness of Ghosts*, Lambda, Tiptree and Locus finalist
Never trust a demon... or a Teren politician
The annual visit by the Teren Throne's representative, the Lord Lieutenant, is merely a symbolic gesture. But this year the Lieutenant has been unexpectedly replaced and Marcia, Heir to House Fereno, suspects a new agenda.

Teren magic is enabled by bloodletting. A Teren magician will invoke a demon and bind them with blood. But demons are devious and if unleashed are sure to create havoc. The Teren way to stop them involves the letting of more of the magician's blood – often terminally. But if a young magician is being sought by an unleashed demon, their only hope may be to escape to Marek where the cityangel can keep the demon at bay. Probably.

Once again Reb, Cato, Jonas and Beckett must deal with a magical problem, while Marcia must tackle a serious political challenge to Marek's future.

ISBN: 9781911409595 (epub, kindle) / ISBN: 9781911409496 (336pp paperback)
Visit bit.ly/ShadowAndStorm

HOWUL
A LIFE'S JOURNEY

DAVID SHANNON

"Un-put-down-able! A classic hero's journey, deftly handled. I was surprised by every twist and turn, the plotting was superb, and the engagement of all the senses – I could smell those flowers and herbs. A tour de force"

– LINDSAY NICHOLSON MBE

Books are dangerous

People in Blanow think that books are dangerous: they fill your head with drivel, make poor firewood and cannot be eaten (even in an emergency).

This book is about Howul. He sees things differently: fires are dangerous; people are dangerous; books are just books.

Howul secretly writes down what goes on around him in Blanow. How its people treat foreigners, treat his daughter, treat him. None of it is pretty. Worse still, everything here keeps trying to kill him: rats, snakes, diseases, roof slates, the weather, the sea. That he survives must mean something. He wants to find out what. By trying to do this, he gets himself thrown out of Blanow... and so his journey begins.

Like all gripping stories, *HOWUL* is about the bad things people do to each other and what to do if they happen to you. Some people use sticks to stay safe. Some use guns. Words are the weapons that Howul uses most. He makes them sharp. He makes them hurt.

Of course books are dangerous.

ISBN: 9781911409908 (epub, kindle) / ISBN: 9781911409809 (200pp paperback)

Visit bit.ly/HOWUL

MILLION EYES
C.R. BERRY
Time is the ultimate weapon

What if we're living in an alternate timeline? What if the car crash that killed Princess Diana, the disappearance of the Princes in the Tower, and the shooting of King William II weren't supposed to happen?

Ex-history teacher Gregory Ferro finds evidence that a cabal of time travellers is responsible for several key events in our history. These events all seem to hinge on a dry textbook published in 1995, referenced in a history book written in 1977 and mentioned in a letter to King Edward III in 1348.

Ferro teams up with down-on-her-luck graduate Jennifer Larson to get to the truth and discover the relevance of a book that seems to defy the arrow of time. But the time travellers are watching closely. Soon the duo are targeted by assassins willing to rewrite history to bury them.

Million Eyes is a fast-paced conspiracy thriller about power, corruption and destiny.

ISBN: 9781911409588 (epub, kindle) / 9781911409489 (336pp paperback)
Visit bit.ly/Million-Eyes

MILLION EYES: EXTRA TIME
Twelve time-twisting tales.

Million Eyes: Extra Time is a compilation of short stories set in the universe of C.R. Berry's time travel conspiracy thriller trilogy, *Million Eyes.*

While the stories in Million Eyes: Extra Time can stand alone, you'll notice that a number of them are strongly linked and follow a loose chronology. The author's advice is that you read them in the order that they are presented.

Available for free download in pdf, epub and kindle formats
Visit bit.ly/Million-Eyes-Extra-Time

Coming soon

MILLION EYES II
THE UNRAVELLER

About Mark Iles

Born and raised in Slough, Mark Iles began studying the martial arts when he was 14 and joined the Royal Navy at the age of 17. A voracious reader he used to devour up to three paperbacks a day – primarily science fiction, fantasy, and horror – by the likes of John Wyndham, Isaac Asimov, Arthur C. Clark, Ray Bradbury, Brian Lumley, Frank Herbert, Stephen King, and a plethora of others. After The Falklands War Mark was drafted to Hong Kong, where he began writing features, for a variety of martial arts magazines, and short stories for a wide range of markets.

In 2012 he decided to challenge himself and undertook an MA in Professional Writing, followed by Diplomas in Copywriting and Proofreading. With over 200 short stories and articles under his belt the book he wrote for his MA Project, *A Pride of Lions* was published by Solstice – followed by two other novels, a short story collection, and four novellas. His latest novel, *Gardens of Earth*, book 1 of *The Sundering Chronicles*, will be published by Elsewhen Press in 2021. Currently Mark is working on the second in the series, as well as another short story collection. Now a 9th Degree Black Belt in Taekwondo, Mark is still involved in martial arts and has also written both a book and an app on the subject.